KAAFIR'S
LOVE

Abhisar Sharma, a reputed journalist, won the prestigious Ramnath Goenka Indian Express Award (2008–2009) for his pioneering work, 'Laal Masjid Ka Safed Sach' (The True Story of the Red Mosque) and was also the recipient of the 2017 RedInk Award in the human rights television category for the story 'Operation Laal Jungle' (ABP News). With over two decades of experience in the news and television industry, Sharma has offered groundbreaking reportage on major international and national events like the 26/11 Mumbai attacks, the Gujarat riots, the Benazir Bhutto assassination, the Jasmine revolution in Egypt, all major Indian elections and the American Presidential elections. Currently hosting the 8PM show on ABP News, the author lives in Delhi.

The KAAFIR'S LOVE

ABHISAR SHARMA

RUPA

Published by
Rupa Publications India Pvt. Ltd 2018
7/16, Ansari Road, Daryaganj
New Delhi 110002

Sales centres:
Allahabad Bengaluru Chennai
Hyderabad Jaipur Kathmandu
Kolkata Mumbai

ISBN: 978-93-5304-048-2

First impression 2018

10 9 8 7 6 5 4 3 2 1

The moral right of the author has been asserted.

Printed by Thomson Press India Ltd., Faridabad

*To my family, my wife Shumana and
my children Mili and Babush*

Prologue

Murmurs of the past, a past as dark as a curse, as an evil spell tears my white shroud with its hideous, gnawed, muck-filled claws. My past is moving with rage towards my face which, until now, had been untouched by its lunacy. How do I shut my eyes to the past that creeps up stealthily and slithers into the unknown dark depths of my soul? Tearing my eyes wide open, I must face my powerful adversary—my past. I struggle hard to shield my face with my blood-smeared hands—a face that still exudes an unscarred, pristine glow. I clench my fingers into a fist, ready to take its punches head-on. I am ready for the counteroffensive. I know I don't stand a chance. How can I? It knows my every move even before I think of executing it. It knows my worst fears and draws from my best strengths, but, ironically, this is the only chance I have. I shall wait. There is no running away. There is no hiding.

The six-foot-one-inch lad with a five o'clock shadow gasped. His eyes grazed past the only opening in the dark room, redeemed by bursts of lights from the bazaar below. Lying on the ground on all his fours, he raised his right hand as he struggled to get up, supported by the wall, its peeling paint much like the raw burnt skin of his tormented soul. Faint sounds from the colossal market down below permeated the room through a rectangular opening barred by rusty iron rods. He closed his eyes, out of habit from his twenty-two years of existence, when he heard the azan from the adjacent Jama Masjid. He heard a faint rustle behind him as he stood up and raised his head, soaking in the hint of breeze and sunlight from the only opening in the room. He felt the blood rising in him once again. He heaved as he exhaled the hot air that burned his chest. His eyeballs struggled to focus on the room—a walnut-wood desk stacked with half a dozen Urdu books; the wall adorned by framed Quranic verses. He remembered what Nasir called them—tughre. The first frame read, *Haza min Fazle Rabbi* (May Allah Be With You). The next frame was bigger and it read *Bismillah e Rehman ur Rahim* (In the Name of Allah, the Magnificent and Merciful). Then, he saw the biggest frame. Nasir once taught him that they were called Yasin, meaning, to ward off evil spirits.

Nasir... He felt a faint stab in his heart as he remembered Nasir. His bond with this world. Then, he heard it again...the faint mumble, almost like a moan, from a corner of the 400-square-feet rectangular room. He jerked himself around to face the sound, his eyes shifting to his left, espying the rusty but powerful two-foot iron rod. He wobbled towards the weapon, making his way through the scattered stuff on the ground. The edge of his toe struck the steel wall decoration as he grimaced and cursed under his breath. His rage only multiplied as he held the iron rod in his hand with finality. He looked at the corner again. The crumbled and broken body in the corner moved, attempting to revive itself one last time. His tall figure moved towards the mass of flesh and raised the weapon.

viii

This is the last chance. There is no turning back after this. If I don't swing the rod, he might survive. But if I swing it, I turn things forever, to a point of no return.

He paused and heaved. His eyes were burning, his breath was swirling in his chest with an intense emotion unmatched by any that he had known in his life. His grip on the rod was unyielding yet he tightened it further. Shutting his eyes, he turned his head towards the small window as the lights from the market shone on his face one last time. It seemed as if they were trying to reason with him and dissuade him from carrying out that single swing of anger. His eyes welled up with tears and his nostrils flared as hot air gushed in and out. The moment had come. There was no turning back. Sameer raised the weapon above his head, preparing to strike.

A year and a half ago…

'You mean Inara? The trader's daughter? That man who has his finger in every pie? You do remember that he is linked to Imam Sahib and has the area's politicians jangling in his pockets like chillar. And you—'

'She is ethereal and has the most seductive smile I have ever seen,' he sighed as he thought of how she had enamoured his senses, just as a mosque is bathed in the luminescence of the moon on Eid.

'But she is virtuous. Don't get carried away by her flirtatious eyes and don't tell me that she smiles at you! Ha! Every boy in the neighbourhood thinks like that and quite a few of them have destroyed their lives thinking she fancies them.'

'Shut up Nasir! I know… I know she does fancy me…you are just jea—'

'Fuck you, Sameer! I am not jealous. Don't play with fire… you are after all a—'

'I know who I am…and I am sure she does too. But you should see how her eyes talk to me. How playful they become when my vision caresses her face. How she pushes that reluctant strand of hair with her tapering index finger above her right ear. Don't you see? How can you not?'

'You're crazy! You are playing with fire… Don't! I am your friend and the best one you have.'

'That I know,' Sameer slapped Nasir's back, shaking the entire configuration of his slender body. Sameer giggled as Nasir frowned, mumbling something uncharitable about Sameer's nonexistent sister.

A smile flashed on Sameer's lips. His light brown eyes shone as he ruffled his unkempt, thick mane of hair. Sameer had a sharp jawline that stood out despite the two-day stubble. His chiselled features accentuated his light brown eyes that were like an open book for people who knew him, people he wanted to reveal his true self to. He smiled, his lips curving into a small arc as he pictured Inara in his mind. Her proud dark eyes, tinged with brown, were capable of unnerving anyone whom she deigned to look down upon. A prominent chin that defined the oval of her face. A slender body and flawless, perfect breasts, their outline clearly visible to his probing eyes through her salwar kameez. Her feet, so spotless and fair that they appeared almost perfectly pedicured; but she never painted her toenails.

He remembered the first time he became acutely aware of her as a woman. Images of that moment flashed through his mind. Her raised hand pushing away a tendril of thick damp hair from her face, on the terrace of her house. Her full breasts jutting out through her white kameez in the soft light of the rising sun, her slender fingers, her sharp and pointed elbow, her flirtatious eyes as she stole a glance at him and hid a smile. How could he have imagined all that? He was certain that she fancied him too. Or maybe he just wished she did.

'I mean it, Sameer! Both situations would be perilous.'

2

Nasir broke the flow of his thoughts with a slap on his back.

'What situations?' Sameer's smile was at once eclipsed by the dark shadow of a frown.

'One...' Nasir raised his bony index finger. 'If you are caught eve-teasing her.'

'And the second?' Sameer knew the answer to that one. He smiled at his best friend in the entire Walled City, rather, in the whole world.

'The second is that she actually falls in love with you rather, you fall in love with each other. Do you know what that would mean?'

'Bliss!' Sameer replied, tongue-in-cheek. This was Sameer's moment of uncontrollable delight. The mere thought of falling in love and his love being reciprocated by Inara was exhilarating.

'It's no bed of roses, Sameer. I mean it.'

Sameer suddenly slapped Nasir's back again as he held on to his skullcap that nearly fell by the impact, 'Just relax, monkey boy! Just having a good time, aren't we?'

'Don't you keep hitting me like this! My bones creak and my spine hurts! My Ammi does not cook as good as Khala,' Nasir growled as Sameer threw his head back and laughed, just like the boy Sameer knew.

'I know, you are a shame to your parents. What kind of a Pathan you are Nasir, *lale di jaan!*'

Nasir shook his head as he revealed his paan-stained teeth, chewing the last remnants of a banarasi in his mouth. He placed his index and middle finger in a 'V' shape around his mouth and spat with full force; the red gooey cocktail of paan juice and saliva landed on the wall of the tailor's house that was already stained red by repeated spitting and had faded scribbles of 'a guarantee of reviving your manhood after consuming Lala ji's exotic herb-based ghutti, Mardani'. Nasir's eyes skimmed over the promise as he dismissed it as yet another false one, like the many others that were constantly being thrown at people of his age.

The two men sat on plastic chairs in front of Nasir's Internet café next to the tailor's shop, on a rare sunny January afternoon. Their world was unfolding in the Walled City, cushioned between haphazard brick-walled houses stacked tightly together, intruding into each other's spaces. A singular lane meandered through this chaotic maze of houses with thatched roofs. It wasn't as if all the houses were in a dilapidated condition. Some stood majestically amongst them, creating, rather demanding, their own space. They were the pakka houses in this slapdash arrangement of a human settlement that had probably remained unchanged over the last millennium. These pakka houses were reminiscent of the fact that some amongst them were the privileged ones. They housed the big fish, the ones placed higher in the food chain: The ones who had access to the bigger fish.

Suddenly, Nasir espied an effusive glow in Sameer's eyes: They first widened and then held the faintest tease of a smile. He followed Sameer's gaze.

There she was. Inara—dressed in a white salwar kameez with a cream-coloured dupatta that was blending with her kameez and a cream-coloured sweater. She stood taller than her five-feet-eight-inch height in stilettos. Her hair was tied in a long plait that snaked across her back. She pushed an errant strand of hair behind her ear with a perfectly manicured fingertip as she walked with an imitation 'Made in China' Louis Vuitton hanging on her slender right shoulder, her eyes fixed on the ground. Sameer could not help but notice a hint of a suppressed smile on her soft pink lips, the lower lip slightly

4

open in an unintended pout and the upper lip, firm, in control of her desires. Her lightly kohl-lined eyes set in the perfect oval of her face, were steeped in pride, with long eyelashes curling at the ends. Her cheeks were tinged with a dash of pink which grew a few shades darker to almost crimson as she approached Sameer. At this moment, Sameer wondered if she was irritated by his overt display of affection or flattered by the attention she was getting from him.

'Where do you think she is going?' mumbled Sameer, loud enough for Nasir to hear.

'It seems she is heading for the metro station...'

He didn't turn his head, but his gaze followed Inara as she walked past them towards the Kashmiri Gate metro station. Sameer suddenly rose from his chair and stretched his arms horizontally, his gaze fixed on Inara. He wondered if she too was thinking about him. He could feel the flow of restless energy in the soles of his feet. His toes quivered as his chest heaved with a sudden surge of nervousness. He exhaled the warm air out of his mouth, opening his lips slightly in an 'O'. He could feel the flow of energy rising up his spine and spreading across his shoulders. He stretched his shoulders back and forth, uncomfortably aware of the effect she had on him. What he did not realize was that Nasir was now giving him a bemused look, fully aware of how one glimpse of Inara had turned his friend into a bundle of nerves.

'What are you doing Sameer? You look...'

'Shut up Nasir!' He was now clearly embarrassed at being exposed, as if he was standing naked there and the whole world had seen his feelings laid bare. It wasn't that he was ashamed of expressing his emotions for her, it was just that he did not want the world, even Nasir, to know the intensity of his thoughts. He turned his head away from Nasir as he saw

Inara walking away, her vision now gradually dimming in the dust kicked up by the jumpy autorickshaws on the dilapidated stretch leading to the metro station.

'I have to go now. I have to follow her... I have to talk to her...'

'Don't get all hormonal, dude! You are embarrassing yourself.'

On any other day, Sameer would have found Nasir's paan-stained, buck-toothed smile adorable, and would have affectionately slapped him behind the head as always, but not today, not now. Right now, his breath felt heavy in his chest and he found it difficult to exhale. He felt like ramming a fist across Nasir's mouth, saving him of all the dental agony he had been undergoing since his childhood.

'I am not hormonal, Nasir! Don't piss me off! I mean it.' Sameer's voice had an edge to it.

'Chill, yaar! It is perfectly normal to feel like that.' Nasir's voice now rose as he spread his hands, even more amused. Sameer did not like it, not one bit. He looked at Nasir's goofy and smiling face and then at his chair. Nasir was lying far back on his chair which was now resting precariously on its rear legs as its front legs were suspended in the air. Sameer kicked the back leg of the chair and

Craaaaash!

Sameer grabbed Nasir's frail frame with a firm hand before he could collapse onto the ground.

Nasir muttered the choicest of expletives for Sameer and tried to take a swing with his free left hand to punch him as well. But Sameer was too fast for him and deftly thwarted his attempts with his right elbow. He was smiling again. Nasir stood up, catching his breath and looked at Sameer. He was not done yet. The slight twinkle in his eyes meant only one

6

thing. He wanted to rag Sameer further, but decided not to. Instead, he spoke gently, 'What is it, Sameer? Tell me what is it that you feel?'

Without batting an eyelid, as if he was dying to tell him, Sameer said, 'She makes me restless. She makes me yearn for her. I have also seen her stealing glances at me, and she is not even apologetic when I catch her in this act of candid flirtatiousness. I have to speak to her.'

'And then what? You know what this means? Remember who you are, and who she is?'

Sameer swept his hand around in the air, turning his gaze in the direction of Kashmiri Gate metro station, just in time to catch a glimpse of Inara taking the left turn towards its entrance.

'I have to go,' he said with a sense of urgency in his voice. 'I have to go *now*, and I don't care about anything else at the moment.'

Sameer started to run towards the metro station. He heard Nasir saying something behind him, but he paid no heed.

Sameer sprinted forward, quickly making his way through cycle rickshaws, autos and nervous cyclists, jumping across puddles of slushy mud and rows of cages stacked atop each other, housing petrified chickens. To his right was a long stretch of shanty shops, mostly kebab and Mughlai food joints. The boys working in these roadside dhabas stood outside, holding menu cards, attempting to lure potential customers, calling out to them aggressively to try out the delicacies of their joints. The aroma of juicy kebabs and meats in tandoors and grillers hung in the air and caressed the senses as burly men with bushy beards and skullcaps stood chatting amongst themselves while keeping a close eye on the simmering kebabs.

Sameer's eyes were unwavering of the path ahead. He had

taken the plunge, unmindful of Nasir's warnings. He could feel goosebumps, and the hair on the back of his neck stood on end as he strode towards the metro station, but it was not with fear or trepidation; it was the anticipation of treading on the hitherto unknown path. It was the ecstasy of finally getting down to speaking to Inara. As he was following her, the thought that he might be stalking her did cross his mind, but he brushed it away just like he had ignored Nasir's warning, 'You know who you are and who she is?'

As he neared the overbridge, his eyes glanced up and suddenly widened in alarm. 'Shit!' he swore. 'The metro train is arriving! Shit! I am going to miss it... And her! I am not going to make it,' he said to himself.

He sprinted up the stairs, climbing three to four steps at a time. He nearly collided with a stocky man descending with his wife who wore a hijab. The man growled as Sameer hurriedly apologized. As he reached the top, his heart sank. There was a long queue at the ticket counter and a longer one at the entrance. He paused and shut his eyes. He could feel the vibration of the train slowing down at the platform. He could sense the sound of restless footsteps around him. He knew it was crowded up there and he still had to climb another flight of stairs to make it to the platform.

He looked at the security guard scanning the belongings of commuters on the screen of the metal detector with a bored expression. He saw the CISF guard physically searching men and he saw women entering the special enclosure meant for them.

All this...and only then can I make it to the platform! He thought.

He bowed his head, raised his right heel, like a cheetah about to make the fastest sprint for his kill. He glanced on his

ABHISAR SHARMA

right and saw his window of opportunity. It was the ticket-swiping entrance booth that lay desolate. There was a red-light sign showing that it was out of order, hence no one was queuing up in front of the booth to enter the station. A ghost of a smile caressed his lips. He licked his upper lip that tasted salty.

The bloody omelette in the breakfast, he thought! And then...

He started running.

A little girl standing next to her mother glanced to her right to see Sameer running. His eyes met the little girl's. She smiled at him and he winked back at her, all the while in motion. Sameer knew that little children did get fascinated by his playfulness. They fascinated him too. He preferred spending time with the kids of the area, playing cricket with them, and Nasir, his only friend in the entire world.

Sameer kept running.

He ran, cutting across men standing haphazardly in a queue for the entrance booth. He swerved to his left, his eyes unwavering of the vacant ticket-swiping entrance booth bearing the 'Not Working' sign. As he swerved again, his brown fake Nike shoes made a squeaking sound and that is when the CISF guard saw him. Suddenly, there was a change in his expressions... From bored and deadpan to slightly more dramatic. His eyes widened in alarm. But Sameer was already near the entrance. The CISF guard glued his eyes on Sameer, anticipating his next move as he neared the booth. Sameer's eyes locked with the guard's. He smiled gently as if trying to disarm him. Then, as if in absolute slow motion, he turned his eyes towards the booth, his left hand rose in the air to grab the metallic board of the booth and he swung himself into the air. His left leg soared in the air followed by his right. In one swift motion, and with a loud slap on the ground, he was on the other side of the booth, his eyes scanning the stairs of the metro station. The CISF guard suddenly got active as his shout was followed by a shower of his saliva.

'Abe!'

But it was too late... Sameer had already reached the edge of the stairs and was running towards the platform like a man possessed. The CISF guard raised his rusty gun to intimidate him but realized suddenly that even an action of taking a shot may result in collateral damage, as men and women, collecting their valuables from the luggage scan machine, crowded in front of him. But he could not let the lad get away unchallenged. So, he pushed a man standing in front of him and he too ran after the errant queue-breaker. Sameer bit his lower lip as he charged up the stairs, eyes narrowed, sweating profusely, and it wasn't only because of the stairs. He knew that he was riding dangerously. At the back of his mind was the possibility that the CISF guard might actually start firing at him. He ran faster. Just for a split second, he looked back and his eyes widened in shock at the sight of the guard with the rifle clasped in his left hand catching up with him. Sameer looked up. He saw the last row of people pushing into the train.

There is no way I can make it!

His eyes also scanned the surroundings for a sight of Inara, but she was lost in that crowd. He ran and climbed faster, gasping for breath, but he did not care. He had to be in the train before the doors shut!

Bloody hell! The train doors are closing! Sameer thought as he sprang towards the train. He jumped like lightning and made it past the closing doors, nearly killing himself in the process. The CISF guard was standing panting at the platform, hurling the choicest of abuses at Sameer, inevitably addressing Sameer's mother and sister. The train started to move. The

guard ran towards the train, his eyes fixed on Sameer, who grinned and winked at him, finally being able to catch his breath. The expression on the CISF guard's face said it all— 'I will get you next time!'

Sameer exhaled heavily as he turned around and felt all eyes on him. He licked his upper lip again and gently tilted his head to his left. Embarrassed at the attention, he started to wade through the crowded bogie towards the ladies' compartment. People were still staring at him as if he was some criminal, a shadow of concern on their faces.

He said loudly, 'Sorry, I did not have money to buy a ticket. Anyone wants to help? I would love to be financed!'

They turned their faces away from him. He ignored their looks as his eyes scanned the crowd for Inara.

She must be in the ladies' compartment, I am sure.

He started to wade through the sea of people—men with obnoxious body odour, women holding cranky children, and those not lucky enough to get a seat, trying to doze off standing, holding to the leather strap tied to the overhead iron bar.

Will I find her? He panicked. *What if she alights at some station before I find her?* A sudden dread engulfed his heart. *I don't even know where she is!* But then he reasoned with himself. *All this scrambling like a madman and putting myself at peril can't be for nothing? I am sure. I am destined to find her...'*

As random thoughts crossed his restless mind, he pushed further, wondering all the time if he would find her in the ladies' compartment. *She has to be there.* He thought. *Why wouldn't she? She is precious and snooty! She would never want to stand in a general compartment with men ogling at her or brushing past her.* As his mind weighed these various possibilities, he made his way through the crowded compartment, careful not

11

to step over anyone's feet, especially the children who stood holding their parents' hands.

Then, suddenly he spotted her. His feet froze and the noise around him faded in to the background. He was shocked at his own reaction. He had heard of such a situation from hopeless romantics, had seen it in many cheesy Bollywood films, and even had Nasir read such scenes to him from Hindi novels. And now it was happening to him. Inara stood a few paces ahead with her back to him, the end of her thick plait caressing her waist. She held the overhead leather strap with her index and middle fingers and clasped an embroidered pink handkerchief between her little and ring fingers.

He stood there watching her from that distance as station after station came and went, oblivious to the pushing and shoving passengers around him. She would occasionally turn her head sideways, exposing the well-defined profile of her facial features, but never once did she become aware that she was being watched by Sameer. Suddenly, the announcer's voice boomed, penetrating his consciousness: 'Next station is Rajiv Chowk... Please change here for the...'

He saw Inara inch towards the sliding doors, away from him. She was still in the ladies' compartment and he was in the one next to hers. Sameer stepped forward towards her, then stepped back when he realized that he was just about to step into the ladies' compartment. He too, made his way towards the sliding doors of his compartment.

Sameer trailed Inara from a safe distance as she emerged from the underground station and walked briskly across the parking space towards the inner curve of shops lined up next to each other, befittingly called the inner circle of Connaught Place (CP) and officially known as Rajiv Chowk. It was Sunday, hence a lot of shops were shut, as a result of which the stretch

was relatively deserted. Sameer was waiting for just such an opportunity to approach her and talk to her without attracting any attention. He knew that if he spoke to her in a deserted place, she would not react dramatically. He was, after all, stalking her. His eyes skimmed the Wimpy's burger joint as Inara gathered pace. She was now exiting the inner circle to emerge at the outer circle.

As he walked out of the inner circle to face the main road, she was nowhere to be found. *Where the hell did she go?* Sameer was stunned. He stopped and started looking around. *Did she cross the road? How can she?* He countered his own thought. *Did she enter the subway? She might have!* Sameer started to walk towards the subway.

'Are you following me?'

Sameer was taken aback by that soft yet firm voice. He must have heard it so many times but this was the first time that she had addressed him directly.

She repeated the question, locking her intense gaze with his, 'I asked...are you following me?'

He could not recall the last time his heart had beaten so rapidly and so hard. He could feel the throb at the base of his throat and suddenly his mouth went dry. His tongue felt as if it was glued inside his mouth. It seemed as if some force within him had overpowered his senses which prevented him from responding. His mouth tasted of their unspoken conversation. He exhaled over and over again. That day, he finally knew what being tongue-tied meant. But what was shocking was the power she had over him at that moment.

She looked at him carefully, the expression in her eyes never giving away what she actually felt. She looked down, a trifle condescendingly, at his dirty brown fake Nike shoes, raking in, with a quick glance, the dusty faded black jeans, the

13

rugged brown belt and the carelessly tucked-in black-and-white checked shirt under a grimy brown jacket. She gently shook her head as she turned her gaze away from him, her eyes softening. She drew out a water bottle from her purse and handed it to Sameer whose cheeks were red with embarrassment by her once-over.

'Have it... I don't want you to faint here, in front of me.'

Sameer gulped the entire content of the bottle to the last drop and smacked his lips, uttering a feeble thanks under his breath.

'So?' She crossed her arms and as she did that, he caught a glimpse of her creamy and pristine cleavage. There was a sudden tingle in his mouth, like he was tasting strawberries. He felt a surge of blood rushing to his loins but he knew that if he harboured any amorous thoughts about her, she would know. So, he bowed his head, his gaze now on his own dirty shoes. He looked up again, this time with renewed confidence and said, 'I am sorry but I wasn't...stalking you,' he finished lamely.

'I think you were!' Her voice now had an edge to it. 'I have been watching you since we neared the station before CP.'

His eyes widened. *She knew all this time?* And then she gave words to his thoughts.

'I knew all this time. I thought it was just a coincidence. But then I also remembered that you and that wretched Nasir were sitting in front of the café and staring at me. I did not in my wildest dreams think that you would actually follow me.'

'As I said, I wasn't stalking you. I just wanted to speak to you. I just wanted to talk.'

'Why?' she asked, even though she knew the answer.

He haltingly breathed out the clutter of his uncomfortable

14

thoughts and said, 'I...uh...I like you...a lot. In fact, you fascinate me.' He drew more strength as he started to speak.

This time it was her turn to blush as her face turned an appealing shade of crimson.

'I have no answers. I just want you to know that I mean no harm. I am *not* stalking you.'

'Stop saying that over and over again!' Her voice was now barely a whisper.

'You know what? Your face radiates the noor of Khwaja Moinuddin Chishti's dargah.'

She raised her eyes and then started giggling.

'No...I mean it,' he continued, 'I would never take His name so lightly. You ooze his...'

'Shut up! Enough of this flattering!' She spoke in the same tone, still unable to muster up enough firmness in her voice to intimidate him. He had disarmed her but not with the compliment. She could sense that he meant every word of what he had said. She was disarmed by his honesty which, as compared to all the other boys who had approached her earlier, had stirred something hidden deep inside her. She was now getting conscious about her surroundings and was aware of the fact that her expressions may attract the attention of the people around them. She was disarmed and vulnerable, so she decided to change the direction of the conversation.

'Well, Sameer, do you know that you created quite an impression amongst the girls of our locality? I guess your exotic looks and enigmatic nature makes you quite the topic of discussion. A lot of girls fancy you.'

He knew what she meant by exotic. He smiled.

Sameer—Sameer Verma—the Hindu boy who lived in a predominantly Muslim neighbourhood ensconced in the Walled City of India's capital. His mother Prabha Bai had been

15

managing his father Sukesh Verma's fruit cart for the last five years. Sameer himself was employed since the past one year, earning his way through college studies. He was working with Atos Original as a call centre executive, drawing a neat ten grand.

No wonder Nasir had warned him. Some lines are not meant to be breached, especially not in the Walled City.

'I did not expect that you would follow me like this,' she exclaimed again, 'I would not have been surprised had it been Nasir or anyone of your other loafer friends, but you...?'

Oh! So, she has a favourable impression of me. Does she approve of me?

What Inara wasn't telling him was that she too was amongst those girls who were fascinated by him, though she could not define it, rather she did not want to define it. She was too proud to accept that she was attracted to him. Even though it was taboo for her to harbour any romantic notions about him, he was a secret fantasy not only for her but for some of her girlfriends too. A good-looking, tall and handsome boy, earning ten grand a month, looking after his family like a good, dutiful son... Wow! What else could a girl want?

And then, he spoke forcefully, breaking her reverie, 'I wasn't, I repeat, *I wasn't* following you! I just wanted to speak to you. But you just jumped on me.'

She started to giggle again, throwing her head back, cupping her mouth with a shapely hand, her fingers tapering to slightly grown but clean and unpainted nails.

'Okay. I have come here because I have a job interview as a copy editor in a travel magazine. You want to come along?'

Does she want me to be her bodyguard? Her pup? He frowned inwardly. The feeling wasn't exactly exhilarating.

But, on the other hand, I would get to spend more time

16

with her and maybe I might even get an opportunity to establish a link with her.

His mind was now working in many directions.

She is, after all, a girl from my mohalla. It is my duty to watch her back, so to say.

But not as a brother!

'Are you coming? I am getting late.'

'Yeah, sure!'

He started walking a few steps beside her to her destination, which was just a few minutes away. But those few minutes were the most wonderful minutes of his life. He felt people eyeing him and he could read the envy in their eyes.

They must be thinking that Inara is my girlfriend! He thought gleefully. He stole a sideways glance at her. Her eyes were fixed on the ground as she walked. Her lips wore a careless smile, but she seemed deep in thought. *Is she thinking of me? Of course she is! This is the high point of my life! Just imagine! Walking beside Inara, masquerading as her boyfriend! It couldn't get better than this!* People could read the high in his eyes and the haya in hers.

As they approached the office of Freebird Publications, she gestured to Sameer, without even looking at him, to wait outside and entered alone. He just stood there, not knowing what to do.

Will she take a lot of time?

What will I do here?

How can she leave me like that and go?

Am I her...?

Restless thoughts kept running in his mind as he paced up and down in front of the office. Thirty minutes passed. The security guard outside Freebird Publications looked at him with curiosity and a hint of amusement.

After a while, the security guard gestured him to stop pacing in front of the office. Sameer paid no heed until the guard raised his voice and called out, 'Aye!'

Sameer looked at him, taken aback by the curtness in his tone. The hint of belligerence in the guard's eyes said it all.

You are on my territory. I decide who moves around here. And I know why you are here.

Sameer felt a surge of embarrassment rise in his chest. What he felt about Inara was something between him and her. Now, this insignificant security guard too, had somehow intruded into that private space and had become privy to his feelings for her. Had Inara not been a part of the situation, the guard would have had absolutely no issues with Sameer standing there. But the guard had touched a raw nerve. Sameer understood that it was just a sadistic kick that the guard was getting out of playing the Khap at that moment.

The guard gestured again and said, 'Move on.'

'Why? What's your problem?'

'Don't stand here.'

Sameer raised his right index finger and pointed to the banner of Freebird Publications. 'I don't think it is written anywhere that I can't stand here?' he retorted.

'That does not matter!' The guard's voice rose aggressively, 'I decide who stands here and who does not! So, move on!'

Under normal circumstances, Sameer would have certainly come back with a befitting repartee, but he felt vulnerable due to the fact that his feelings for Inara lay bare before the guard. He could feel the heat rise within, but he felt weak at the same time. He wanted to teach the guard some manners, but he also knew that, for Inara's sake, he could not create a scene.

He glared at the guard and then lowered his eyes, knowing that he had conceded defeat. He started walking away from the office, each step heavier than the previous one. Random sounds of the weekend traffic, strains of a Bollywood number blaring from a music shop in the distance, the yelp of a stray dog kicked by one of the ragpickers and the subsequent guffaw... All these sounds assailed his ears as he sauntered through the lanes of Connaught Place. He did not know where he was headed to, but he wanted to get as far away from Freebird Publications as he could. He wanted to erase the feeling of helplessness that overwhelmed him. His jumping over the ticket counter at the metro station and endangering his own life, his following Inara all the way to CP and baring his feelings before her without even speaking a word, and then, being rebuked by the security guard... He had never behaved like this before, ever! The initial high of the adrenaline was now replaced by this ineffable, overpowering feeling of vulnerability that clawed at his chest.

❦

'You did not go to work, did you?' Her voice was barely a whisper. Her eyes were lined with wrinkles, her lips were parched, and her teeth were tinged with yellow. She wore a mud-coloured sari, a tattered black sweater, and covered her head with a black shawl that also enveloped her emaciated bosom. Strands of salt-and-pepper hair with traces of orange, thanks to henna, peeped out reluctantly from underneath the part of her shawl that covered her head. Prabha, Sameer's mother, had a thin, bony, almost skeletal, frame of barely five-feet two-inches. She was 48 years old but she looked no less than 60. Raising Sameer and looking after her bedridden paralytic husband for the past two decades had aged her before time. Every moment, every experience of her life could be seen seeping through the crevices of her wrinkles. But her eyes told a different story altogether. Expressive, intense, mystical and weary, they seemed to be hiding a dark secret, yet they exuded a silent stoicism which comforted Sameer to no end. He grew up under the shadow of that comfort and unexplained mystery. He had inherited his mother's eyes and fair complexion. Even though Prabha's skin tone had faded to a dull-brown-parchment paleness but it still lent a glimpse of its once-pristine translucence. However, a suntanned existence was now her reality as a fruit seller.

Sameer had just entered his two-room first-floor house and switched on his hazy coloured television set, when his mother came and placed her slender right hand on his shoulder. Without looking at her, he mumbled, 'I have a night shift from tomorrow.'

'But it's getting cold now. Will it be safe, beta?' she asked, a worried frown creasing her forehead.

'Oh, come on Ma! The office cab picks me up and drops me back too. Where's the risk? You just have to worry yourself, I guess! You just need an excuse to bother yourself,' his voice had an unapologetic curtness to it.

Prabha raised her right hand and started caressing his thick black hair and continued in the same tone, 'Why are you getting irritated? I just asked a simple question, didn't I?'

'Yeah, but do you have to ask me a question to which you already know the answer?'

Prabha smiled and patted her son's back, 'I think you are mad at something and hungry too. Let me get you some food. It's nearly lunchtime now.'

Sameer knew that his mother was right on both counts. He was simmering with anger but was at a loss to understand whom to focus it on: Inara, the security guard or himself.

20

But in his heart, he knew it was Inara. Only she was responsible for his troubled state of mind. Why did he ignore Nasir's advice and just run after her the way he did? Initially, he had cloaked his action by justifying it as bravado, but now he knew what it was sheer stupidity!

Ma could very well have been mourning over my lifeless body lying in the mortuary of Fatima Memorial Hospital near the metro station, had the CISF guard fired at me, thinking I was a terrorist.

He was lucky no one had hauled him up at the next station or the station after that. Sameer drew in a deep breath and exhaled heavily. He was still very restless. He got up and started pacing across the fifteen-by-fourteen room that was linked with the kitchen on one side and the toilet on the other.

The room was dark, barring the fleeting and rare sunlight filtering through a solitary precolonial design window, caressing the rough and unevenly cemented floor. In one corner of the room sat a TV set bought by Sameer's earnings from the Atos Original BPO company. A wooden table lay in the centre of the room and three chairs lay haphazardly around it. One corner of the room, diagonally opposite to the TV, housed arm-long idols of Shri Ram, the Hindu deity, along with his revered wife, Mata Sita, and the loyal Lord Hanuman. Burnt-out incense sticks lay scattered at the floor, by their clay feet. A mat was neatly placed next to the idols. Prabha would religiously pray every morning before she drowned in her daily chores that started with preparing food for her son and then walking half a mile to her fruit stall.

There was no grand plan for the future here. It was just the existence of two people. Yes, two. A garlanded photograph which hung under the window was that of a man with a near-skeletal face drawn in a tired and somewhat forced grin. Sukesh

Verma, Sameer's paralytic father, had died three months ago due to a fall from the stairs of their first-floor house. The garland of flowers around the framed photograph was fresh as Prabha changed it daily.

Sameer wanted to drown this unsettling feeling in sleep and it wasn't difficult for him to doze off at any part of the day, considering that he worked in a BPO centre. Since he had started working, sleep had become a luxury for him. He could hear the gentle jangle of utensils in the kitchen, the sound of a mass of dough being slammed on the kitchen slab, the rolling out of the dough under the belan, and the clank of the steel spoon in the vessel containing potato curry... The sounds and smells emanating from the kitchen had a lulling effect and his tired and bloodshot eyes began to droop with sleep. He reclined into a chair and rested his legs on the table.

Within a minute, Prabha heard the sound of feeble snoring coming from the adjacent room. She shook her head and smiled. She knew that now the food will only be consumed after Sameer woke up.

∽

'Smell the air, Sameer? I think it's going to rain,' Nasir said, taking in a long deep breath, his hand on Sameer's shoulder.

'Dhakkan, it's a clear sky, how will it rain?'

'Can't you smell it in the air?'

'I don't smell anything,' retorted Sameer.

'Ah, she has engulfed your senses, you can't smell anything but her,' teased Nasir.

Sameer raised his middle finger.

'Same to you, brother,' winked Nasir.

Nasir paused and then his expression suddenly turned

22

solemn. He looked towards the Jama Masjid to his left which was bathed in the pristine moonlight that late evening. Both Nasir and Sameer were standing on the terrace of Nasir's house. It was a fog-free, clear evening after weeks but there was still an edge, an uncertainty in the air. The market below was bustling with activity as shopkeepers and dhabawallah's aggressively pursued customers walking across the untarred, kuccha street.

'I think you are in love with Inara.'

'Don't even go there, Nasir.'

'But it's a fact, isn't it? That is why you are so restless! Look at what she has done to you even before she's even responded to your advances.'

Irritated, Sameer turned towards Nasir and said, 'What is it that you want? Do you want me to leave now? You are right, I am restless and that is why I came up here! I just wanted to...' Sameer's voice petered out and he looked away as he ran his fingers through his hair, tugging at a tuft of hair in the middle of his head. Nasir opened his mouth to say something but stopped himself. He knew that Sameer would start talking again on his own. He did not have to wait long.

'I have no clue why she makes me so restless. I have never felt like this before, and that episode in CP... That was like a rude eye-opener. The terrible feeling of being watched, of your feelings being exposed before someone hostile,' Sameer spoke, his tone denoting his inner turmoil.

'That is why I ask you to nip it in the bud. You are playing with fire, Sameer, and you know very well what I mean.'

'Are you jealous, Nasir? Do you also have a crush on her? Being a Muslim, do you think you have a better chance with her?' retorted Sameer.

'Do you even realize what you are saying and how you sound? Me hoping for a chance with Inara? She is the daughter

23

of Imtiaz Khan, the biggest trader in the community! Do you think she or her father would even acknowledge the existence of a nobody like me? You still have the looks and the charm, you know how to talk to people. I can't talk to anyone except you and Ammi and Abbu. This is my small little world.'

Sameer lowered his head and shut his eyes, gently cursing himself under his breath. He had no right to speak to Nasir like that. But he was helpless, bruised from struggling to disentangle himself from a web of his own making. He knew that Nasir was right. He was the Hindu boy living with his mother pat in the middle of a sensitive Muslim-dominated locality. He was the minority within the minority. Their lives had just started getting comfortable after he had started working with the multinational BPO. Earlier, theirs had been a life where it was a struggle to barely make a living, so much so that even making sense of it all was a big struggle. Getting through the day was a big struggle. Now, they were just about inching toward their comfort zone. Once he became more secure financially, he planned to move to more spacious quarters. So, the last thing he needed in his life was drama with an explosive twist!

❦

Meanwhile, the following night...

He ran, gasping for breath, every step now heavier than the previous one. His breathing was now turning erratic. The clean-shaven, slim-built man's mouth was half-open and a sluggish stream of saliva dripped from one end of his cracked lips. His steps fell on the ground as if in a drunken stupor. He had been running for the past one hour and he kept looking back

24

to see if he had indeed dodged *them*. As he ran, he would throw his head back intermittently, opening his mouth wide to suck in air, emitting distressed wheezing sounds along with some senseless babble. He was trying hard to focus on the streetlight-lit road ahead, which lay deserted, spare a few shivering footpath-dwellers gathered around the dying embers of a bonfire of trash, struggling to keep warm. He could barely make out the bend ahead in the road, his eyes streaked with red due to exhaustion. He started running faster but he knew that he was running out...of energy and options. At the bend, he momentarily shut his eyes and...

Crash!

The man slammed into an electricity pole, his nose crashing against the cold hard and unforgiving cylindrical structure. He fell back on the ground with a loud thud as a gush of blood spouted from his nose. He groaned in pain. He raised his right hand and touched the tip of his nose gingerly with his fingers. The sight of dark red blood still unnerved him, in spite of what he had done that evening. He tried getting up, but he could not. His strength was now ebbing away. He looked at the dark skies, his eyes shutting down slowly. He raised his right hand, still trying to gather strength to get up, but gave up soon. He lay still, panting, as his chest rose and fell heavily. Sounds of approaching footsteps caressed his mud-stained ears. He turned his head towards the sound. All he could see was hazy silhouettes of some men running towards him. He tried to get up again but he could not. In a few seconds, the three men had converged on him; all three men were wearing skullcaps. His vision of the sky was now blocked by the men looming over him. One of them bent down and asked him something, but it was inaudible to him, it sounded like echoes from a distance. And then, he shut his eyes. He had given up.

25

The next morning...

Nasir was right about the impending rain.

As the constable pushed the tailgate of the police truck with his right foot, he looked at the merciless skies that had been pouring down constantly for the past four hours. As he jumped from the edge of the truck, his gumboots landed on a slushy cocktail of dirt and mud, his black raincoat fluttered as the brazen wind struck his body like the hostile claws of the locality he had just landed in. A fresh battalion of jawans followed him as they too tentatively jumped from the truck, in rows of three, holding their rifles and their black raincoats. The battalion stood in haphazard rows as they deboarded the truck, and the constable who had alighted first, gestured to the driver to move on. They were about to join the four battalions that already stood on alert at the doorstep of the Jama Masjid. The entire stretch leading to the mosque was now occupied by cops in black raincoats and OB vans of TV news channels parked randomly in the narrow and muddied lane of the Walled City. The reporters sat inside their OB vans, as the relentless rain continued to interfere with the signals of the uplink to their studios.

A reporter spoke into his phone, 'Well, Namita, I can tell you that the situation is really tense here. From where I stand, I can see that hundreds of policemen are standing at the boundary of the Jama Masjid mosque waiting for orders from their superiors. Meanwhile, young and angry youth, presumably Muslims, are blocking their entrance and are sprawled across the stairs leading to the doorstep of the mosque. This morning, a group of four policemen had come here and had to beat a hasty retreat after they were threatened by violence from none other than Imran Khan, the maverick and short-tempered

26-year-old son of the Imam of the mosque, Zulfiqar Khan. I can see that he is not present there with the youth of the locality, but my sources tell me that he is inside with his father. I am also told that Imam Zulfiqar Khan is not happy with the turn of events and is finding a way out of the current impasse.'

Namita, the agitated news anchor from the TV studio asked, 'But how can Imran Khan interfere with police investigations yet again?'

'Namita, Imran Khan has had several infamous brushes with the police and the media in the past and every time he gets away purely because of the patronage he receives from the government at the centre and his father's position as the undisputed leader of the capital's Muslims as well as the greater part of northern India. No political party worth its salt would like to tread on this path or rather cross paths with Imran Khan. The confrontation that is unfolding behind me is because of the new Assistant Commissioner of Police, Yashwant Mohite. Instead of consulting with his political bosses, which police officers normally do in such situations, Mohite has actually decided to take the bull by its horns. It's an eyeball-for-an-eyeball kind of situation between Imran and Mohite and none of them seem to be in the mood to budge. Meanwhile, my sources tell me that Shivkant Singh, the Member of Parliament from the Walled City, is having regular consultations with the Police Commissioner of the Capital, Neeraj Asthana,' replied the reporter.

Suddenly, there was heightened activity as policemen started asking media personnel to move their vans ahead. The reporter could see that someone important was arriving. It was none other than the man of the moment—ACP Yashwant Mohite.

'Namita, I am afraid I will have to hang up now as ACP

27

Mohite has just arrived here for the first time and it seems that the confrontation is about to cross the threshold frequency,' said the reporter as he disconnected the call.

'For those of you who have just joined us, this is the culmination of the incident that took place in the Khan Market area of the capital yesterday, when a man shot a female Israeli diplomat at point-blank range. Susanna Sharon now lies in a critical condition at the All India Institute of Medical Sciences. Police have reason to believe that the assailant has taken refuge in the Jama Masjid mosque and some eyewitnesses are even saying that a group of men had carried away a man to the mosque late last night after he had reached here while being pursued by the police,' intoned news anchor Namita.

As Yashwant Mohite reached the footsteps leading to the mosque, his jaws tightened. Through his dark glasses he saw the surge of skullcaps lined across the stairs, thwarting any move by the policemen to enter the premises. He realized that the daggers were drawn. No one was ready to bite the bullet and make the first strike, but time was running out and so was Mohite's patience. He stepped out of his white Ambassador car and walked with pronounced intimidation towards the first line of defence.

'Sir, pardon me, but what is the plan? Are we entering the premises? And if we are, have we factored in the consequences? What are the seniors saying, sir?' The look of concern on the face of the middle-aged constable said it all. He wanted to be out of the action as soon as he could. He knew that Mohite had already gone too far by bringing the situation to the brink. No one would have dared to cross the Imam and his son, but Mohite was from a different mould. Raised in a conservative Marathi family, he had little patience for bullshit and the duality that existed in the lives of people from his profession. He had just been posted in the area after clearing the civil services exam a year ago; political correctness was certainly not one of his strengths. He was a rare breed of a man, the likes of whom were on the verge of extinction.

'Our seniors don't have the balls to face Imran Khan. His father carries them in his pocket like loose currency. They are looking for a way out and I will not give it to them by bowing before Khan. The man responsible for the attack on the Israeli diplomat is in the mosque. I have my reasons to believe it. Now it is just a question of who blinks first. I am just waiting for his men to raise the tempo. Aai shapath, I will not disappoint Imran Khan.'

Mohite's hard talk was unnerving for the constable who had not bargained for this situation. Mohite had crossed the laxman rekha. He had dared to step into a zone where police officials wouldn't dare to tread. Careers would be destroyed if anyone dared to antagonize the Imam. Politics of this area centred around him. Parties with national ambitions and with a presence in Uttar Pradesh would not dare to annoy the crafty Zulfiqar Khan. His political acumen was legendary and he swore by the art of the realpolitik. The fact that he was also a religious leader was an added bonus, like the extra sheen to a sword's edge.

The athletically built, five-feet-nine-inch tall and clean-shaven Yashwant Mohite was now standing in front of the first line of defence that had the burliest men defying the police. A shadow of nervousness crossed their faces. They knew Mohite would not hesitate to push the envelope. They could sense the impatience in his eyes. Suddenly, a wave of restlessness rose among them, starting from the first row and drowning down to the last. There was a sudden edginess in the gathering as if someone had dropped a big rock on the surface of perfectly

29

still water. Mohite's sharp jawline tightened as he tilted his head a bit to his left.

'Imran Khan should be ashamed of himself, hiding behind these brainwashed men! Is this the reality of the man I have heard so much about?' Mohite provoked.

A man with a shaggy beard retorted, 'We will not tolerate a word against Khan sahib.'

CRACK!

The echo was sharp, like the hard snap of a whiplash. Mohite's response to the retort by the Muslim youth was instantaneous. The back of his right hand swung in an arc of 45 degrees and landed straight at the lower jaw of the guy. He crashed back, to the shock of the people around him. Mohite had just raised the bar. He crossed his arms and a smile played on his battle-scarred face. A wave of shock passed around him. The hearts of the policemen started to beat fast. They knew that now the dice had been rolled to a point of no return. Nervous and curious faces watched the scene unfolding at the edge of the Jama Masjid from their terraces and the Mughal-style windows of the crumbling houses all around.

'See! I have just shown you that I have zero tolerance for bullshit! I will not be intimidated by scumbags like you or that Mafioso.'

Suddenly, there was a roar among the mob facing Mohite. The Prince had just arrived. There was a cleft in the crowd as the gathering parted bang in the middle and Imran Khan walked down the steps of the mosque with a man holding a black umbrella behind him. Mohite raised his head to size up his adversary. Imran Khan gingerly placed his feet on the slippery steps of the mosque, while the men around him formed a human chain to protect him as he made his way down to the edge, the spot where Mohite stood. The 26-year-old slim

Pathan, peaking at six-feet three-inches, had a neat French-cut beard with a light brown tinge. He wore a woollen hard-shell Islamic kufi, a red skullcap embroidered on the edges with white. Dressed in a traditional Pathani suit, the beige buck-string trouser and kameez and a black woollen jacket, his swagger did not reveal the slightest of panic that he might have felt at the back of his mind. The raised eyebrows that symbolized his arrogance were now a permanent feature of his face. A man with a fair and radiant complexion, his intense brown eyes added to his aura. The flock of young men suddenly grew restless and even brazen, the boldness emanating from the arrival of the leader, the Prince—Imran bhai, as he was commonly addressed—the man who would be King someday.

Mohite could read the eyes of the agitated pack. They were fidgety, their anger waiting to be unleashed. The initial tentativeness had now vanished completely. They were now in the mood to fight. The confrontation now seemed inevitable.

Imran was standing just an arm's length away from Mohite as he spoke firmly in a deep but taunting voice, 'Must be quite a burden on your soul! You must, I presume, be spending many sleepless nights. After all, unleashing your borrowed sarkari power on innocent men and women can hardly give a high to a real man, a man worth his salt!'

Mohite was quite the contrast to Khan. He did not possess his striking personality. His voice could never inspire a gathering, but he was a fighter. His slightly guttural voice was no match to Khan's baritone, but it was firm and had a rebellious edge to it, 'My power may be sarkari, as you say, but I have worked my way up here. At least it is not inherited shamelessly from my father.'

'How dare you speak to Imran bhai like that?' roared a man standing to the left of Imran.

31

'Shut the fuck up! Don't you see I am having a conversation with your bhai?' Mohite turned his face back to Khan and said, 'I have just given a taste of my medicine to one of your men. It would be advisable if they avoid speaking out of line or not at all, unless asked. I am not here for some personal mission. I am just doing my job and I will not hesitate to use my sarkari power, if I have to.'

'If any one of my men dies, this entire locality will burn. If half a dozen of my men die, this city will burn. But,' he paused, looked around and then went on, 'if a dozen of my men die, your country will burn.' Imran's retort was the warning that Commissioner Neeraj Asthana was talking about. If Mohite had taken permission from him before making the charge, Asthana would never have let him go. But Mohite knew about the politics at play here. He knew that if he had any chance of nabbing the attacker, it could only happen if he laid a siege of the mosque. But there were certain lines even he could not cross. In this case, it was entering the historical Jama Masjid without permission from the higher-ups and of course, the man of the moment, Imam sahab, Zulfiqar Khan.

'This brazenness that you are desperately trying to fake in front of your brainwashed men, betrays the fear that lurks in your heart. I am sure you know what it means to be responsible for the death of those dozens.'

For the first time since his face-off with Khan, a smile caressed Mohite's face. He knew that it was to hide the nervousness that was creeping steadily up his chest.

'So bring it on, ACP Mohite,' Imran Khan now pointed his index finger to the dome of the mosque, 'I dare you to make the first move, but I can promise you that we will not let you step on the stairs leading to this mosque, even if it requires us to wash the stairs with the blood of every pious individual standing here, ready to take on your firepower.'

A constable holding a black umbrella started running from the Ambassador car that Mohite had arrived in. He held a cell phone in his right hand as he carefully manoeuvred his way through the horde of nervous men in uniform about to take charge.

'Saab! It's Asthana saab on the line... He wants to speak to you, now!'

A flash of irritation and disdain crossed Mohite's face, but he turned his back to Imran Khan and started walking towards his Ambassador car, grabbing the phone in his right hand.

Police Commissioner Neeraj Asthana bellowed from the other end, 'Do you want the city to burn, Mohite? That too because of some misplaced enthusiasm of yours? For some cheap bravado that you wish to parade in front of the goddamn press? What do you want?'

'Sir, I'm just doing my job.'

'Fuck it, Mohite! Leave the job to me! You have neither the experience nor the maturity to handle such a situation. You should have taken me into confidence before making this move.'

Mohite's ears had turned beetroot-red. He was breathing heavily, unable to speak a word.

'You will not step inside the mosque. We have already got in touch with Imam saab and we shall sort it out in an hour or so. Ask your men to move back a few steps, rather push them at least 50 yards away from Imran Khan's men. Is that clear, Mohite?'

'Clear as crystal, sir!'

'There will be no further confusion in this matter. Not anymore! Not one bit! Ask your men to back down! No confrontation! None at all! Am I clear?'

'Yes sir!'

33

THE KAAFIR'S LOVE

In a far recess, hidden behind the prayer room of the mosque, where all the volatile action outside seemed like a distant echo, like a faded memory, the man in question sat before the TV, watching a minute-by-minute update of the crisis at his door. Imam Zulfiqar Khan, aged 66 years, held his khandani hukkah, which had been in his family for nearly five generations, in his right hand, his upper lip lazily resting on the mouth of the hukkah's inhaler. His thick mane of white hair, back combed, extended up to his shoulders. He was wearing his reading glasses that were perched at the edge of his sharp beaklike nose; his intense brown eyes, flecked with grey due to cataract, were focused on the hukkah's tube. Long faced, his fair skin, though shrivelled, still had a glow to it. He firmly clasped the remote with the long slender fingers of his wrinkled left hand. Observing his hands, anybody would say that Imam sahab had the fingers of an artist. His perfect white beard had just been polished with olive oil and it rested majestically on his chest. Kept warm by the heater at his feet, he wore a cream-coloured sherwani with light brown embroidery criss-crossing at the chest. Imam sahab was a tall man, peaking at nearly six-feet-two-inches. However, old age had shrivelled him up by an inch or two.

Without looking at the help standing in attention at the door, he said, barely raising his voice, 'Haroon, I want Imran in this room in exactly five minutes.' Haroon understood that that voice meant business and he quickly scampered away, hurrying through the long hallway towards the exit of the mosque, crossing the prayer room. It was clear where Imran inherited his deep baritone from. However, he still lacked the finesse and control possessed by the old man. Imam sahab reached for his cell phone and looked at the previously dialled number which read—MP Shivkant sahab.

ABHISAR SHARMA

'Singh sahab, you have yet again asked me to shoulder a responsibility that is too heavy for my frail shoulders to bear... The burden to maintain tranquillity, to maintain aman—peace.' A ghost of a smile played on his frail lips as he pressed the red button on his remote.

The man on the other end, Shivkant Singh, a two-time Member of Parliament from the Walled City squirmed and let out a sycophantic cackle, 'Even in the Shivpuran, it was Lord Shiv who had to swallow the poison. How else would the devtas drink the amrita, the nectar of life?'

'You can't beat me in religion, Shivkant ji. I know that ultimately the devtas drank the nectar, but have you forgotten the two asuras: Rahu and Ketu? They too drank the nectar of life and became immortal. Don't—and I say don't—send such asuras to my doorstep,' his voice now had an edge to it, 'that I get tempted to slay them and chop off their heads.'

As he spoke on the phone, an agitated Imran entered the room, shaking off drops of the merciless rain from his face and black jacket. His eyes were streaked with red veins. The Imam gestured to Imran to shut the door as he continued to murmur into the phone, letting out an occasional gentle laugh. As he disconnected the call, he kept staring at the blank screen of his LCD and then without looking at his son, said with finality, 'I want that man in front of me...now.'

'What do you plan to do with him, Abbu?'

The Imam turned his gaze upon his son. The look was as comforting as it was intimidating. He knew very well what it meant.

I know what to do. I don't like it when you ask such questions because it seems that you are questioning my authority and with it, my wisdom.

The Imam spoke firmly, 'I plan to do just what you should

THE KAAFIR'S LOVE

have done a few hours ago instead of sheltering him in the mosque. In fact, I feel that it is best for this man, something that would set him free.'

In a few minutes, they brought the fugitive to Zulfiqar Khan. His face had blue-black bruises from the previous day. His bleary eyes were swollen from crying all night, though they weren't tears of repentance. Fear, maybe, but not repentance. Fear of realizing that he had committed an act in a moment of passion and now his family will have to pay the price for his actions for the rest of their lives. Shooting someone point-blank, that too when the victim is looking straight into your eyes, isn't easy. The look in those eyes haunts you forever. Just before and immediately after he had pressed the trigger, he had felt intense hatred for the Jewish diplomat he had never even met before. He did what he did out of a general sense of hatred. But now it was all over, the hatred had disappeared. He tried hard to latch on to it, but he could not. His mind was like a landmine, booby-trapped by remorse, fear and guilt. He sat in front of the Imam and immediately buried his face in the Imam's lap and started crying uncontrollably.

The Imam caressed his unkempt and dusty, cobweb-smeared hair, his eyes unwavering of the crumpled man before him. He kept mumbling something under his breath; it was an aayat of the Quran to comfort the nerves of the man.

'Do you have any family?'

The nameless man raised his head, nodding in the affirmative, his eyes red, and tears streaking down his cheeks. Muck and watery fluid oozed from his nostrils. He mumbled, 'I have two daughters,' as his chapped lips struggled to hold the words together.

'Are you afraid?' The Imam's voice was firm, but tinged with a hint of compassion.

He knew he could not lie, not in front of the Imam.

'Are you a true Muslim?'

'Ye…sss….every bit of my exis…tence…' he spoke haltingly, but with greater confidence.

'Do you know what the Quran says about attacking women? Do you think you did a noble thing by attacking her? Of course you did not! But I don't see any contradiction in your belief that you are a true Muslim and your action.'

The man kept looking at the Imam's face and then again drowned his face in his lap. His shoulders started to shake as he said, 'Help me, Imam sahab, please help me out. Help me find…a way out of all…this.'

The Imam raised his face and cupped it in his wrinkled yet comforting hands, 'Do you promise me that you will follow my advice?'

'Every bit of it,' the man spoke with a note of finality in his voice. For the first time, he had seemed to find his voice and his confidence back.

The Imam withdrew his hands from the man's face and leaned back on his cushioned chair. He raised his right hand, his index finger pointing to an exit of the room that led up to a staircase.

'Just follow that path and you shall be free. It is an exit from this mosque.'

The man's eyes followed the direction to which the Imam's finger pointed. His expression turned solemn. He wiped his tears and muck with the sleeve of his right hand and stood up.

'Is this a safe passage?'

The Imam nodded as his son stared at him in shock. Imran was flabbergasted. He knew where the exit led. He had no clue what his Abbu was up to. His eyes moved back to the man who started wobbling towards the stairs.

37

It was a narrow staircase that coiled upwards. The man looked up. The stairs seemed to stretch up to eternity. As he placed his first step on the treacherous rung, it wobbled a bit. His heart shook and a lump suffocated his throat. He began to place one step after the other gingerly. The Imam kept staring at him as he disappeared in a few seconds, the echo of his steps fading gradually.

'I have never questioned your wisdom, Abbu, but what is this freedom that you have promised that man? What is running through your mind? You could have let him escape through a hundred secret passages out of this mosque that lead to the city, beyond the siege.'

Zulfiqar, angry at being rudely questioned by his son, raised his voice a pitch higher, his tone bordering on the condescending, 'And then? Then what? What next, Imran?'

Imran looked at him with a film of anger in his eyes. He was not convinced.

Meanwhile, the man climbing up the stairs started panting a little. Now and then, he would stop to look down. The climb seemed unending. He raised his neck up, espying the hint of light ahead. It was dark, but the wall supporting the stairs had small bulbs which emitted a dim light. As he climbed further, he felt a sudden whiff of air strike his face. The end was nearing. He could soon feel the caress of fresh air on his face. His heart felt comforted. But nothing could prepare him for what he was about to see in the next few steps...

The cold winter breeze struck his frail frame like an electric shock. He clasped his weak and emaciated body with his mud-stained fingers. He shivered as he emerged, his eyes scanning the view in front of him... Majestic, but cruel. It was the highest point of the minaret as well as of the Jama Masjid. He held on to the ancient cemented bars that supported the

ABHISAR SHARMA

dome of the minaret and looked around. It was the most beautiful view he had ever seen in his life, which started moving rapidly in front of his eyes. To his left was the entrance to the mosque where he could see policemen squatting in droves. He could also see the youth with their skullcaps spread across the stairs, guarding the mosque. Beyond them, were countless media OB vans parked haphazardly with reporters barking continuously into the cameras at various nooks and crevices of the area. Curious onlookers stood at the rooftops of their houses, anticipating the next move of the police and the men defying them. The man smiled. Words from the wise old man came back to him.

Just follow that path and you shall be free...

He clasped the bars supporting the dome tightly as he gently shut his eyes. He was now at peace. He raised his head and then opened his eyes for his Maker, a gentle smile caressing his chapped lips. He moved ahead, stepping on to the edge of the minaret.

Suddenly, one the constables looked up and his eyes widened in alarm at the sight of a man stepping on to the edge of a minaret of the mosque. However, his look of alarm quickly changed into horror as the man took the next step, or rather, took a leap of faith—thus, ending the siege. This was the Imam's master stroke... A confrontation was averted and a martyr was born.

An hour later...

Curious onlookers now crowded around the body as the police drew a long perimeter around the site of impact, which was outside the mosque, as the minaret was at one edge of the mosque. The siege was over. People gaped in horror at the

sight. Never in the history of the mosque had they witnessed such a horrific incident. Sameer and Nasir pushed and shoved their way through the crowd to reach the edge of the perimeter. Their eyes reflected the horror and disbelief that engulfed the Walled City. At one point of the crowd, that was being regularly pushed back by a handful of khaki-clad policemen, were the womenfolk and among them stood the fear-stricken Inara. Sameer could spot her even in the mayhem that overwhelmed the swell of people gathered there. Her eyes were fixed on the shattered body of the man. He was covered with a shroud but even the white shroud could not conceal the red blood oozing from every crevice of his corpse.

Even in this moment of turmoil, Sameer could not help staring at Inara, who looked stunning despite the melancholy stalking her face. The intensity in her eyes was unnerving as was the shadow of fear in them. Her vulnerability was so enchanting to Sameer that he wondered how the past two encounters with her could have been in such unsettling circumstances. He wondered if that was a sign. Nasir looked at him, followed his gaze, and smiled. Sameer stared unwaveringly at Inara, hoping she would look his way. His prayers were finally answered. She looked at him and caught him staring at her. Her gaze rested on his face for a few moments before she looked away, but she turned back and gazed into his eyes again. Sameer could read her expressions. If she could have spoken to him, she would have said, 'How unabashedly you stare at me? Have some fear of the Almighty, or the Angels of Hell will notice your inappropriate behaviour as they descend on Earth and turn Heaven into Hell.'

Another hour later...

That evening, Zulfiqar Khan elucidated to his son the biggest question in the latter's mind—why?

Gently stroking his silken beard, he said, 'I could have let him escape if I wanted to and he could have squeezed a few more days out of his life, but what after that? The police would have caught him, eventually, come what may! Then? Then what? They would have made him sing and he would have named his sponsors. He just had two choices: Lead a disgraceful life in prison or die like a rabid dog by a bullet in his head. Either way, his soul would rot. Why did I do what I did, you ask! I accorded him the dignity he deserved. I gave him a third option. You have to understand that what he did was napak! It was haram! Attacking an unarmed woman? Even if she was a Jew! His intentions were driven by passion, a passion for his belief, the same belief that has enmeshed the Islamic world...the Ummah, the belief of community bound together by religion! You will see in a few days that the investigation will reach a dead end with his death. I will see to it that his family never suffers. I will see to it that his daughters are accorded admissions in educational institutions run by our missions just like so many other destitute and yateem children. See, I am a man of my word. Look at that Hindu boy, Sameer. He came from a penniless family but I took care of his education. He went to one of our English-medium schools, and you can see the results. He works in a multinational firm and speaks flawless English. All because of your Abbu whom you should learn to trust!'

⌣

Zubeida

Inara had never felt like this before. Her mind kept going back to the sight of blood seeping through the shroud...and Sameer's eyes boring into her. She could not sleep the previous night and the siege had kept her awake during the day. Her mind went back again to Sameer.

Doesn't he have any shame? How could he still stare at me, knowing what was unfolding in front of our eyes? Shameless and rude! Yes, rude! When I had asked him to wait outside Freebird Publications, he just vanished and now staring at me in front of everyone! How could he? He is such a weirdo! That's what he is! Yeah! A weirdo!

Inara could not understand what was troubling her more—the dead man lying spreadeagled at the edge of the mosque or Sameer's insolent behaviour. What was it about Sameer that made her so anxious? Maybe she was expecting him to be waiting for her at the door of Freebird Publications after she had finished her interview... Maybe. She needed answers for his behaviour. A sudden thought crossed her mind but she was too proud to even tread on that path.

Did he abandon me?

Inara dismissed the thought as soon as it came to her mind but she could not completely scrape off the feeling.

No boy would ever do that to me!

Zubeida, Inara's best friend, could sense her discomfort. The two were sitting, cross-legged, on Inara's bed in her room, covered by a quilt. Pushing her round-rimmed spectacles that rested at the edge of her nose, Zubeida poked Inara with her index finger, 'I have never seen you so restless, that too for a guy!'

With a hint of irritation in her sleepy eyes, Inara reached

out and clasped Zubeida's hand. She rested her head on her shoulders.

'Awww, you are indeed a mess, aren't you?' teased Zubeida.

'Shut up!' Inara mumbled, her voice barely a whisper.

'Even your hands are shaking...'

'It's because of the cold Zubeida, you imbecile!'

'But you love the cold, don't you? The ice maiden is finally melting, isn't she?'

Inara dug her fingernails into Zubeida's soft and warm hands, which elicited a feeble yelp from the latter.

'Why do you even need to lie, Inara? You have never been the one to be afraid to speak your mind?'

Inara's eyes suddenly turned intense as her gaze paused at the sight of the crimson sun, her head still resting on Zubeida's shoulder.

'Because he is forbidden, isn't he?' she said softly.

'Allah, so you are attracted to him, aren't you? The ice maiden has finally met her match!'

'No, it's nothing like that...'

'Yes, it is! You are attracted to him! You are...are, are, are, are!'

'I am not, not, not, not!'

'My, my, you are like totally attracted to him! You want to kiss him, you want to make love to him, you want to have a thousand of his babies!' Zubeida giggled uncontrollably, still trying hard to control the pitch of her voice. She knew that Inara's parents were in the next room.

Inara pursed her lower lip under her teeth as the shadow of fondness flashed across her face.

'Zubeida,' she paused before continuing, 'Have you ever...?'

'What? No! Never! I have never...'

Inara raised her head from Zubeida's shoulder, her eyes

locked into hers and asked, 'What do you think I am asking?' Her gaze held a lingering mischief.

'Whatever it is that you had in mind!' Zubeida retorted, barely able to conceal the discomfiture at broaching a discussion on the 'S' word.

'Shut up! Even I know that you have never had sex! I am just asking, have you ever kissed a guy?'

'No, never!' Zubeida's tone had a tinge of protest.

Inara exhaled and said, 'I wonder...'

'Wonder what?' asked Zubeida.

'I wonder how it feels when they do that tongue thing, you know, the French kiss,' Inara's voice, now barely a whisper.

'It's so unhygienic! Most guys don't even brush their teeth properly! The guys in my class are ideal case studies for Zafar uncle's dental clinic,' Zubeida giggled.

'Well, he didn't...' Inara left the last word hanging, realizing that she was probably pushing the envelope way too far.

'You kissed him, Inara?' Zubeida's eyes were open wide now, enmeshed with a childlike curiosity.

'I did not! I just walked next to him for a few minutes... and you know I wouldn't hide it from you. It's just that I was wondering how it really feels. His lips were so...pink.'

'Yes! I have noticed that,' Zubeida said.

Inara locked her eyes again with Zubeida's. She kept looking at her intently for a few moments after which her gaze dropped down to her lips. She kept looking at her mouth, defined by the pout of the lower lip. Suddenly, an awkwardness crept up Zubeida's bosom as she noticed where Inara was staring. She licked her upper lip and then the lower one, puckering them under her teeth.

'I was just wondering...' Inara's whispered tremulously, 'if you would...you know...you would like to...try...'

'Try what?' Zubeida could feel the warm and moist grip of Inara's hands tighten around her arm. She could feel her ears turning beetroot-red.

'Just...' Inara's gaze was now fixed pointedly on Zubeida's lips and her breath was slowly caressing Zubeida's.

Zubeida swiftly looked behind her, fearing someone might just walk in. Sensing her discomfiture, Inara too looked back at the slightly ajar door. She pressed Zubeida's hands tighter and got up, placing her right foot on the cold floor. She walked gingerly, her arms crossed, as she felt a shiver run up her body, her heart throbbing rebelliously. She locked the door and looked back at Zubeida who seemed stupefied, with the hint of guilt on her face for a crime she had not yet committed. Inara curled up inside the quilt, her gaze never leaving Zubeida's eyes.

'I am just...I don't think...I mean...I just want to know how it feels. I am sure you must be curious as well.'

Zubeida's breath was erratic and her chest heaved with each one. Her mouth opened slightly of its own accord. Inara moved quickly ahead, her eyes at Zubeida's lips that were trembling. It seemed her entire body was throbbing with a rhythm that was defined by the subtle panic engulfing her heart.

Zubeida squeaked, 'Are you sure...?' Inara nodded. She shut her eyes, her mind already anticipating the sensations she would experience with the impending kiss.

Inara was now provocatively close to Zubeida's lips. She gently nudged Zubeida's lower lip with the tip of her nose and then gradually moved sideways, encircling the edge of her lower lip, moving up, towards her cheek. Zubeida had closed her eyes too and was now breathing rhythmically as she felt Inara's moist lower lip around her chin slowly moving up. As Inara moved further up, the rim of Zubeida's glasses poked her. Inara smiled sheepishly but before she could do anything, Zubeida removed her glasses and kept them on the side table. Inara started running her lips across Zubeida's cheeks, tasting her. Zubeida moaned feebly, her heart racing so fast that she thought it would explode. She turned her lips towards Inara's and their lips touched for the first time. Their lips intertwined with each other and they relished each other's taste with desire. Inara dipped her tongue inside Zubeida's mouth and she responded with yet another moan. Zubeida entwined her tongue with Inara's who raised her hands and cupped Zubeida's face. She started nibbling Zubeida's lips before Zubeida's tongue entered her mouth again, this time probing deeper. The pleasant sensations that had engulfed Zubeida's chest now travelled down, across her stomach to her navel. It lingered there for a while, teasing her, and then travelled down further. Another moan escaped her mouth— this time louder—as she felt a mild tremor between her thighs. The feeling was exhilarating; it was novel and unfathomable. Their embrace had become suffocatingly passionate as their lips relished and discovered each scent and flavour of the other's mouths... Two nymphs were locked in lyrical harmony.

The craving was intense but both had their own different reason. While Zubeida was locked in this embrace with Inara and revelling in the feeling, her partner had someone else on her mind. As she explored every nook and crevice of Zubeida's mouth, flashes of Sameer's smile kept jabbing at her heart.

And then Zubeida pushed it further. She withdrew her mouth from Inara and whispered, 'Touch me down there.'

'What?' Inara looked at Zubeida, shocked. She was panting heavily, barely able to catch her breath.

'Touch me there,' Zubeida repeated. She held Inara's right hand and drew it between her legs, but Inara snatched her hand back, 'No! Why? I just wanted to know how it felt to kiss!'

46

Zubeida lowered her eyes, mortified. Her breath caught in her chest, the hint of a tear in her left eye.

'I just thought... I thought you would feel good and would want to,' Zubeida's eyes welled up. Tears hovered over the threshold of her lashes, threatening to spill over.

Inara was high on adrenaline and felt as if she had been on a perilous adventure. But as soon as Zubeida asked her to touch her, she felt numb and confused. Even though the taste of Zubeida's lips still lingered on hers, it was only Sameer who felt closer to her than ever before. She looked back at Zubeida, who was staring down at her own hands, and said firmly, 'This is the first and last time. I am not selfish. So, I will not leave you high and dry. You are my best friend. But remember, this is just an experiment, nothing more. Okay?'

Zubeida nodded, her head still lowered.

Inara looked at the door, checking to ensure if it was indeed locked properly. She then turned her eyes back on Zubeida who finally raised her eyes and they locked into each other's arms again.

Midnight, at the ACP'S residence

The dead calm of the night was broken with gentle sounds of rhythmic moaning. Yashwant Mohite was in bed. Pinned under him was a high-class prostitute with credentials of charging 25,000 rupees an hour. As he approached the last few thrusts of the act—his face contorted and flushed red, his forehead dripping with sweat, his hands clawing her waist, much to her physical discomfort—flashes of Imran's face kept stabbing his memory. Every time he pictured Khan's face, dripping with sarcasm, he plunged harder into the woman below him who moaned in pain, asking him to slow down, but Mohite kept hitting her harder, like powerful waves on a rocky shore.

'Please, be gentle...aaaannnnhhh...slow down! You are hurting me...aaaannnn,' she begged. But her begging only provoked him further. 'Slow down...Yash...'

And then, just like the strike of a thousand-volt electric current, like the power of a controlled explosion within a small perimeter, he burst inside her. He heaved and gasped, unable to control his breath, saliva dripping from the arc of his contorted mouth. His eyes were bloodshot with red veins standing out and his breath burned with the hot air he exhaled, like the flow of lava up a narrow shaft.

He pushed the tall, dusky, naked and voluptuous woman away as she looked at him with hurt in her kohl-lined dark eyes. He lay on the bed, chest down, his back rising up and down like waves in a turbulent sea. She caressed his warm back with her slender and long-nailed fingers and curled next to him, scared to snuggle up to him, but trying to approach him nevertheless. She felt like she was at the mouth of a volcano that could explode any moment now, but she was ready to take her chances. Then, he mumbled something, barely audible, his mouth buried in the white sheets of his rumpled bed.

'This is how they fuck the morale of a man who is just doing his job! This is how they kill us from within. And all for that fucking Pakistani [although he was a Muslim], that bastard! Bloody cowards!'

Drawing strength from his words and his reluctant effort to strike a conversation, she drew closer to him and said, 'You can tell me, Yash. I am there for you.'

'Shut the fuck up! You are not my lover. You are just a who...'

And then, without warning, Imran's face with his sarcastic smile and raised eyebrow flashed through Mohite's mind again.

Mohite turned around and jerked himself up. His chest

48

was heaving animatedly as he started to move back and forth, gritting his teeth. The painful memory of his fall from grace kept clawing at his heart. But he should have known. He did push the envelope. He dared to tread where his seniors would not. He should have known that pride was a small price to pay for what he had done.

Mohite was a different kettle of fish. There was no space for pretence and shallowness in his scheme of things. In his eyes, the Khans were guilty of sheltering a terrorist and they should have been tried under the law. The only solace was that he was the new hero for the Internet Hindus on various social media platforms and for the middle-class Indians who watched television. The authorities could not touch him for fear of media glare because touching him would raise a furore across the country and the right wing Sanskari Party would leave no stone unturned to embarrass the beleaguered Secular Party government at the centre.

That day Mohite made himself a promise and his witness was his favourite high-class prostitute whom he had been fucking since his posting in the Walled City:

I know I can't win as long as I play by the rules and as long as you cross your lines and violate my territory, but I shall wait. And that's a promise, Imran Khan! I shall wait for that moment when I can rub your nose on the ground in front of the Jama Masjid, in that muck-filled lane infested by insects of your kind. Aai shapath! I shall wait for that day when I shame you; when you will have tears in your eyes and your life will be at my mercy. I don't care what price I have to pay for it. I don't care if I have to make a deal with the Devil himself! I promise you that.

The next day...

Yesterday was the weirdest day of my life.

As Inara walked towards the metro station, her mind was reluctantly drawn towards the unorthodox fifteen minutes she had spent with Zubeida last night. She could still taste Zubeida's lips and smell that awful odour of her vagina. It made her cringe. She had always shared a friendly bond with Zubeida but this bizarre turn that their relationship had taken, unnerved her. She believed it to be a one-off instance, but what worried her was the fact that maybe Zubeida didn't think so. It was too much drama for her to handle in a single day. And if there was a person who was responsible for all of this, it was the man who was sitting outside the Internet café at the bend of the road she was about to take.

As Inara turned the bend, she nearly collided with a man on a cycle carrying empty chicken cages. Instinctively, she cursed the clumsy man who did not even bother to look back and with the same rage on her face, she locked her gaze with her tormentor. That was the first time Sameer had seen anger on her face. At first, Inara turned away from him, the irritation writ large upon her winter-scarred face. Her jaws tightened and her nostrils flared slightly as she tilted her head sideways. Then, her eyes locked back with the subject once more. There was something unnerving about that look on her face and Sameer knew why. He could sense that she wasn't happy with him leaving her like the way he did that day!

She thinks I abandoned her!

For Inara, it was beyond that now and more. He had changed things for her, forever. Though *forever* was indeed a strong word for her, but not at that moment. This was the most compelling reaction she had ever had towards any individual

50

in her life. For the first time, there was someone who had made an indelible impact on her, someone who had ruffled her composure. Even though she was too proud to accept it, she could sense some feelings take shape for the Hindu boy. Adding to her predicament was the realization that her feeling bordered on lust at the moment! And the problem with lust was that it was always downhill after the big burst, the colossal moment. It was easy for her to ignore him forever, but she couldn't understand why he bothered her so. She had to sort him out before she could move on.

She thought of him as an irritant, but she was wrong. She should have just walked on and ignored him. But the forbidden inevitably draws you in, it entices you, conspires against you and then lunges at you. Inara should have seen it coming.

She walked a few steps past Sameer and Nasir, when she suddenly paused. The heel of her left foot raised and she turned back with her head down. She was walking straight towards Sameer; his heart started to pound.

She is coming straight at me! God! What is she going to do?

Nasir's eyes now started to oscillate between the two. Inara and Sameer... Sameer and Inara... Inara and Sameer... Sameer and Inara...

She looks pissed! But why?

He was going to discover the answer to the question in just a moment.

'Could I have a word with you?' It wasn't a request, it was a bloody order, rudely disguised as one! Her eyes, narrowed down on her subject, and her face, slightly tilted upward, indicated an innate hauteur. God help him had he been busy or had answered in the negative! He tried to swallow the sudden discomfort in his throat, but could not.

I will have to though, if I want to respond coolly.

His heart was now thumping with the ferocity of a thousand beats and he could feel it right up his throat. His tongue seemed glued to the base of his mouth.

'Are you going to say something?' Inara asked him pointedly.

'Yes, I will. I mean, yeah, please go on,' he fumbled pathetically.

She shifted her gaze to Nasir. The cold stare sent a shiver down his spine. That look meant just one thing: You are unwelcome! The bony and apologetic Nasir got up nervously, sending the plastic chair crashing down to the ground. Without moving a single nerve in her face, she raised her right eyebrow. This was sarcasm at its best.

Nasir fumbled his way across the lane in front of his Internet café as he took the left turn to his house, giving one hard look to Inara who had by now trained her eyes back on Sameer.

'You vanished that day. I thought you would wait?'

Sameer bowed his head, his gaze now scanning his dust-kissed brown shoes, and noticed that the lace of his right shoe was on the verge of coming undone.

He raised his eyes, 'I…uh…I just left. I am sorry but I felt uncomfortable.'

'Uncomfortable?' Her voice rose a notch higher, but her gaze softened and held a hint of curiosity in it. 'Why?'

'It had something to do with the guard, but forget it! You tell me? How did it go? You got the job?'

'I will!' The confidence was unmistakable. She looked intently at him and spoke, 'I will. The result will be out soon. Today, I am going to Jawaharlal Nehru University. I am applying for a course in Spanish.'

That last bit of information was unnecessary and Inara

realized it as soon as she said it. Confused, she wondered why.

Why did I say that? Why does he need to know where I am going today?

Inara felt stupid, more like an imposter. It seemed as if her actions and words were perfectly in her control but she was still letting them slip—deliberately—and then acting all 'holier than thou!'—as if she got a kick out of it. She could see through her own pretence. Her pathetic hypocrisy stood exposed. Her aloofness was not fooling anyone anymore.

'So you are going to JNU today,' he smiled knowingly and that smile said many things. 'All the best for your entrance exam. I am sure you will rock it!'

Without acknowledging his words, she turned around and started walking away, her eyes fixed on the ground that was slipping below her feet. The chaotic market and its sounds caressed her ears without permeating them. The high-pitched echo of a hen's shriek at being drawn out from the cage to her inevitable and obvious fate, the burst of a motorbike at a garage nearby, the hiss of the grill as the chef slammed slabs of meat over it and the aroma that hung in the air were not potent enough to wean her away from her thoughts that were a maze, a collage of unstructured memories of the last 24 hours.

'So? What are you going to do now?' Nasir's curiosity was getting the better of him. 'She must have meant something when she said that she was going to JNU?'

'I know. I mean why did she tell me? Unless...unless she wanted me to come over?'

'Or maybe, we are reading too much into this?' Nasir pondered.

Sameer looked hard at Nasir, 'You know what is your problem, Nasir? First you said that she isn't interested in me. You said I was imagining things. Now you can see the proof

53

unfolding right in front of your eyes, and you still don't believe me. Do you?'

Nasir had not even responded when Sameer suddenly got up and started walking towards the metro station. Nasir shook his head, a wry smile on his face. He knew that Sameer was now treading a forbidden path, a path of no return. He was worried because he suspected that Inara reciprocated Sameer's feelings, because he had just seen a glimpse of that fire in Inara's eyes too. Nasir turned his gaze towards the Jama Masjid and shut his eyes, a reluctant and unfamiliar prayer on his lips.

Four hours later...
At the Jawaharlal Nehru University

She sat on a cemented bench in the small green park in front of the Narmada hostel, munching on a vegetable sandwich. Her eyes were wide open, observing a red beetle trying to push around a mass of soil. It would flap its wings as the push got harder or a blockade interfered with its path. Inara's eyes unblinkingly followed the path of the beetle, but her mind was elsewhere.

Her mind was still oscillating between the disastrous entrance exam she had just given and the man she thought was responsible for it. She was distracted throughout the hour and a half she was in the examination hall and kept looking out of the window. Then, her eyes scanned the people getting out of bus number 615, the one coming straight from Connaught Place. Her heart would start beating fast every time she saw someone remotely resembling Sameer. She would bow down her head and then steal a glance to find out if it was indeed him. Chewing her sandwich, she shook her head and scoffed at her actions that defied common sense and logic, both of which were her most trusted allies, until now.

This is not just a crush! This is way beyond that!

She was honest enough to accept the truth now but this realization only aggravated the feeling of discomfort in her chest. She exhaled. But the feeling still besieged her. She exhaled deeply again but her breath, though warm, failed to give her any respite. She gave up and gazed randomly at the students and the day boarders walking along the tarred roads of the campus. She bowed her head, her gaze now pointed at her perfectly pedicured feet. She had taken off her sandals and was poking the moist winter-scarred soil with her big toenail, the beetle nowhere in sight anymore.

It must have entered its jungle: The shrubs!

Removing a stubborn speck of mud from her toenail, she raised her head, gazing at the tree above her. Excited squirrels jumped from one branch to the other chasing each other. A blue jay flew out of nowhere and landed in its nest. Inara tilted her head to get a glimpse of its fledglings. But all she could see were hungry beaks poking at the roller that had just landed and was precariously perched at the edge of the nest, trying to feed its young the pulp of worms in its mouth.

Suddenly, from the corner of her right eye, she saw someone at a distance, looking at her. A tall and lanky lad in blue denims and a matching jacket was staring straight at her. At first she decided to ignore him, like she had done so many others before. But she stole a glance discreetly...

What the!

Sameer was panting and running his fingers across the buttons of his denim jacket nervously. He had been frantically searching for her across the university campus and now that she was in front of him, he was stupefied and did not know what to do next!

Should I just walk up to her? Should I wait for her to notice me? Or should I keep watching from a distance and leave in a few minutes?

He could not dare walk up to her. The sheer audacity of his act that bordered on stalking, prevented him to approach her now that she was right in front of him.

Inara stared at Sameer, but, surprisingly, her heart wasn't pounding anymore. She wasn't shocked or even surprised. She had been preparing herself to see him all this while. Otherwise, why would she even tell him where she would be? She was wondering whether he would walk up to her or keep standing like that.

There's no way he would turn back now...now that I have seen him! Well, he better not. Especially after giving me so much grief today and yesterday!

The chill in the air suddenly rose as a gentle breeze wafted in from the ridge. Inara crossed her arms, her gaze fixed on Sameer, who lowered his head and started walking towards her. When he raised his head again, she noticed that a thin film covered his right eye as the chill struck at his chest like a stab of needles, the jacket hardly a protection from the unforgiving winter chill. Suddenly, he saw her rising from her bench, arms crossed, her gaze piercing.

It was clearly the most magical and the most comforting moment of his life, one that he would never forget. As she rose, she smiled. Her lips, like the arc of the crescent moon. Suddenly, the uncertainty and the discomfort faded. Sameer started to sprint towards her, a renewed confidence in his stride. He could not stop smiling himself as he approached her. Inara sat back on her bench, watching Sameer as he walked towards her.

'So, now you are stalking me?' Her head was still lowered,

ABHISAR SHARMA

her voice barely a whisper.

He looked at her and smiled, 'I thought we were way past stalking. I thought we had sorted this out.'

'Really?' The pitch of her voice now rose, 'Just because I spoke to you gives you the licence to follow me here? This is not stalking?'

'I guess it is not!' Sameer stabbed the inner wall of his right cheek with his tongue, 'I have decided not to pretend any further. Now, it is time for you to decide when you want to stop pretending!'

'I am not pretending! I just can't wear my feelings on my face like you, for the world to see and for my parents to discover... That too for a Kaafir.'

She was trapped. She was trapped the moment she uttered the words. And there was no turning back now. She was right. She wasn't pretending. Not anymore. She did not want her parents or the world to discover what she felt for him. She did not want him to discover it either. But he knew now. Even the word Kaafir seemed so lyrical coming from her.

Kaafir. He had heard the word in the past for so many years of his existence in the Walled City. It was a tribute to what he meant for the people around him. This word created a wall around him, separated him from 'them'.

She had uttered the word rather nonchalantly, in keeping with the manner in which it was used by Muslims for Hindus of that area, and the way she had heard it being used by her parents and her other Muslim friends. However, she immediately realized her political incorrectness and cursed herself under her breath—her head lowered, her ears turned crimson, and her toes curled. The surroundings suddenly turned chillier. A gust of wind struck her bosom and she shivered. She crossed her arms, digging her nails deep into the flesh of her arms as if punishing herself for her insolence.

'Kaafir, huh? So, that's what you think of me?'

'No, I am sorry. I did not mean...'

Absolute silence.

The chirping of the fledglings slowly rose in decibel. The wind swung in an unusual arc as Inara found herself being drawn towards Sameer. A storm of restlessness swept across the spaces between them, the spaces that were not meant to be breached—the forbidden spaces. She held the edge of the cement bench with her right hand, the fingernail of her little finger gently caressed Sameer's hand which was firmly holding his end of the bench. His first reflex was to withdraw his hand, but he paused. He looked at her hand. Conscious of the attention she was drawing, she slid her other hand under her thigh. Sameer smiled. He gently held the edge of the cold cemented bench. Through the corner of his eye, he saw her hand and his, as if they were striving for an intimate embrace. She slowly raised her head and caught him looking intensely at her hand. She curled her fingers in a grip. He was studying her closely. She could feel a surge of restiveness across her chest. It was an uneasy feeling. Even though she did not feel awkward on being caressed so intimately by his eyes, the judgement was still out on whether it was a pleasant feeling. As she gently blew out air from her lungs, she could hear him release his own nervousness. The synchronized release of their breaths tickled her, as her lips stretched into a smile. Realizing that her tormentor was as tormented as she was, she raised her head and looked at him.

'It's a pleasant day. You want to take a stroll?' she asked.

'I know of a great place around here!' He suddenly latched on to her words.

Amused by his enthusiastic retort, she raised her left

58

eyebrow and asked, 'What place?'

'There is a place called the Parthasarthi Rock...'

'You mean the Lovers' Rock? You want me to go there with you?' There was an edge to her tone and Sameer knew that she wasn't some brainless ignorant girl who could be herded wherever he wanted. He bit his inner cheek hard, cursing himself but still oblivious to the turn this conversation was about to take.

'Why would I want to go to this shady place with you?'

Taken aback by her sudden outburst, he fumbled, 'No! I...I...I just thought that...'

'You thought you could take me to some shady place and just because we are in JNU, I would not mind a bit! Is that so?'

'N...No, you are getting me wrong! Absolutely wrong!'

Inara sprang to her feet and stood right in front of Sameer, her eyes filled with a thousand accusations, 'Really, Sameer? Either you think I am naïve or you are so twisted, so moronic, that you think you could say that to a girl on your first meeting?'

Stunned by her insinuation, Sameer rose slowly to his feet, his eyes locked with hers. He could feel a stab. He understood that he was standing at peril's edge, that he was in danger of losing her forever. He had blurted out 'Parthasarthi Rock' innocuously, having taken a few girls from his office there. He did not even realize what Inara would think about his intentions. It was just the 'guy instinct' when he spoke about Parthasarthi Rock. But now, Inara had latched on to that.

'Have you been there?' Enmeshed in trepidation, his voice was now barely a whisper.

'Where? Parthasarthi Rock? And why would I want to go there? Do you really think that I need to go there to know why people go there and what they do there?' The aggression in her voice was now rising, but the pitch and tone remained

59

stern, calm and unwavering

'Please, just hear me out! If you don't like what I say, you can walk away.'

Inara crossed her arms, as if telling him, *'Your time starts now!'*

Sameer exhaled and then bowed his head, closing his eyes for a moment as if trying to think, knowing fully well that one wrong word and this may all be over.

'I just wanted us to go somewhere where we could sit comfortably without being watched by anyone, some place where I could talk to you without the nagging feeling that someone might be watching my discomfort, my hesitation. My feelings for you are meant to be judged only by you, not by someone random, some passer-by.'

Sameer looked into her eyes, intently. Inara, as a reflex, bowed her head. After a while, she looked around, her eyes fidgeting at the random montage of people, spaces, greenery and structures around them.

'Maybe I just blurted out what came to my mind, but you have to believe me when I say that I can't even dare to think of something offensive, something licentious about you, even at a place like Parthasarthi Rock! Though, it's not as bad as you think. Yes, lovers or couples do go there, but I just wanted our first date to be special.'

She raised her perfectly-arched eyebrows and said, 'Our first date? There's no *us!*'

Shaking his head, with a wry smile on his lips, he asked, 'So why did you ask me to take a walk with you? You were the one who talked about being afraid of displaying your feelings for a Kaafir. What did you mean by that? You want to judge me from your perfect little world and expect me to be perfect as well? Well, I have got news for you, I am anything but perfect.

60

But let me tell you what I am not. I am not pretentious. I can't wear hypocrisy as many do!'

Her jaws tightened and her ears turned a deep shade of red. Inara bowed her head, digging the ground with the pointed edge of her sandal. At that moment, realization struck her.

She was trying too hard...trying too hard to tell him that he did not matter to her, that he had not unsettled her perfect little world and that he had not been the single source of uneasiness that engulfed her over the past few days.

She sought some form of respite from her anxiety and the person she wanted it from was her tormentor himself. She knew that her pretence would not work anymore.

Then, another thought struck her fragile mind.

I should not have encouraged him in Connaught Place or met him today.

But surprisingly, instead of clinging on to that thought, she let it slip away and drown in an ocean of unstructured misery, the misery that defined her at that moment. She stood there, stupefied, unable to move, unable to decide.

Finally, she spoke, 'I am sorry, I did not mean anything derogatory when I used the word Kaafir. I know it was harsh, but my intentions weren't wrong. Believe me when I tell you that a lot of my friends are Hindus. It's just that, and I am being honest here, there are words and expressions that are a part of my existence, part of the surroundings that I have been raised in. But I have never subscribed to these rigid notions of existence because I believe that there is a world beyond our walled and cracked existence, and someday, I will cross the threshold to find my own footing in that world. Someday...' her eyes were glazed with the abstraction of her desired existence.

She turned her gaze back to Sameer, only to find him looking at her intently, 'I don't judge people too, but someone

would be extremely naive if he or she claims that these prejudices aren't a part of our existence. Just look at how you Hindus think about us Muslims! Hmm, Sameer? And pardon me for saying this, but the prejudices that exist amongst the Hindus are outrageous. For you people, every skullcap, hijab-wearing person is a suicide bomber!'

Sameer interrupted, 'Why am I being subjected to this sermon? Why do you think that I deserve to be told all this? Let me tell you a few things about myself. I have grown up listening to the sounds of the azan. I have walked my first steps on the rise that leads to the Jama Masjid. That's where my father held my hand and taught me how to climb the stairs. Shutting my eyes to the sound of the azan isn't something I have had to practise over the years, it is my belief. It is what defines me. I owe my existence to Imam sahab. It was because of him that I could study in an English-medium school, otherwise I would have struggled to complete my education even in a government school, the one that my best friend Nasir studied in. It was that sponsorship that helped me complete my education in Fatima school where rich kids like you study. And never during those years of my education was I made to feel that I was a child of a lesser human. Never. You seek liberation from this walled existence that you call suffocating, but I was made to feel the pinch of being a fruit seller's son, only after I stepped out of the Walled City. The city is my cocoon, a protective layer that cushions me like Amma's embrace. Why would you identify me as a part of those you condemn? Is it because it is convenient, or is it because you share your contempt for me like some of your brethren? Honestly speaking, even their contempt does not matter to me. I know their premises. I know where they come from, but you? What is your grudge?'

'The list is very long,' she mumbled dismissively, 'but this

62

isn't a time for me to talk about that. I agree that I overreacted. Now,' she raised her eyes to look straight at him, and whispered with a hint of a smile, 'can we walk or do you intend to provoke me further and make me utter other politically incorrect inanities?'

They sauntered on the footpath next to the road with buses and cars whizzing past them. The air was laden with the fragrance of mogra flowers. Shouts of 'pass pass' echoed in the air from the basketball court of the adjacent Kendriya Vidyalaya in the JNU campus. They were quiet, but the silence was helping in erasing the uneasiness of the past few minutes. Inara looked at the students walking around, dressed informally, a bit unkempt, some with dishevelled hair and an aura of casual and lazy elegance. It was something she found very appealing. She craved to be a part of that crowd, she desired for an existence like that, but she could not dare tell that to her Abbu, knowing how he would react. She had taken the entrance exam for a purpose and that had caused a minor storm at her house. Feisty that she was, she had argued passionately with her father who had to finally give in to her demand with a few riders; the most important one was that she would not insist on continuing to work after marriage and that it would be subject to approval from her in-laws. Inara had agreed, knowing that she would fight that war some other day. Her flow of thoughts was suddenly interrupted by Sameer's question, 'Why Spanish, if I may ask?' His voice was heavy with a specific curiosity that had been bothering him since she had informed him about the entrance exam.

'Well, that's a long story, but to cut it short, my father wants me to work in Freebird Publications as a copy editor. The interview that day was just a formality as the owner of the agency is a dear friend of Abbu's. So the interview was just an eyewash. Now, my uncle works for the Spanish Embassy minority section. They will be hiring a few people soon to present a more humane face of the country to the Muslims and to initiate a dialogue with them, and for that they need people like us, you know, Muslims. Now, I would not miss this opportunity because that also involves a lot of travelling to Spain and other Latin American countries. I thought of learning the language and the Latin way of life before joining them.'

Oh Lord! Is this a coincidence?

'Atos Original, my company, primarily interacts with Latin American clients. There are so many Spanish language professionals in my office. So many of my seniors have been posted to Latin American countries and someday I too may have to go,' he said, enthusiastically.

Then, he went on a creative overdrive which was his favourite sport. Imaginative was something he certainly was.

This can't be a mere coincidence. It seems our paths are leading to the same destiny. Is it possible? Amma talks about destiny all the time. She talks about how people who are meant for each other transcend all boundaries, spaces and prejudices to be with each other. Is it possible that someday, we would get married and settle down in some beautiful Latin American country or maybe even Spain? Our house would overlook the sea. Amma would sit in the backyard, resting on a chair with the sunlight on her face! Our child, wide-eyed, would be fascinated by the waves crashing on the shore just beyond the threshold of our house! Inara calling out to me with irritation on her face, asking me to stop the little one, who is refusing to be controlled by his mother...'

'Phew,' he breathed out. *There I go again!* A wide grin on his face, Sameer tried to catch a glimpse of Inara from the corner of his left eye, careful not to be caught this time by her. There was a shadow of calmness on her face as she gazed at the lush greenery around them. Her eyes widened with curiosity, as if she wanted to soak in every moment that breezed past her. It seemed to be her wonderland indeed. He now understood what she meant by escaping the walled existence. This was the prelude to her fantasy...and his.

'I think, this is where we turn back,' Inara suddenly stopped, jolting Sameer out of his dreamy existence.

'Why?'

Sameer should have looked around him before asking that question. They had now reached the edge of Parthasarthi Rock, and once more, that moment of awkwardness came upon them and even the simple act of turning around needed some strength.

'Yeah, you are right! Maybe some other day!'

What the hell? Some other day? Why did I say that? Is this some kind of death wish? She is definitely not meeting me after this!

Sameer cursed himself under his breath.

'I guess we can turn back and the walk to the right will take us to the bus stand,' he said, trying to salvage the situation.

'I think that is indeed a good idea. Your first one since morning!' she teased him.

Sameer accompanied her till Rajiv Chowk metro station and from there on, they pretended that they did not know each other. He kept watching her from a distance during the metro ride up to Kashmiri Gate. She would steal a glance at him too and if their eyes met, she would pretend it was accidental. But deep down, she knew that she was way past all the pretences. Soon she would have to shed all of them. They were sucked into this vortex and the ride, though perilous, was exhilarating nevertheless.

A pall of unease coupled with a shadow of guilt descended upon her as soon as she reached home and faced her Ammi who opened the door. But without indulging in any small talk, she rushed straight to her room. Shutting it from inside, she opened the window overlooking the Jama Masjid from another side. Inara shut her eyes as she held the windows apart, letting the gush of wind strike her face. It was breezy and the force of the wind was hurting her, but she wanted the restlessness to ebb away. Her plan was failing miserably. She wondered if her tormentor felt the same.

But what if he forgot about me the moment he entered his home or sat down with that good-for-nothing Nasir? Well, he had better not! That Kaafir! He has given me so much grief that I can't even erase him from my thoughts!

These thoughts further compounded her misery.

Then, she realized something belatedly, something that left her with a tinge of guilt... It was the fact that she wanted to be with him and it only him who could erase that swell of uneasiness besieging her heart; that she wanted to indulge with him in a reckless act of lovemaking; that she did not even need to shake his hands or touch him to know what he felt like, what he smelled like; that she should not have turned his comment about Parthasarthi Rock into such a big deal; that she should have walked on; that she should never have taken that right turn to the bus stand.

Something about that thought tickled her. She could feel the adrenaline rush through her, at the thought that if not today, she would soon visit the legendary Parthasarthy Rock with him, someday. A charge of roused curiosity reverberated across her body. She opened her eyes and looked at the colossal market and the staccato-like existence of shanties and houses surrounding the mosque. It was unusually crowded that day. She tried to look for diversions, something that would obliterate her confused feelings. But she could not. And then she saw something...

A thin film of tears covered her right eye as she gazed at the dome of the mosque with the crescent moon shining above. She could hear her mother calling from the kitchen below but it felt as if she was calling from far away. Everything seemed inaudible except her own heartbeat, her own muddled thoughts. She cursed Sameer under her breath.

May Allah impart the same misery on him! Maybe worse!

The diversion that she so desperately needed did come in the form of her mobile which started ringing. The name that was flashing on the screen was Zubeida.

'Hi!'

'Are you at home, Inara?'

'Ermmm, why?'

'No, just asking.'

'Yes, I am...'

'Can I come over?'

Silence.

'Hello?'

Silence again.

'Inara, are you there?'

'Yes...I am sorry, I am a bit a distracted! Sure, come over... I will be waiting.'

The awkward feeling of last evening rose between them as soon as her eyes met Zubeida's. But Inara had a suspicion that Zubeida did not share her discomfort. In fact, she looked besotted. The silence between them further prolonged her present predicament.

'Listen,' Inara spoke with the hint of decisiveness in her

67

voice, 'you are my best friend! I don't want to lose you because of one strange evening. I was in a state of mind which I can't explain. It was weird. He makes me restless and that is an understatement. You know, I met him again!'

'You did?' Zubeida's voice was barely a whisper, as she turned around to face the door.

'Could you just go and shut the door? I don't want Ammi to be privy to this conversation.'

As Zubeida came back and sat on the edge of the bed, Inara lay down, resting her head on the pillow, her eyes fixed on the white ceiling. She noticed that the paint was peeling off at the corners, indicating a probable leakage in the bathroom of the floor above.

'So, I met him...'

'You did? Where?'

'JNU. I had to take the entrance exams for Spanish...'

'So, was it a date?'

'No, no... I was there and he had come to meet me.'

'If he is stalking you, you need to speak to your Abbu.'

Inara turned her head away. An array of photographs from her childhood, some recent ones, a life-size poster of Hrithik Roshan, and a rectangular frame of the Mecca with a faint light from the window bathing its glassy surface stared back at her from across the room.

'Is he stalking you, Inara?' Zubeida asked again.

'I am afraid he is not. It's not so easy.'

'Inara? You do remember who he is? Do you know how your father would react in case...'

'Yeah, yeah... I know that,' she spoke dismissively, knowing that Zubeida was stating the obvious, again.

'So what are you even doing?'

Inara jerked herself up and looked straight at Zubeida,

with a hint of disdain in her eyes.

'I have told you I am aware of the repercussions. But it's just that…I don't care. He makes me restless when I am with him, but in a pleasant sort of way. I crave him as soon as he is out of my sight, but the restlessness still remains, like a constant throb on a wound. I have this craving for him that ignites so many of my fantasies and I am not even ashamed of them.'

Wide-eyed, Zubeida just looked at Inara, studying her every emotion, every twitch on her face, the nervous fidgeting of her fingers, the occasional biting of the lower lip by the sharp upper tooth, the scratch of the winter-kissed cheek by the nail of the index finger.

'How long has it been since you have had feelings like that for him?'

With a slight hesitation, she said, 'I have been really curious about him for as long as I can remember. Even when I was a child. I always remember him running along with the other boys wearing a skullcap, standing in line to collect goodies from Imam sahab on Eid, holding his mother's hand while walking with her to Kashmiri Gate metro station and of course, during his father's death.'

She paused to draw in a breath before continuing, 'I still remember the grim expression on his face, but not a drop of tear, walking in front of his father's funeral procession, holding the jute rope tied to the clay vessel with smoke rising gently from within, head shaved, with the worry of uncertainty that lay ahead.'

'Inara,' spoke Zubeida with unconcealed shock in her voice, 'I am afraid, it's not him, but you who seems to be stalking him. You are obsessed! Do you realize that?'

'And you know the best thing, Zubeida? I don't care! I don't care how Abbu or Ammi will react when they come to know about it. I am not even afraid.'

'Are you sure, Inara, that you have not trodden on a path of no return?'

'What do you mean?'

'I mean, have you in any way indulged him?'

Inara protested as her voice rose, 'No...no...Ya Allah...no! If walking with him in JNU is indulgence or if sitting next to him in a bus is indulgence, then maybe! Or trying to steal a glance at him in the metro, knowing that he knows that you are trying to do so... I hope that does not qualify as indulgence?' she asked, incredulous.

'But that marks the beginning of it, doesn't it?'

'As I said, Zubeida, I don't care, I really don't!' She turned her face away from Zubeida, shutting her eyes so that she could clearly see him.

A long, uncomfortable pause followed as Zubeida stared at Inara with a hint of desire in her eyes.

'Inara...' whispered Zubeida.

'Hmm...'

'I have been thinking about last evening. I don't know why you have disowned that moment. But I thought it was one of the most beautiful moments...'

'Don't even go there, Zubeida!' Inara retorted without opening her eyes. She was dreading that question. She realized that Zubeida had not moved on and had held on to the last evening as something special. But she also knew that she had only one person to blame for it...herself.

A few houses away...

Nasir's father had often warned them not to light a bonfire on the cement-floored terrace. But did Nasir ever bother? No!

70

A small bonfire was lit up in the middle of the terrace as Sameer and Nasir sat on a jute charpoi besides it. While Nasir's back was to the mosque, Sameer faced it in all its pristine glory. The lights from the mosque and from the market below shone on his face. A wooden slab was placed in the centre of the charpoi, with a sumptuous assortment of kebabs and curries piled on top of it. As Nasir wolfed down the kebabs without even looking at Sameer, faint sounds of a qawwali reached their ears from the music store at the far end of the lane. A sufi number echoed from another end as a bawdy and cacophonous Salman Khan song blared from an adjacent restaurant. The music was as varied as the assortment of kebabs that the two were having; rather, the emaciated Nasir was gorging on. Sameer was absent-mindedly rolling the naan in a bowl of mint chutney and benignly looking at Nasir with a hint of amusement and fondness.

It didn't take long and Sameer's mind flew to Inara. She wasn't just a distraction anymore; now, after their walk together, he was completely enamoured by her. He wondered why she inspired such extreme emotions in him. There was a moment in JNU, when he had nearly decided to walk off. But he couldn't. It was not just because of her beauty, her persona. It had to be something else, something deeper. His mind was still sending him a warning, but he had decided to let his senses prevail. Metaphorically speaking, every step he took towards Inara was like a rush of adrenaline, like an beast waiting to be unleashed. He was irrevocably drawn to her, and was tying himself in knots that would soon be inextricable. At the same time, there was a thoughtless sense of triumph that he was at least entangled with her.

'That silly grin on your face has become so predictable, Sameer sahab. And it's spoiling a perfect evening with kebabs

71

and a bit of borrowed Khusro.' Nasir meant the sufi songs being playing loudly from the lane below.

'Oh, if you mean gorging on the kebabs, like a certain famished Nasir sahab is doing, then maybe the evening is on the verge of, as you say, getting spoilt. But try to look at it through my eyes: A perfect winter evening with the light of the Almighty bathing my face, the smell of galouti kebabs and sheermaal naan, the lilt of a sufiana number, and last but not the least, the company of my best friend.'

Without looking at Sameer, Nasir pushed another bit of kebab in his mouth, and said, 'Alas! My best friend is present just physically as someone else has engulfed his senses. I am now jealous of her.'

Sameer latched on to the last sentence and teased him, 'Oh, Nasir, please! Now don't start with a love triangle. I can hardly handle one!'

'I wish I was indeed your lover. Then, I would have driven some sense into your head and saved you from certain disaster...' Nasir's tone turned solemn.

Sameer gently shook his head, 'I know what I am doing, Nasir.'

'I am afraid, you don't! You don't, bhai! I pray that either you get over this phase and move on, or—and I know that it's impossible—you find your fairy-tale ending with...' he paused before adding with some distaste, 'her.'

'Inara, her name is Inara. God, you are indeed jealous of her! In fact you detest her, it seems! You don't even want to name her,' Sameer slapped Nasir's shoulder with a playful twinkle in his eyes.

'How does it matter what I feel about her? You are my best friend but she means nothing to me. Maybe if it weren't for your feelings for her, she would have just been a fantasy

ABHISAR SHARMA

for masturbation.'

'Screw you, Nasir!'

'Same to you, bhai! The feeling is mutual!'

They laughed aloud as bit by bit, the night sucked in all the sounds, smells and colours, before it dragged itself to a predictable ending.

The morning would bring yet another day in Sameer's life, and in Inara's, whose life was just a little more complicated than Sameer's at the moment. She woke up the next day with the thought of seeking a closure to her 'affair' with Sameer. But as they say, destiny is a bitch. Inara should have known better.

A month later...

She was trying hard and was succeeding it seems. It had been nearly a month since she had last met Sameer at JNU. She had often walked past Sameer and had pretended, quite successfully, that he did not exist. On the other hand, he wasn't sure how to react to her targeted indifference to him. He started getting restless. Around this time, she had also joined Freebird Publications in Connaught place.

On the way down, at the steps of the Kashmiri Gate metro station

That day, Sameer had finally decided that he would confront her with his misery, but he chose the wrong place.

'Inara,' his tone was hesitant, hence, at first, she could not hear him. However, when he called out to her the second time around, a worried look crossed her face which progressed to a look of sheer panic. She decided to walk on as Sameer called out her name for the third time.

73

'Inara, please stop.'

'What?' she said through gritted teeth. Her tone displayed a subtle irritation.

'Can I have a word with you please?'

'And can we not, please?'

'I just want to know what happened. Why are you ignoring me like this? What have I done?'

'What is there to ignore? I don't owe you anything, Sameer! What is it that you want?'

'I just want to know if I have said or done something to offend you because I can't understand how one day we take a walk in JNU and the next day, you behave as if I do not exist even on the periphery of this planet?'

She kept walking as he tried to keep pace with her, looking around for unexpected reactions from curious bystanders.

'How many times do I have to tell you there is no *we*? And taking a walk with you in JNU means nothing! Absolutely nothing!' she hissed.

'I just want to know if I have offended you.'

'You haven't! So now, could you please stop following me? I will get into trouble, we are nearing our mohalla.'

Sameer looked ahead and saw the bend that marked the beginning of the lane leading to her house, but he was clearly not satisfied with her response to his question. He needed answers and it wasn't actually about ignoring him. That day in JNU, he had started believing that it was the beginning of something beautiful with Inara but it turned out to be something quite the opposite.

'I have to tell you something Inara...'

'I am afraid I don't wish to hear anything, Sameer. And please, we are nearing our locality. I will get in trouble if I am seen walking with you.'

'Could I meet you just once? Just this one time...'

The irritation on her face was growing as she started to walk faster, 'I don't want to meet you! Why don't you understand what I am trying to tell you? Please, for Allah's sake, just turn back. You will get me in so much trouble,' she pleaded with him as they took the turn around the bend.

'You are behaving as if I am stalking you. Please listen to me...'

'But that's what you are doing! You are indeed stalking me!' As she spoke the last words, her eyes widened in horror.

She paused for a moment, and then with the same look of horror writ all over her face, she started walking faster.

'I am done, Sameer. Now, I don't have anything else to say to you. Abbu is standing right in front of Saleem chacha's shop. So, please, please, just leave me alone! I beg of you.'

Imtiaz Khan, Inara's father, was a man of wheatish complexion and medium height peaking at five-feet-seven-inches. He had a wispy beard, shrewd, probing eyes, and he always wore western attire. In an obvious attempt to flaunt his new Rolex, he rolled up the sleeve of his beige-coloured coat and pushed the sweet paan in his mouth. Hearing the sycophantic praise coming from the paanwala, a complacent smile appeared on Imtiaz Khan's face. His detractors had nicknamed him Dracula, probably because of his uncanny resemblance to the legend. Just as Dracula sucked his victim's blood, Imtiaz Khan has this ability to suck money from his unfortunate borrowers. Not only was he the most influential trader in the entire Walled City, his links extended much beyond, further up to Western Uttar Pradesh. Imtiaz Khan dabbled in everything, right from pure Kashmiri shawls to dry fruits, and even a rumoured railway contract near Azamgarh.

He was also a generous donor to Imam sahab's charity work and the mosque.

Inara started walking faster, her eyes fixed on her father who was standing perpendicular to the market lane. If he had stood like that a little longer, she would have probably gone unnoticed, but she was not that lucky, and neither was her father.

'Imtiaz sahab, why is that Hindu boy walking next to your daughter?' asked the paanwala, his voice barely a whisper; he was unable to conceal the scandalous delight in his eyes.

Sameer knew that it was probably too late to take a U-turn. Meanwhile, her arms crossed, holding a blue file close to her chest, Inara bowed her head and started walking with an added urgency to her steps.

Imtiaz turned around and saw his daughter being followed by Sameer.

This was the perfect angle for them.

Them.

On a bike.

The man riding pillion raised his right hand, the nozzle of his revolver perfectly aimed for Imtiaz Khan's temple.

His finger was on the trigger.

The motorbike encountered a slight bump in the treacherous lane.

Press.

Bang.

The bullet entered Imtiaz Khan's face, first cracking his cheekbone and then exiting at exactly the same point from the other end. A splatter of red splashed onto the small platform of the paanwala's shop as Imtiaz Khan slumped to his right, his eyes still fixed on his daughter. The paanwala stared, open-mouthed at Imtiaz Khan's crumbling frame on the platform of

ABHISAR SHARMA

his shop, as his eyes widened in horror. He clasped his ears and gasped aloud, 'Allah! Khan sahab!'

The man riding pillion on the bike raised his hand and fired a few more shots in the air as his driver accelerated the motorbike, now moving towards Inara. But it wasn't Inara, whose eyes were steadily fixed on the ground, who noticed it all. It was Sameer.

Since Inara had warned him a few minutes ago, his eyes were continuously fixed on Imtiaz Khan, hence, the entire scene played right before his eyes, as if in slow motion. As he saw the men approaching Inara, he lunged forward and pushed her aside, sheltering her with his body, and stood facing them. The man driving the bike swerved sharply, trying to avoid Sameer, nearly toppling in the process. But luck was indeed on their side that day. Inara's gaze swung from Sameer to the paan shop. Her father was now sprawled on the ground, with the paanwala standing over him and shouting hysterically. She watched transfixed as men in skullcaps ran towards the shop. The reality of what had just happened suddenly hit her.

'Abbu!' she let out a painful shriek, which seemed to echo till eternity, as powerful as the echo of that lone bullet that had just been shot at her father.

With his eyes on a distressed Inara, Sameer ran towards her father. At the back of his mind was Nasir's Internet café and Nasir's motorbike. As he ran towards the paan shop, he saw a curious Nasir emerging from the Internet cafe. He roared, 'Nasir! Go and get your motorbike!'

His mind was now working at breakneck speed. He knew that every moment mattered if he had to save Imtiaz Khan's life. His first priority was to take the wounded man to the nearest hospital and he knew that during that time of the day with the traffic at its peak, the only way to get there was by a

77

motorbike. He saw Nasir kick-starting his motorbike and then he shifted his gaze to Inara's father. He noticed the blood that was gushing out from the exit hole of the bullet, as Imtiaz Khan gaped motionlessly at the skies. The entire scenario was macabre. He bent down and raised Imtiaz Khan's head to his lap. He could see the entry and exit holes of the bullet. He looked right and saw Nasir riding the bike, wobbling a little, on the cracked street of the Walled City, carefully dodging the small rocks and rubble spread across his path. He looked back at Inara, who stood there, frozen with shock, unable to move, her hand over her mouth. She had just started to walk towards him when Nasir reached him.

Sameer raised the wounded man with a grunt and mounted him behind Nasir. Blood dripped from Imtiaz Khan's wound with a vengeance on to his checked shirt. The flow of blood was alarming and that shook him to act faster. Imtiaz Khan's eyes were wide open, yet motionless. He knew that look from countless Bollywood movies.

He must be dead!

But he brushed that thought away, for Inara's sake, who was now standing next to them, holding her father's shoulder, mumbling incoherently, and weeping profusely.

'Nasir, drive with all your might!'

Two hours later...

In just a matter of one hour, they descended upon the Walled City. Their landing was synchronized to perfection with the rest of their tribe. The media tamasha unfolded with all the jazz that comes with it: The long serpentine wires coming out of fancy red, blue and white Live OB vans, the restless shuffling and contorted faces of the sound byte soldiers clasping

ABHISAR SHARMA

the ultimate weapon—the mike with the loud logos, the burly and dark complexioned cameramen mouthing the filthiest of abuses to the sound assistant and pushing the onlookers away from the camera. The drama was being played out to dazed onlookers who were, until now, unmindful of the attack that had just taken place. Now, they stood behind the reporters who were doing their respective pieces on camera. Like flies crowding in on a sticky soggy handful of jaggery, the bystanders were smiling, waving into the camera, pushing that unyielding strand of hair behind their ears, some talking on the mobile phones, probably telling their mother, 'Hey Mummy! I am on TIMES, can you see me?'

'The Walled City is again in a state of shock and as you can see behind me, this was the spot where Imtiaz Khan was shot at by unknown assailants who escaped on a motorbike. Fresh patches of blood are still visible as the police have cordoned off that small area where the shooting took place. Let me remind our viewers that Imtiaz Khan was the cousin brother of the notorious Tabrez Khan who is currently serving a sentence in Tihar jail for financing the bombing that took place in Lucknow which had claimed a dozen lives a year ago. I would remind our viewers that during that attack, the target was the dreaded Don and Hindu radical mascot Munna Shukla, who escaped with grievous injuries. Our sources tell me that the attack on Imtiaz Khan may be an act of revenge, but there is still no proof of any direct links between Tabrez and Imtiaz Khan.'

Anchor Deepti asked, 'Rahul, could you tell us about the present situation in the Walled City?'

Rahul, coughing and clearing his throat, replied, 'Well, Deepti, the situation is tense and the locals are angry at the incident as Imtiaz Khan was an influential man of the Walled City.'

79

The camera zoomed in on the faces of a few boys waving at the camera.

Rahul continued, 'The police presence is heavy, considering the scale of the attack that took place. I am also told that the MP from the Walled City, Shivkant Singh, has reached the hospital and is now with the family of Imtiaz Khan.'

'Rahul, could you tell us more about the actual incident...' asked Deepti.

'I am told that Imtiaz Khan was at the paan shop, this one right behind me, and this is usually where he stops during this time of the day, which clearly points towards a detailed reconnaissance done by the assailants. As soon as he was shot, two youths from the area carried him to Fatima Hospital on a motorbike. Khan's family was rushed to the hospital minutes after that. The old man, Imam Zulfiqar Khan, is still inside the mosque with his son and all eyes are on him now.'

Imam's room, somewhere in the recesses of the mosque

'Abbu, how long are we going to pretend that this is some random attack? It was a cowardly Hindu attack on a Muslim man! That's what it was and that's how we need to treat it! We need to send out a message to the youth who are now restless for retribution!'

The Imam was worried. There would come a day when he would no longer be in control of his faculties, his senses—a time when the baton will have to be passed to his son Imran Khan, the restless protégé. He was shocked not just at Imran's impatience and extremist views, but also because he feared that Imran may never learn the art of diplomacy that even a man of God like him needed to practise now and then.

The Imam's eyes were bloodshot and streaked with red

ABHISAR SHARMA

capillaries, the telltale signs of anxiety. The Imam sucked in a lungful of vapour from his hukkah and then released it, slowly, distracted but also clearly irritated with his son.

'I am afraid that we will not be able to stop our men this time,' Imran said.

Devoid of any emotions, the Imam retorted wryly, 'Then what do you plan to do?'

'Pardon me, Abbu?'

He turned towards his son and this time, his voice rose, 'Then what, huh, Imran *bhai*? What then?'

'I am not asking for retribution in terms of blood, but I want this city to know that we exist and that we cannot be trampled over again and again and again.' Imran's voice had conviction and this was the moment when the Imam knew that he could not prevail over his son.

'We have to send a strong message to the outsiders. We have to at least take out a procession across the city, in the heart of the political establishment, so that they know what we are capable of! Yes Abbu, revenge is what I seek and revenge is what I shall get.'

The next day, 9.12 a.m.
4 Aurangzeb Road, in the heart of Lutyens' Delhi

Raj Narain Pandey, oval-faced and bald with white hair sprouting above his ears, was a 76-year-old Jan Sangh veteran, now with the principal opposition party, the Sanskari Party. He pushed his gold-rimmed glasses up the bridge of his nose and started stroking his thin white moustache as he saw the drama unfold on the huge LCD fixed on his wall. The defeat at the hands of Shivkant Singh, his arch rival in the last general elections, still rankled him. The next Lok Sabha elections were

fast approaching and he realized that time was running out. He needed to take some desperate measures to turn the tide. He knew that the Imam would have a crucial role to play, directly or indirectly. He was banking on a few false steps taken by the wily Imam that would set the motion of polarization, which would ultimately benefit him. He had his reasons to believe that the two incidents in the Walled City would provide the perfect ground for the schism he was hoping to create. Huddled with Gupta ji, his chief strategist, Raj Narain Pandey raised the remote and pressed the red button.

'So, what do you think?' mumbled Pandey, his voice cracking.

'Sir, my sources tell me that this time, Imran Khan might have his way and that he is planning to raise the issue in a big way. His men talk about revenge and retribution. Apparently, he had a meeting with his father and he seems to have prevailed upon the Imam.'

'But what do you mean by revenge? I am sure even a hothead like him can't be that rash?'

'Pandeyji, if Imran had his way, he would have converted India into a colony of the Islamic Republic of Pakistan, but that's a separate issue. Any action by him would only propel us towards a certain victory in the next elections in the Walled City. The Hindu votes made all the difference last time. They voted for the Secular Party. We are hoping that the recent incidents will create an atmosphere laced by insecurity and instil a feeling among the people that they are living on the edge. But for that, we shall have to wait for the Imam and his son to take the first step. Now, this step could either be in the form of a retaliatory attack somewhere, orchestrated by them or their cohorts, or it could be some form of disturbance around the area. In any case, that's just the trigger we need!'

'So, what next?'

'I am told that the father-son duo are, in fact, going to address a press conference this evening, so all eyes on that!'

Noon, at the Fatima Hospital, Intensive Care Unit

His eyes were drooping with fatigue and lack of sleep, yet, Sameer stared unblinkingly at the woman just outside the ICU who was dressed in a white salwar kameez. Her head was covered with her shawl as she bent down to sit on the beige-coloured mat to pray. However hopeless the situation seemed, she looked calm. She must have been over 45 years, but she did not look a year older than 35. She was Inara's mother, Rukhsar Khanum. Age and a regular dose of red meat had taken a toll on her figure, but her face radiated a placid glow as she turned her face towards his direction to pray, her eyes closed.

Her lips parted slightly as she murmured an aayat from the Quran.

Sameer continued to scrutinize her, wondering at the realization that Inara would look exactly like her mother when she grew old...

with me.

His heart added to the thought...

Only that she would be fitter and not the bulky woman her mother had turned into.

He smiled at the thought. The corridor leading to the ICU was now teeming with men and women, faces flushed with worry and suspicion. Some of the men were holding something hidden inside their pathani suits, maybe a concealed weapon, and were looking around warily for any unwarranted presence amongst the friends of Imtiaz Khan's family. Everybody was a

THE KAAFIR'S LOVE

suspect in their eyes. Weapons and men present in such large numbers were not allowed in the hospital, but no one would dare to say anything to them. Not now. Nasir had left last night itself, but Sameer had decided to stay put.

Suddenly, he saw Inara emerge out of the bathroom, her face streaked with water that she must have just splashed on her face. However, it was unable to hide the trauma of the past 20 hours, her hair was dishevelled, her dupatta hung lazily across her shoulder, brushing the hospital floor. She came and sat down next to her mother on a bench. She leaned back, rested her head on the wall and slowly shut her eyes. She could feel a sudden rise of panic in her chest, coupled with a searing pain across her spine. The murmurs of the aayat should have soothed her, but it was further accentuating her agony. She knew why her mother was praying. It wasn't just a normal prayer. It was a panic call to Allah.

At that moment, Sameer wished that he had been married to her; he would have walked up and sat down on the bench next to her. Then, he would have held her soft and warm hand and bade her to rest her head on his shoulder.

For the first time, he saw Inara being surrounded by many young men, probably cousins; many of them, her possible suitors. He could see that even in those moments of grief and uncertainty, they were leaving no opportunity to outdo each other in extending a helping hand to the Khans. For the first time, Sameer also realized the competition he was up against.

Just then, Inara's mother rose from her namaz. As she got up, she gave Sameer a fleeting look, pausing on him for just a hundredth of a second. Someone, probably a relative, came and asked the mother and daughter to come to the other room. He could hear Inara speaking in a strained voice, 'I don't feel like eating anything, mamu. Just leave me alone.'

84

The mamu murmured something in her ear as Rukhsar, her mother, stroked her daughter's hair and said, 'Come, they are saying na, your Abbu is out of danger.'

Inara broke down again, 'I want to see him walking around as he used to earlier.'

Reluctantly, she got up and was taken to the room next to the ICU, the same room that Inara and her mother slept in the previous night. As she disappeared, Sameer started to trace the uneven crack that stretched from one end of the wall to the other, wondering at the same moment, if this would be the same hospital he would have to bring her to when she became pregnant. He grinned stupidly to himself.

Here I am, stuck in this sea of grief and all I can think about is...

If anyone could hear his thoughts, they would have shot him by now.

Shot...

Suddenly, he was back on the motorbike. He recalled how clinical he was while putting Inara's father on the motorbike and getting him to the hospital. Not once did he panic. The only thing that had played in his mind was Inara and her well-being. On second thoughts, it was this clinical approach that had probably saved her Abbu's life. He remembered how he had pressed the exit wound with his right hand as blood kept gushing out in spurts, smidgens of which had even entered his eyes. He suddenly realized that he must smell awful.

Just then, someone tapped his shoulder. He raised his eyes to see one of Inara's aspiring suitors with a grim expression on his face, 'Please wear these clothes after you take a bath. Then, I shall take you to eat something. Rukhsar khala will meet you after that.'

An hour later, as Sameer was stuffing a sandwich and a

THE KAAFIR'S LOVE

boiled egg into his mouth, he was taken to the room where Inara and her mother were staying. As he entered the room, he could see a white linen curtain separating the bed from the sitting area. That was where Rukhsar Khanum sat, pensive, lost in a trail of her own thoughts. She raised her immaculate kohl-lined eyes up at him and her gaze softened. She smiled tiredly, though her eyes were weary due to lack of sleep. Interestingly, he could not trace a single tear or any other sign of agony that the family had been undergoing, almost as if she was prepared for this day. Sameer stood before her and she gestured him to sit down.

Her voice cracked as she started to speak through blocked sinuses which had been bothering her for a long time now, 'The doctors tell me that had Khan sahab gotten delayed by even fifteen minutes, he would not have survived. They were praising you tremendously for stopping the flow of blood. I now realize how Allah sends his angels when people are in distress.'

Sameer bowed his head, embarrassed and at a loss of words.

'Inara just told me how you emerged out of nowhere and brought her Abbu to the hospital.'

Emerged out of nowhere? Is that what you told her, Inara?

He bit back the half-smile that played upon his lips.

The stalking messiah would have been more apt!

'I should be thanking you for what you have done, but I know, son, that nothing and no act of kindness can repay what you have done for this family. But I would still like to know if we could help you in any way...anything at all! You just have to say it!'

Inara.

He almost spoke out aloud.

Just let me court your daughter. I promise you that I shall

be the best son-in-law you could ever have hoped for.

He smiled inwardly.

What if I had actually said that!

The thought tickled him, but he bowed his head again and said, 'I never thought of anything when I carried him to the hospital on that motorbike. I would have done that for anybody. In fact, anyone would have done that. There were many people there. It was just that I reacted quickly...'

She interrupted him, 'That was what made all the difference between life and death... Those crucial fifteen minutes and your presence of mind in blocking the flow of blood. Your mother must be very proud of you.'

Believe me, you will share her sentiments and that will make two: The mother and the mother-in-law.

He clenched his jaw, smothering the smile that was about to embarrass him.

'It has been hard for Inara. She is very close to her father. I guess the shock of seeing her father shot like that has unnerved her too much. The doctors have just given her an injection. I hope she recovers soon.'

She continued to speak, as he listened for another fifteen minutes, her faint voice echoing across the corridor. As Sameer emerged out of the room, a man accompanied him to the exit door at the end of the corridor. Inara was still asleep under the effect of the sedatives administered to her by the doctor when he left. He walked out of the hospital and as the sounds and the smells of the hospital faded away, he realized how much he was in absolute control of her. He wondered how she felt about him. It wasn't an entirely pleasant feeling. Not the usual heady, love kind of feeling, but a feeling laced with the guilt of longing for the forbidden as well as the feeling that this may be a one-sided affair.

How does it matter?

His chain of thought was broken when he heard someone call out his name from behind.

'Sameer!'

Shivkant's Singh's residence, Safdurjang Lane

Huddled with his core team of strategists, the MP from the Walled City knew that this incident was going to be a game changer. All his efforts to speak to the Imam had failed. He had even sent a messenger who was turned away politely. Shivkant Singh knew that if the city came to a boil, his political stock would plummet dramatically. The last thing he needed was an incident that would dramatically polarize the electorate. The police was already on a standby and the neighbouring Hindu dominated area was tense. The entire matter was now gradually turning into an 'Us versus Them' matter.

'He is calling a press conference in two hours,' a bearded man in khadi said, glancing at his mobile as it beeped, an SMS from a pet TV journalist, perhaps. Shivkant stared fixedly at the blank screen of the TV, his face expressionless, his lower lip protruding in a pout, his eyes unblinking, scarred by lack of sleep. Originally hailing from Bihar, 63-year-old Shivkant Singh was a short man, with a pronounced belly. His spiked and perennially oiled white hair and a thin white moustache could be misleading, but his political acumen had won him many admirers cutting across party lines. He was an old hand and a traditional Secular Party man through and through but recently he had fallen out of favour with the high command. Hence, he was removed from the cabinet and shifted to 'strengthen the party' at the organization level.

'What are you thinking, Singh sahab?'

88

Licking his parched lips, Shivkant Singh picked up the copper glass and gulped down some water. He looked at his confidant of 24 years and said, 'I am stuck. If I react and stop them, I will antagonize all the Muslim voters. If I don't, the Hindus will flock back to Raj Narain Pandey.'

He paused as the men around him weighed each and every word.

'But I hope, for his sake, hot-headed Imran would not do anything reckless. I hope the Imam prevails upon him. I seriously hope so.'

'That is, provided Imam sahab wishes to prevail over him. We have no idea, no clue whatsoever, as to what or how the Imam is thinking right now.'

'So we wait. Subhash, turn on the TV,' Shivkant Singh gestured to a tall man standing next to his bearded confidant.

The bearded man named Javed Khan glanced at his mobile as his eyes widened, 'I am afraid, sir, the News Broadcasters Association (NBA) has decided to not telecast the press conference live. But I am told that a few webcasters associated with the Imam's son will be showing it live on their portals.'

At the Press Conference

The Gulfaam community centre in the backyard of Jama Masjid was literally bursting at the seams with cameramen and reporters jostling for space in the rectangular hall. A long table, with three chairs, was placed at one end. A huge photograph of Mecca was hung as a backdrop of the dais. Cameramen were shouting at print media photographers, warning them not to block their view upon the Imam's arrival. Reporters were on their phones, connected to the newsrooms, coordinating with the assignment desks, and giving them animated accounts of

the latest developments and the time that Imam Zulfiqar Khan was supposed to arrive.

Suddenly, there was a commotion behind the cameramen. A tall muscular bodyguard of the Imam, accompanied by half a dozen young men, had just slapped a cameraman who was standing at the entrance to the hall to film the Imam's entrance. Tempers flared as other cameramen abandoned their posts and went to the rescue of their comrade. The bodyguard and his minions were suddenly in the minority.

'How dare you raise your hand on him, bastard?'

Push, shove, slap... The tussle reached a crescendo with the cameramen giving the bodyguard and his supporters a dose of their own medicine, forcing them to beat a hasty retreat. However, the bodyguard threatened them of dire consequences when he came back. It was just the perfect beginning to the press conference that would decide if the city would get sleep that night.

A few minutes later...

This time an old man with a flowing white beard in a brown salwar kameez and a black Nehru Jacket entered, appealing the media to maintain calm. He was also apologizing to the reporters for the trigger-happy bodyguard's scuffle with the cameraman. As the reporters and a few cameramen responded animatedly to the old man, someone shouted, 'Imam sahab is coming.'

The old man warned them with finality in his voice, 'No more ruckus as Imam sahab arrives, or we shall cancel the press conference. No shouting and no heckling, specially the cameramen.'

The warning worked, but only partially. The voices died

down but the decibel of the incessant clicking of photos by the print media a.k.a the still photographers rose, as electronic media cameramen glared at them while shouts of 'Still...still....' echoed in the room. Zulfiqar Khan arrived, accompanied by his son Imran Khan. Their clique of bodyguards made an oval enclosure around them to enable them to reach the dais. Reporters whispered into their mobile phones, informing the respective assignment desks that Imam sahab had just arrived.

Zulfiqar Khan, dressed in a black khadi sherwani and white khadi trousers, appeared solemn as his son Imran Khan scanned the room, gently smiling and nodding at the familiar faces in the press corps. His deep and intense eyes defied the upward arc of his lips. But there was anything but cheer in his heart.

Zulfiqar Khan and his son settled down in their respective chairs, leaving the third one vacant. Reporters noticed the empty chair, wondering who could be the mysterious third on the dais. The people accompanying the Imam requested the print media photographers to stay at the periphery so that they didn't block the view of the cameras filming the event.

Considering the sensitivity of the event, the News Broadcasters Association had decided not to telecast the press conference live, but three different web portals were telecasting it live across the world. So the purpose of the NBA stood defeated as the target audience was already acquired.

The grand old man speaks...

'I am a man of God.'

He paused. His pause was followed by the sound of a few clicks of the camera and a beep on a mobile.

'I am overwhelmed when people address me as Imam

sahab. More than the respect, it's the burden of a million aspirations that gives me sleepless nights. Every step you take, every word you speak is idolized by so many of your followers. And it is not because of my own qualities. I am just carrying a legacy that was entrusted upon me by my forefathers. I am here and I speak with the sense of that...' the Imam raised the index finger of his right hand in the air, 'responsibility...the burden of which rests on my frail shoulders, which someday I shall pass over to my son here.'

Zulfiqar Khan placed the same hand feebly on his son's shoulder.

'But today, I come here to condemn the cowardly attack on Imtiaz Khan, a namazi, a pious man who has a unique place in the community. The attack on Imtiaz Khan is an attack on the community.'

There was a sudden buzz in the hall as reporters slammed the keyboards of their iPads and mobile phones or scribbled on their notebooks. The Imam was just about to raise the stakes.

'We had been asking the police to provide security to Imtiaz Khan but all our requests had fallen on deaf ears. The mosque and the entire city itself is vulnerable to terror attacks with absolutely no security. The CCTV cameras do not record anything. It was a disaster waiting to happen. The attackers came and left without being challenged. And even now, more than twenty four hours have passed, and the police have no clue whatsoever about the identity of the perpetrators. We are men of peace, but we are being provoked, I repeat, we are being provoked!' This time the old man raised his index finger in the air with greater firmness.

'But I can see through your dirty games... We were provoked during the shame of 1992 and the outrage of the Gujarat genocide, but in both the unpardonable satanic acts,

ABHISAR SHARMA

I asked my people to maintain restraint. The anger still rankles in their hearts, but they have learnt to suppress it. Our patience should not, in any way, be construed as cowardice. No! But as I said, I can see through your dirty games.'

He paused and took a sip from the glass of water on the table.

'I would like to ask a question to the media here. How many of you can claim full knowledge of the attack that took place on Imtiaz Khan? You have just been reporting that an influential trader in the Walled City was attacked, owing to his relations with the jailed Tabrez Khan. But does anyone here know who took him to the hospital? Anyone?'

Another pause.

'The man who took Imtiaz to the hospital, the man who was the difference between his certain death and life, was a Hindu boy called Sameer Verma, a resident of this area. A Hindu boy who grew up in these by-lanes and I am proud to introduce this brave young lad to you.'

The Imam raised his hand, gesturing to someone standing behind the cameras. Sameer emerged, his face a mix of nervousness bordering on shock. He had just been airdropped at the press conference for the Imam's master stroke.

'Sameer Verma, come and sit next to me.'

Sameer hesitantly sat next to the Imam who was now flanked by Imran on his right and Sameer, 'the item number', on the left.

'Sometimes, the real story lies between the uncomfortable spaces that we dread to explore. This is the story that needs to be told to the world, the story of how the presence of mind of this Hindu boy, who is integrated in to a Muslim dominated locality, gave Imtiaz Khan a chance at life. Sameer may not be my biological son, but he assumes an importance far greater

THE KAAFIR'S LOVE

than my own son, Imran. Let me explain how...'

Imran sat next to his father, with a stoic expression, as if he knew what was coming. Reconciled to his father's big game—his master stroke—he now understood why the old man had fans cutting across party lines. Why the chief minister of UP would come running to him every time he was in Delhi. Why the clerics across the country would not take any decision without consulting him. Why he was such an important fixture in all important functions of the prime minister's office.

'Sameer is the son of a fruit seller. His family was in dire straits on the economic front. It would have been impossible for him to seek education even in a government school. But we decided to sponsor his entire education right from school to college and as a result, Sameer is now working in a multinational company. My son Imran is carrying out my legacy as I have done, but my other son...' The Imam now raised his left hand and placed it on Sameer's shoulder. Sameer still looked very uncomfortable, his eyes now merely slits, with camera flashbulbs shining on his face.

'My other son, Sameer, has made a place for himself in this society. He is an ideal example of what inclusivity can do to a society. We are proud of this son of the soil.'

As the flashbulbs blasted across the room, TV news channels cut in live to the press conference. The narrative had changed dramatically. Raj Narain Pandey was banking on a possible outburst by the Imam and his son, something that he needed to reinvent his own political comeback in the constituency, but the Imam could see through all of it. He even had his reasons to believe that the assassination attempt on Imtiaz Khan was orchestrated by forces close to Pandey. No one would ever know of that for sure, but the Imam could see the big game behind the entire plan. Like always, this time too, he prevailed over his son. That night he forced his reckless son to see the logic behind his thought and the 'Sameer Verma' trump card that he planned to play before the press. The general elections were just 18 months away. He knew that this was the perfect time for the polarization that the rightist forces would have desired—one incident and it would have ignited the whole of North India. The socialist government in Uttar Pradesh had drastically started losing its appeal amongst the electorate within a short time of their assuming power. The central government was enmeshed in its own issues, mainly related to its credibility, after the plethora of scams that beleaguered it. All the rightist party needed was communal polarization and a split of the Hindu-Muslim votes. Zulfiqar Khan wanted to avoid this at any cost and he knew that he, alone, was capable of doing it.

Meanwhile at Raj Narain Pandey's House

'It was just bloody brilliant, Gupta ji!'

Pandey mumbled, his voice barely audible, his eyes unwavering from the TV channel that he had just switched off after watching the rerun of the entire press conference on TV.

'I have always believed that men of God can be brilliant politicians, provided they keep their eyes, ears and the horizons of their thought wide-open to accept the viewpoint of the opposition. This man,' Pandey pointed his index finger at the screen with decisiveness, 'can be the difference between us and more than two dozen seats across North India, and you know what?'

Gupta stared at his master blankly.

'You can't touch him.'

Gupta took a deep breath, suppressed a burp and said

hesitatingly, 'There is a strange buzz going on...'

'And what would that be?' a faint smile spread across Raj Narain Pandey's face as if he knew what was coming.

'I think you know it...'

Pandey retorted, his eyes still fixed on the blank TV screen, 'I want you to say it.'

'That...uhm...that you orchestrated the attempt on Imtiaz Khan's life.'

'Well, well, well. Gupta ji, you are my closest confidant, you should be knowing all this,' Pandey's smile grew wider as he teased his political adviser.

Gupta ji smiled sheepishly and shook his head.

'Be careful of what you think Gupta ji. If I fall, you will automatically bear the brunt for it. It has happened in the past. It will happen again. Political advisers and secretaries always take the fall for the deeds and misdeeds of their masters.'

Gupta could not understand what Pandey meant by that last sentence. Was it a confession, a joke or a threat? He knew that it could be a threat and was implicit only if it was a confession. He could have delved deeper, scratched further, but he knew that muck was all he would have discovered, so, he shut his eyes and let it pass.

A week later...
2.33 p.m.
At Inara's House

Beep...beep...beep...beep.
beep...beep...beep...beep.
beep...beep....pause...

Disconnect!

Beep...beep...beep...beep.
beep...beep...beep...beep.
beep...beep...pause...

Disconnect again!

Her fingers trembled as she dialled his number and disconnected just at the last moment. A shadow of guilt overwhelmed her as she saw the number in her phone book. She had obtained that number from the hospital directory, when he had taken the bloodied Imtiaz Khan to the emergency ward. Simply storing it in her handset had given her a rush, a strange high, like the dawn of a reckless adventure. But as she disconnected for the third time, she asked herself,

Why would I not speak to him, knowing I have procured his number in my full senses? Why should I be afraid of speaking to him?

But she knew that it wasn't just speaking to him; it was what she wanted him to do.

'To hell with it,' she said it out loud.

The unknown number rang on Sameer's mobile as he first gazed at it and picked it up on the second ring.

'Hello...'

No answer.

'Hello...?'

No answer again, just a faint whiff of a breath.

Sameer smiled; he was also pleasantly surprised. Meanwhile, Inara's heart was beating so fast that her head started spinning. Her throat parched, she grabbed the bottle next to her table and gulped it in one go. All of these sounds carried over to the person on the other end of the phone.

'Inara, is that you?'

97

THE KAAFIR'S LOVE

He thought that she would not respond, but what she said next, stunned him out of his senses.

'Can you come over to my place?' she said, panting, barely able to control her breath.

'What?'

'Be there in fifteen minutes. Use the back door. No one uses that lane. I am waiting, come as soon as you can. I am alone...'

Then, she hung up.

The question that struck his mind first was not the logical one—*why is she calling me*—rather, it was...

How does she want me to get in without anyone noticing? What if I get caught? Would I get a beating from some enthusiastic relative?

Even he knew that saving Imtiaz Khan had not given him the licence to enter the house, especially when the daughter was all alone. Sameer started pacing across the small drawing room of his dilapidated house, his toes numb with fear, excitement and anticipation.

She doesn't know what she is doing.

She is probably stupid.

...maybe reckless too.

But then...no one is home...

How would anyone know that I am there?

Well, it's a disaster waiting to happen...

Maybe she just wants to thank me 'properly'.

We haven't spoken after that incident...

So, what's wrong even if someone discovers me at her place?

But then, she is alone! Dude, she is alone! Do you know what that means?

Sameer groaned, grabbed his hair and pulled at them hard.

'Fuck it!' He said aloud, 'I am going!'

98

The lane behind her house was much narrower than he had anticipated. A mere arm's width, it only had space for a bicycle to go through; it was so cramped that one could stretch out one's arms and touch both sides. He knew that the fifth door was hers. He just had to knock it once and get in and hope that no one would see him enter.

As he stood in front of the back door, he wondered if he should call her mobile or just tap the door. His hands were trembling and he could feel a surge of electricity course through his calves and toes.

'Phew,' he breathed out and raised his hand to knock at the door.

'What are you doing?' She opened the door even before he could knock and pulled him inside by grabbing his collar.

'Are you mad?! What were you waiting for? I was peeping through the keyhole and I saw you standing there for like a thousand years!'

'No, I...uh...I...' His throat was parched and he felt faint as a sudden panic attack engulfed him. He exhaled heavily and looked around. It seemed like a dark storeroom with huge trunks piled over each other, covered and tied with a jute rope. Some had markings and inscriptions in Urdu which he could not understand. In that musty, dimly-lit storeroom, he saw a rectangular framed black-and-white photograph of a woman in a burkha sitting on a chari, her face revealed, a child on her lap, and a clean-shaven man standing next to her. The man looked similar to Imtiaz Khan. Before he could deduce anything, she said, 'Did anyone see you come in?'

'I don't know. I guess not...I mean I don't think so...'

Through the faint light coming from the door behind, he saw Inara looking simply beauteous, her hair plaited neatly, reflecting an effusive golden glow. For the first time, he saw

THE KAAFIR'S LOVE

her in a casual black T-shirt and baggy capris. Though she was standing against the light, he could see the outline of her oval face with her wide and curious eyes that looked pale brown in the light. He didn't know whether his mind were playing tricks on him or it was because of the abstractness of the situation that he was in, but the moment was indeed surreal.

How else could anyone define this moment?! Here I am standing in her storeroom and she...just a breath away.

In fact, he could feel her warm breath on his chest. Maybe he was imagining that. But how did it matter? He was with Inara, in her house.

'Ok, just follow me.'

She turned around and started walking and Sameer followed her. Soon, he was in their kitchen which was bright, spacious, fully-equipped and bigger than his whole house. The smell of biryani assailed his senses as he saw a big black semi-oval deep vessel with scraps of flavoured and coloured rice sticking to its surface.

Biryani indeed! That's what my lady had for lunch.

They crossed the kitchen into another small room, what seemed like a buffer between the main drawing room and the kitchen. It had a table with a steel utensil, covered by a plate and going by the steam that covered its rim, the food inside was piping hot. A white plate with a fancy blue design on the rim was kept aside neatly.

That was where she stopped, turned around and gestured him to sit.

She was quiet for almost a minute, as if thinking what to say and how to start the conversation. She looked uncertain, a far cry from the picture of confidence she always portrayed.

'I have never been ashamed of admitting that I love my Abbu more than my Ammi. Though they say that I am a spitting

ABHISAR SHARMA

image of my mother...'

They are damn right!

'As I saw you hoisting him up from the ground that day, I was sure that he will not survive. How could he, I remember thinking! A bullet had entered his face and exited from the other end, but it is nothing short of a miracle that the bullet grazed just an inch below his brain. I remember that night. My heart was pounding so hard, I thought it would explode! I thought that I would die before him. But he survived,' she said, tears welling up in her dark and kohl-lined eyes. She wiped away the single drop of tear that had crossed the threshold of her eyelashes, with her index finger.

Then, she raised her eyes, locking them with his. He felt disarmed and slightly dizzy, as she continued to gaze deep into his eyes. For the first time, she had let him come this close to her, to see her vulnerability. That was what that moment meant for him...special.

'Surely a miracle had happened,' her voice was now barely a whisper as she bowed her head, lightly tapping the edge of the dining table with her beautiful fingers.

'And it was you,' she raised her head, 'that made that miracle happen. You...Sameer Verma.'

The pause that followed was the strangest single moment of their lives. Both had their heads bowed, not even looking at each other, their minds were numb, and their words, that seemed to have been glued to some far recess of their soul, were refusing to be uttered.

'My Abbu lived and it was only because of one man. It was because of you...'

Sameer smiled. He felt overwhelmed that she had just put him on a pedestal. He felt tremendously aroused too, maybe it was because of her vulnerability at that moment, that look

101

of surrender in her eyes, though there was still not complete capitulation.

'I have never cooked for any other man in my life, except for my father, and I had made a promise to myself that if I ever cook for anyone else, it would only be for my husband.'

Sameer listened to each and every word, his gaze moving between her lips and her eyelashes.

'But I never knew that somewhere in between, there would come a man who would assume such an important place in my life, probably the most important one by the sheer impact of his deed.'

Without looking at him, she turned her head to the utensil on the table and uncovered the lid. A whiff of sumptuous chicken biryani filled his senses...the delicious aroma, the smell of the chicken and the long rice laced with chicken stock, the subtle fragrance of the cloves, the cardamom and the saffron. She elegantly placed the plate in front of him and with equal grace, stirred the biryani with the serving spoon. Steam rose from it, further enticing his senses. Hungry that he already was, this was just heaven. As she served the biryani, he gazed at her intently, with his mouth slightly open. She was probably waiting for him to ask her to stop. But he was lost in a different plane of existence. Inara smiled, her eyes still not meeting his.

'That's all,' he fumbled over his words.

She raised her eyes, her lips stretched into a smile. This time, she was playing the perfect hostess to an important man in her life.

'Thanks...it tastes amazing,' he spoke as he pushed the first spoonful in his mouth.

The next five minutes were awkward for him and amusing for her because the munching sounds he made, broke the silence. She was staring intently at his mouth all this while.

102

Suddenly, she got up, saying, 'Let me get some water for you.'

As she disappeared, Sameer ate the remaining biryani with a vengeance. He had to finish it before she came back. The ordeal was too much for him to take. And lo and behold...

'Allah! You've already finished the biryani! Do you want some more? Did you like it?'

Sameer responded, moving his head sideways, his mouth full with the last huge morsel. He looked as if he had just run a hundred-metre sprint.

'Thanks,' he mumbled, with biryani still stuffed in his mouth. Inara smiled again.

'God, were you hungry! You ate so fast? I was away for like three seconds,' she giggled.

'I'm sorry, I'm a fast eater,' he smiled nervously. This was followed by an embarrassing hiccup. He reached for the glass of water and gulped it down immediately to save himself from further embarrassment.

An awkward silence followed.

'I wanted to thank you in the most special way I knew, Sameer. And I...'

Sameer interrupted, 'You could not have said it in a better way.'

Inara bowed her head shyly, fidgeting with a handkerchief, rolling it between her fingers.

Lucky bastard, that handkerchief!

She looked into his eyes and said, 'I just want to say one more thing.'

But before she could tell him, the doorbell rang...

The romance in the air suddenly evaporated as their eyes widened in alarm and their hearts started beating fast.

'Who the hell could it be? Shit!' she cried. Inara jumped up from the chair and started pacing the small space of the

103

buffer room, her mind in panic, wondering what to do next. Sameer just sat there, shocked and certain that this would be the last day of his life. Then, dramatically, she grabbed his hand and dragged him to the storeroom. Even in that moment of extreme panic, the warm cushion of her soft but firm hand was so comforting. This was the first time they had locked hands like that.

The doorbell rang again.

She went to open the door and heard faint voices from outside. She bent down and peeped from the keyhole and her eyes widened in horror.

'Shit! The neighbours have opened their back doors and are chatting with each other!' she squeaked. The doorbell was now ringing again insistently. 'I am so finished!' she looked around wildly, wondering where to hide him.

'Listen, just hide somewhere you think you wouldn't be found out easily. I don't know what else to say.'

Inara turned back and started walking towards the drawing room. With panic setting in, Sameer looked around for a space to hide.

'What took you so long?'

The sight of Zubeida standing on the threshold was a tremendous relief, but this was a secret she would not even share with her. Inara's cheeks and neck were red. Her ears and her heart were pounding rebelliously. She was panting as if she had just run a marathon.

'You okay?' Zubeida asked as she forced her way in to the house, looking around quizzically. Inara's condition had sown the seed of suspicion in her mind.

'I am fine, but I want to be alone.'

'Why? What happened?'

'I don't feel well, that's why!' Inara's voice became high-pitched with panic, as she saw Zubeida's inquisitive eyes scanning the house for the intruder that she suspected was hiding somewhere.

'But you have never asked me to leave before, even when you have been unwell! What's wrong?'

'*Zubeida!* Nothing is *wrong!*' The emphasis on *Zubeida* and *wrong* was obvious, underlining the curtness of her tone. Inara wanted to convey clearly that Zubeida was not welcome and she needed to get the hell out of there.

'Why are you being so rude to me?'

'I am not! You are just irritating me!'

'I am not irritating you, Inara.' The look of hurt in Zubeida's eyes did not match her actions. She still seemed to be searching for the intruder.

'Is there something you wish to tell me? Is there someone...'

She paused, looking intently at Inara. Zubeida was trying to get a confession of guilt out of her but Inara was now getting brazen. She knew that she could not be defensive anymore. She knew that Zubeida *knew*.

'Is he in the house, Inara? Is Sameer here?'

Silence.

'You won't even deny? Allah! Inara, you are playing with...'

'Zubeida!' Inara retorted, 'It is best that you leave now, you are getting too imaginative for your own good. Please leave!'

'All I am asking of you is to stop playing with fire. He is, after all, a Kaafir.'

'Shut up, Zubeida!' This time her voice echoed loud enough to be heard by Sameer, who was cowering in a dusty and cobwebbed corner of the storeroom.

'You have never spoken to me like that! Ever! And all for that...' Zubeida didn't dare complete her sentence and speak that forbidden word again. She kept looking at Inara. She would have felt hurt in any other circumstance but she knew that she had caught Inara on the wrong foot. So, she turned around and exited the house in a huff.

It was now Inara's turn to feel miserable.

She walked back to the storeroom, anger and irritation writ large on her face, her mind unable to erase the look of sadness on Zubeida's face. Warm air filled her chest when she tried to exhale heavily as Sameer emerged from his hideout.

'I think your neighbours have left,' Sameer gestured towards the back lane, 'I don't hear any voices now. I even heard the shutting of a door. Actually, I heard two distinct sounds which means, it's safe for me to open the door.'

'Come here.'

There was something strange in Inara's voice. Her words were laden with vulnerability and a hint of desire.

He stood transfixed in front of her, just a breath away. She first bowed her head and then moved closer to him, her head touching his chest. As a reflex, he stepped back, but she immediately clawed his shirt, undoing one of the buttons. For the first time, she saw the naked bronzed skin of his slightly hairy chest. Her breath rising, she moved her index and middle finger inside the small opening created by the unbuttoning. He was warm as his chest rose and fell. She could sense the panic in him. Inara raised her eyes and looked deeply into his. A thin film of sweat glistened over his upper lip as nervousness paled his face. Sameer was stunned. Never had he been engulfed by two emotions—two radically different emotions at the same time—arousal and fear. Inara withdrew her fingers from his shirt and slowly placed her head on his chest. Her hands now uncomfortably dangled sideways. His heart enmeshed in panic, Sameer raised his right hand and placed it over her back. She stirred but didn't move away. Instead, she raised her arms and clasped him. Miraculously, both could feel the panic ebbing away. But a new feeling was taking its place and Inara was the first one to feel it. Sameer could feel her warm breath caressing his chest as she tightened her grip around his waist.

Trying hard to control her breath, she said, 'Hug me tightly; don't let go.'

Their bodies were now intertwined, as his arms cocooned her. She drew closer to him and Sameer felt her breasts tease his chest, their breathing now perfectly synchronized. They stood like that for some time as a pleasant dizziness overcame both of them. Inara shut her eyes, tempted to doze off. It was so comforting and warm in the cocoon of his embrace, but the sounds of the world outside suddenly permeated her ears. She knew he would have to go. Then, she did something that surprised them both.

Inara stood on her toes and gently pressed her lips to his. A faint moan escaped his lips, as she felt his lips encircling hers, the moistness of his mouth now hers to relish. His eyes shut, Sameer stood numb. Flashes of intense desire struck him from within, as she started enamouring his senses. It felt like biting into a sweet, juicy strawberry, like the first bite of a ripe black grape, like slowly relishing the fruity exterior as you can feel the juice gushing out from the core. On an impulse, Sameer moved his tongue in her mouth. The first bite wasn't enough. She moaned feebly as she felt his tongue in her mouth. And then...

She pushed him back.

'Not the tongue thing,' she said, barely able to catch her breath.

'Please,' he pleaded longingly.

'No, not now, and,' she giggled, 'you smell of biryani. I can even taste it in your mouth. Just go now. I am afraid someone

107

THE KAAFIR'S LOVE

else might drop in and then we will be in serious trouble.'

She stared at him with the glint of playfulness in her eyes.

'Let's not spoil this. All I wanted was to thank you. And I think you are stretching it a bit too far.'

'Am I seeing you again? Rather, when am I seeing you again?'

'Sameer, go! The lane is quiet.'

'Please, just tell me.'

'You have my number, now just go! Please.'

The 'please' wasn't a request. It was sheltered by a smile.

The Imam's residential quarters, inside the mosque

'Abba will never trust me! He never says it, but I can read it in his eyes. He thinks that I am unfit to carry on his legacy.'

Imran Khan was with his mother, Afshan Begum, 51 years old, whose henna-dyed orange hair peeked through an abundance of black streaks. The dark circles under her eyes were carefully hidden by a generous application of concealer. In a dark red sari and white blouse, the round-faced, pleasantly-plump Afshan Begum sat on a teak-wood rocking chair, carefully listening to her son, though her eyes were fixed on the pair of colourful blue jays jumping restlessly inside the cage hanging near the window of her sunlit room.

'You are restless, Imran. You need to think like your father.' Her voice was calm and soft like the pleasant sunlight on a cold winter morning. Afshan Begum did not let the birds out of her sight even as she tried assuaging the wounded pride of her son.

'Your father is like a clever politician. His responsibility is even bigger than the politicians who represent our constituency. After all, he represents faith...'

ABHISAR SHARMA

'You don't get it, Ammi!' Imran retorted with a hint of anger in his voice, 'Abbu's style of working is over. The Muslims of this country are getting restless. We need leaders who can address their cause. Look at Kashmir, look at the scores of Muslims who have picked up the gun and are walking the path of jihad.'

'Are you justifying that form of violent jihad? Are you trying to say that people who pick up the gun and go on slaughtering the innocent are correct?' Afshan Begum countered.

'I am just saying that such youth have no place in Abba's discourse! They never had! He dismisses them as aberrations! They are, after all, a part of the ummah. We shall have to seek answers for Islam through the acts of their restlessness.'

Afshan Begum was a woman of her convictions. She had been with her husband long enough to understand his brand of politics. She could see the divergence and she could see the long-term implications of her son's recklessness.

'But this agitation cannot be the excuse and it can never be used as a gun to be pointed at the head of an entire community for the voice of the restless to be heard? You want to turn the entire argument on its head! You want *them*, the restless, to lead the agenda, the dialogue with the world?'

'Why not? Can you afford to ignore them? You say that I am different from Abba? Well, yes, I am, and let me tell you what my problem is with his school of thought.'

Imran paused. He kept staring at the floor and then turned his eyes, locking them with his mother's.

'I have issues with Abbu's school of thought because I see him as a closet politician though he seems to be unashamed of admitting it! I see that the lines between religion and politics seem to have blurred for him. That's my problem with him.'

Suddenly, Afshan Begum's help, Naeema, a young, dark

109

THE KAAFIR'S LOVE

complexioned and petite girl opened the door and stood before them, apologetically, with her head bowed, 'Imam sahab is on his way.'

Imam Zulfiqar Khan entered as soon as she finished announcing him, as if waiting for a cue to come in. After entering the room, he did not acknowledge any one of them, leave alone look at them. He just strolled to one corner of the room and sat on his favourite cushioned chair, the one that only he could use. Imran raised himself up on his chair as a mark of respect for the old man as Afshan Begum stared at her husband calmly, without any sign of panic or urgency on her face.

Zulfiqar Khan sat on his chair and shut his eyes, but anyone could see that there was a storm unravelling inside him. One could see that his eyeballs were constantly moving sideways, typical of a man trying to clasp something but unable to put a finger on it.

'You know what my problem is with your version of Islam, Imran?'

The gentle and the silken voice of the Imam had a hint of steel in it, something both Imran and his mother dreaded. Now they understood that the Imam had been listening in on their entire conversation, standing just outside the room. Zulfiqar Khan opened his eyes and then turned his head towards his son.

'The problem with your version of Islam is that it drives, and when I say drives, I mean something violent, you see; it drives a wedge between Hindus and Muslims of this country. To be fair to you, I know that these are two different entities and they can never find common cause on the grounds of religion. As long as they interact, religion shall continue to play a dominant role, and both entities will seek solace and shelter in their respective religions. Hence, the vicious cycle of confrontation shall never end. When you think about it, it is really simple: Interaction means religion and religion leads to confrontation! But having said that, it is human emotions superseding religious beliefs that bind them together, there are innumerable simple and daily examples of such a bonding. That's the only hope for them. As long as we stay together, we will need such emotions and examples to bind us together. Now, coming back to your version of Islam.'

The old man paused and then shut his eyes, resting his head on the headrest of the chair.

'My problem arises with this puritanical approach you have towards religion. Unconsciously, you strive to divide the Muslims further into Shias and Sunnis! Segregating the Ahmadiyas, branding them not Islamic enough, even branding them Wajib-ul-Qatal (fit to be murdered). This Salafi ideology arising out of the sands of Saudi Arab that brands some Muslims as Kaafirs! This Takfiri school of thought is my problem!'

He raised his head again from the headrest and locked his eyes with his son, 'And this, my son, is precisely what is leading to the genocide of Shias in Pakistan. I mean look at Pakistan! In 1947, the country had minorities, the non-Muslims comprising 23 per cent of its population, and now it is reduced to an abysmal 2–3 per cent! That is what your school of thought strives to do!'

Imran shook his head, a wry smile caressing his lips.

'Correct me if I am wrong! Don't you dare patronize me like that!' his father thundered.

'Patronize you, Abbu? I thought that was your favourite weapon against me? I just speak for Muslims who have been slaughtered like lambs by those harami Kaafirs. I speak against those who roam around freely, nurturing ambitions to subjugate us as second-class citizens and turning India into

111

a Hindu Rashtra. My blood boils when I see my Abbu, who can make a difference, make a weak and impassioned plea for maintaining peace! Peace? Peace, Abbu? There is no peace!'

The Imam was listening carefully to each and every word of his son. It's not that he did not see reason in Imran's anger. It was just that he knew that the anger would only make him unhappier. He was worried that his son was pushing himself further to the edge, and that was the last place he wanted to see the future influential leader of the community.

Eyes unwavering from his son's distressed face, he said, 'You think my blood does not boil when I see Muslims getting slaughtered in Gujarat or Assam? You think I have never ever been haunted by the cries of Muslim women who were raped by the lunatics of Bajrang Dal and their types? You were not even ten years old when they brought down the Babri Masjid. I know your uncles tell you tales of how I appealed for peace and how they wished that I had made a call for retaliation instead! It was because of my appeal for peace that lives were saved. Had I made a call for retaliation, we would have been pushed further to the edge, and that is just what the Sanskari Party wanted! I had seen the fires of Partition. I know what hate is capable of. Yes, you are right! There is no escape from all of this, from the truth! But then there is another truth that you need to understand... The chance for the utopia that you so fervently desire came way back in 1947 and look what they did to the paradise that was Pakistan, the Land of the Pure; rather, now I should call it the Land of the Puritanical.'

∾

Sameer and Inara had faced their desire for each other, but there was only one fear that lurked in Inara's mind... not

the fear of being discovered by her parents, but the fear of Zubeida, her once best friend turned stalker. There was an undercurrent of hostility between them. In any other matter or circumstance, Inara would have been the catalyst herself to flare up the hostility. But this time was different. She knew that she was on the defensive and she also knew that Zubeida was aware of this.

Inara had joined Freebird Publications. It was a typical 10-to-6 job. After attending his night shift, a bleary-eyed Sameer would take a bath, take a small nap and then head for Connaught Place. He would message her on his arrival. If she could, she would always come out and meet him. Her one-hour lunch break was always spent with him. He would spend the day waiting for her to emerge. There would be days when she would get free earlier and this would only mean either a movie or a visit to Lodhi Garden. They went to any place where they could get cosy. Parthasarthy Rock was still taboo because of the discomfort it had created, but the first threshold—the laxman rekha—had been crossed when they had kissed at her house. In those dark and cosy cinema halls, where they purposely chose flop movies or movies that would have thin attendance, they would hold hands, fingers intertwined. They would touch each crevice, each crease of the other. They would feel and cherish the warmth, even the moisture of their hands. Initially, Inara would hesitantly tilt her head towards him, but never place it on his shoulder. Sameer noticed it happen a couple of times during the first movie they saw together. Then, as they approached the climax of the movie, he raised his right hand, the one away from Inara, and gently pressed her head to his shoulder. That was the reassurance both of them needed. The first movie they saw together also led to their second kiss.

As they exited the near empty cinema hall, he clasped her

right arm and gently pressed her to the wall of the corridor that led to the exit. It was dark and they were the last ones to leave. First, she gasped. Then, he pressed his lips to hers as she instinctively pressed her palms on his chest. They stood motionless for a minute and then her mouth melded into his and they started to relish the nectar of each other's lips. Inara moaned as he nibbled her lower lip. He could feel her breasts rising and teasing his chest as he moved closer to her. This was the closest they had ever been yet. Sameer moved his lips along her chin and then to her cheeks. As the tip of his nose touched her right ear, she quivered. It was the trigger that broke down all the protective walls she had built around herself. Realizing what the mere sensation of his nose had done to her, Sameer moved towards her ears and started licking her earlobes, tasting, teasing and dipping his tongue inside her ear.

A pleasant shock ran through Inara's body that culminated below her navel as she reluctantly and unsuccessfully tried to push him away. He had discovered her trigger and wanted to stimulate it further, and slide deep down into the maze of her desires. After struggling for a minute, just when she realized that she was in danger of losing her senses and control, she gasped, 'Please.'

Sameer glided his right hand across the curve of her waist and just when he was about to rise further, he paused. He could still feel her breath caressing his chest, her breasts touching his chest. He knew that she was vulnerable and her frontier had been breached. The *please* was a feeble cry for mercy. He understood that what he wanted was something that she still didn't desire with all her heart. He slowly moved back to her lips as she panted heavily. The sweet smell of her mouth, like strawberries, a hint of popcorn and Pepsi, a caress of the moisturizer on her cheeks, Sameer stood there just inhaling her fragrance. This went for another ten minutes till they heard footsteps from the side of the screen. Hurriedly withdrawing, they started walking towards the exit door as Inara dabbed her lips with her pink handkerchief. That day on her walk to the metro station, she did not look at him. She knew that he was walking behind her. Her heart was beating really fast. She was sure of one thing. The feeling that besieged her wasn't shame. It wasn't even repentance. It was her desire that lay naked before him. There were no pretences between them now.

Sameer would always accompany her back home in the metro and get down one stop before. This way the chance of getting spotted together was minimal.

This was the time when Inara's mother's time was spent mostly in the hospital where Imtiaz Khan, her father, was still recuperating. The family detested relatives coming and staying in their house, so Inara was mostly alone during the day, when she was not working, and evenings. With the entire house to herself, she was often tempted, but she dared not repeat that folly of calling Sameer over again. However, she would be on the phone with Sameer, sometimes for hours. Inara's mother was too busy with her husband, hence there was no way to notice the change in her daughter.

Where Inara's interaction with Zubeida had come to a naught for obvious reasons, tragically, Sameer's evening chats with Nasir over kebabs and chai had also dramatically decreased. Sameer was uncomfortable with Nasir asking, and regularly warning him, about Inara, so he started avoiding him. Nasir first thought was that it was just a phase or probably extra work in office, but then one day, he saw Sameer with Inara in Connaught Place. His immediate reaction was to confront him, but looking at them together, he knew that it was too late now. So, he decided to wait for Sameer to tell him about

Inara himself. He knew that his best friend would come to him eventually.

～

Four months had passed since Imtiaz Khan had been shot. The summer was unrelenting. Nature had unleashed its fury. It seemed like the Walled City was in for preferential treatment by the intense heat. Not only the dogs, but even the people had started behaving in a strange manner. They were snapping at the slightest provocation. Fights were breaking out at the flimsiest of reasons. There had already been two minor fires at the restaurants and both were caused by a short circuit. The trickle of sweat, travelling from behind one's ears to the neck and then down the back, felt like a sharp claw tracing its path down the spine. Children would just not stop scratching the boils caused by heat, hence causing further agony. Women forced to wear black burkhas even in that heat, were stinking from a distance of three feet. Khansamas, or cooks at kebab and curry shops, stood in front of the tandoors and the boiling pot in ill-fitting, sweat-soaked vests, with their bellies wobbling, scratching their armpits and throwing orders at the timid helpers who cowered before their masters in fear.

The lovebirds had been taking new strides every day and even the unforgiving summer did not deter them. They would continue to roam in the outer circle of Connaught Place, at times, cutting through the by-lanes and the backyards of various shops. There were times they would cross a desolate stretch. Sameer would look around and if no one was around, he would grab her arms and kiss her. Inara always anticipated Sameer's move the moment they entered a lane that was a bit isolated. As they kissed, with one eye on the lane, their hearts would race, the adrenaline unfathomable, the feeling simply indescribable in words. After kissing each other, they would walk with unsuppressed smiles on their faces, as if wanting to break free in laughter. A mutual acceptance, that the person walking next to them is the most special person right now, was their joint code. These would be the moments when they would not speak to each other, but Inara would always love to steal a glance at him, just to know what Sameer was thinking, only to find him looking right back at her. It was just magical.

A thought often bothered them though. They had not made an effort to define what existed between them. They had still not used the word *love* ever. How could they? It was not supposed to be everlasting, as both knew that it was in the realm of the forbidden. But something that felt so magical and made them so restless could not just be a mere passing attraction? They wondered. Both needed answers. It was just a matter of time when they would have some.

The Central Park, cushioned right in the middle of Connaught Place, was always buzzing and you could find all sorts of people—unemployed men, government babus lying under the shade, families who had just emerged out of Janpath and Palika Bazaar having lunch, college students with their unabashed 'I don't care' attitude, lovebirds grabbing their own space at the peripheries of the park and so on. One of the many couples jostling for space was Sameer and Inara.

Both sat cross-legged, facing each other, as Sameer stared at her immaculately pedicured feet and a lone black ant moving towards them. When it reached the edge of her salwar, Sameer brushed it off, hurling it back into the oblivion of thick grass, the ant's dreaded jungle. But he did something else too. He caressed her soft, tender and spotless feet, all under the pretence of brushing off the insect from climbing her feet. Sameer raised his eyes. She was looking right at him. He pursed his lips, failed hopelessly and ended up smiling.

'What's so funny?' she enquired, a hint of curtness in her silken voice.

'Nothing,' he said, as he shifted his gaze back to her feet. Inara curled her toes, dropping her dupatta over her feet which were under intimate scrutiny.

'Why did you do that?' he protested.

'Do what, Sameer?' The way she uttered 'Sameer' felt like a gentle stab.

'Can I touch your feet?'

'You want to touch my feet? Why?'

'Ainwain! Just like that...'

She turned her gaze away from him and bowed her head as she mumbled, 'That's too personal and intimate.'

'And kissing is not?' he teased her, as if testing her patience.

'It is, but I think touching my feet is more intimate!' She sounded irritated and had discomfort writ large on her face.

'Let's change the topic, please,' she mumbled.

'No, in fact, this is the perfect time to talk about a few things that have been bothering me,' he insisted.

'Don't ever think that those things are bothering only *you*!'

'Oh! So you know what I wish to speak about?'

She said nothing, but smiled back with a touch of sarcasm in her eyes.

'Don't patronize me, Inara! You have no right to do this.'

'What did I do?' Her voice broke into a shrill protest.

'That look on your face! You always do that!'

'Do what, Sameer? Here I am, sitting with you, out in the open in Connaught Place, unmindful that some inquisitive relative might spot us and report this back home. I meet you daily, at times, ignoring my work, knowing the perils of what

ABHISAR SHARMA

might happen if this gets discovered.'

Sameer interrupted, 'Is it only about you, Inara? Am I not shamefully ignoring my work and living on the edge too, risking my very existence in the Walled City?'

'So why? Why are we doing this? Why are we playing this dangerous game which could change so many lives forever, which could bring grief to so many people? Why?' A film of tears covered her eyes.

'It's not a game.'

'Shut up, Sameer!' She clenched her jaws, 'I just meant it as an expression. Don't take what I say, so literally! All I am asking is...why are we...'

'You want to know why, Inara?' The gravitas in his voice meant only one thing. This was going to be dramatic.

'It is because I have never known a bond in my whole life that has given me such a pure and unblemished feeling. Nothing. I have seen the worst sorrows of my life in the most pious relationship of my life: My relationship with my Amma! But with you...'

The reluctant teardrop stood entangled in her beautiful eyelashes as she looked at him in rapt attention.

'With you, I don't care, even if my existence in the cocoon of the city is threatened, even if the strongest bonds of my life are violated. It's not a fling! I have had my share of those. Remember what I said when we met for the first time? I would like to repeat it again, your face radiates the noor of Khwaja Moinuddin Chisti's dargah,' he paused for a moment and then whispered softly, 'that noor and that peace is my cocoon when I am with you, so why would I bother about the world?'

The warm air suddenly froze. The chirping of the sparrows, the guffaws of the college kids, the sound of smoke-spewing cars, all the sounds around them were suddenly muffled. It

THE KAAFIR'S LOVE

seemed as if everything had quietened down on purpose, as if the world conspired to hear what he was saying and what she wanted to hear.

'I don't remember ever having felt like this for anyone! Anyone in my life! Today, I would like to say something in my full senses.'

'Don't…Sameer,' Inara knew what he was going to say and trembled at the thought.

'I love you and I have loved you from the day I saw you looking at me with a thousand questions in your eyes in school. I have loved you ever since I saw you looking at me with pain, when I carried the ashes of my father to the Yamuna. I have loved you ever since you caught me trailing you, here, in CP.'

With trembling hands, he caught and held her hands in his own. As his warm hands sheathed hers, she could sense the vibration travelling from his trembling hands to her heart. Inara closed her eyes, as tears started rolling down her cheeks.

His voice now barely a whisper, he said, 'Now it is your turn. I have laid bare my feelings for you, yet again.'

Inara bowed down her head, her mouth agape, lips parted, unable to breathe. Her chest rose rhythmically, incapable of controlling her breath. It was a different thing to be in a relationship without defining it, and it was a totally different thing after you give it words, lend it a name. Sameer had just defined his feelings for her, something that she knew all along, something that she did not wish to accept, something she felt for him as well, because she knew that once the word *love* became a part of the lexicon, it would become a one-way street with no chance of a U- turn.

'I am still waiting.'

'I have nothing to say.'

Sameer tilted his head and said, 'You have nothing to say?'

120

'And certainly not in this crowded place,' she retorted.

'So where do you want to say it?' he probed her face with his desire-laden eyes.

Inara raised her eyes. A thin film of tears was covering her eyes. The moment had overwhelmed her. She blinked once and asked, 'How many girls have you taken to Parthasarthi Rock with you?'

'What?' Sameer was stunned and a little taken aback by the unexpected question. He replied haltingly, 'Errrm...why? How does that even matter?'

With firmness in her voice, she repeated her question, 'How many girls have you taken to Parthasarthi Rock with you?'

Sameer bowed his head and then smiled, his eyes on the grass burnt brown by the unrelenting summer.

'I am waiting for your answer.' She was adamant.

'But how does it matter now?'

'Because, I want to know what space I occupy in your life, as you had insisted on taking me there on our very first meeting. I deserve to know the truth and nothing less.'

His hands froze and his head felt heavy. It seemed as if something was gouging his heart out with its pointed nails. He felt riddled with the burden of guilt and a rancid feeling of having committed a sin. He raised his eyes just to look into hers for a moment, like the hundredth of a second, and bowed his head again. Just moments ago, he had bared his soul to her and he knew that he could not lie to her now. He also realized that only truth shall set him free.

'I...' he trembled, 'I have taken a couple of girls to Parthasarthi Rock with the intention of...you know...' His voice petered off.

She was watching him with a sadistic sense of empowerment that he could not lie to her. She wanted the truth and the truth

121

THE KAAFIR'S LOVE

was what she would have.

Sameer exhaled. Suddenly, the wall of guilt that overwhelmed him cracked. Streaks of anger shone through the crevices and punctured nooks of the wall. He started breathing heavily and raised his eyes. She could see him rebelling but she was unnerved.

'I took them to the isolation of those rocks because I had desires and so did they. We could see through our pretences of a healthy friendship. Afterwards, we drifted apart because there was nothing more that we desired beyond those intimate moments. I saw the futility of continuing that charade by calling it friendship.'

'You had sex with them?' Her voice dipped as she uttered the word 'sex'.

'No, I did not...'

'You are lying! You did!' she replied as her jaw tightened.

'I don't need to lie. Neither do I feel the need to justify myself for my actions. Quenching a desire isn't a sin. It takes two to tango.'

'And you see me as your third trophy at Parthasarthi Rock?'

Sameer suddenly got up and walked a few steps away from Inara. He could feel the warm air rising up his throat as a storm of uneasiness swirled in his chest.

'So you see me as a trophy, don't you?' Her tone was accusatory.

His eyes were now streaked with red, 'I don't think that even warrants a response.'

'That doesn't answer my question,' she persisted.

Before Sameer could respond, Inara's mobile phone started ringing. Her eyes widened in fear as soon as she saw the name on the phone. It was her home number.

How is this possible? Ammi comes back home in the

evenings! How could she come back so early? Has someone noticed us sitting here in CP?

'Allah,' she said, panicking. 'It's a call from my home! But how can it be? Ammi is not supposed to be back so soon.'

'Now, don't panic. Just answer it!' Sameer reasoned.

'Just shut up!' She raised her index finger and said, 'and don't say anything. Please...'

Inara took a deep breath and then pressed the green button on her mobile.

'Hello...Ammi? Yes, I...I am here only. I mean, I am at work. No...I mean...what? How...when did this happen? Okay...I will be there soon!'

She hung up.

'What happened?' The suspense was about to claim its first victim in the form of Sameer as a thick layer of sweat glistened on his forehead and his throat had suddenly gone dry. He licked his lips and looked at Inara, whose eyes were now moving sideways as if trying to figure out what might be happening.

'Don't just sit here like that; tell me what happened!'

'Abbu is back home, Ammi had just called and was asking where I am. But Abbu was not supposed to come for another month at least! The doctors must worked some miracle, I presume.'

'So that's good, isn't it?'

'I did not like her tone. It was very accusatory. I...'

But before she could complete her sentence, Sameer's mobile phone started ringing. The look of horror was back, this time on Sameer's face.

'What the fu...! It's the number you call me from, you know, your home number.'

Inara cupped her mouth with her right hand yelping a faint 'Allah' under her breath as Sameer kept staring at the screen of his mobile, his hands now shaking. He raised his right hand and placed the mobile to his ear.

'Hello? Yes...yes Aunty? Yes...oh! That...that's great!' Sameer looked at Inara, panic covering his face as he wiped off a layer of sweat from his face.

'Ok...but, no...no...this is unnecessary. It's okay! Please don't, please...'

A long pause followed after which he said 'okay' at each and every word from the other end, the panic now ebbing, giving way to a nervous smile.

'Thank you, aunty. I will be there!'

'What?' she lunged at him, 'What was that about *I will be there*? What happened?'

A faint smile played on his lips as he poked the inner wall of his cheek with his tongue—mischief!

'Your Ammi wants to meet me.'

'Why?' She was clearly irritated at the answer and wanted a more definitive explanation from him, to put her out of her misery.

'She wants you to get engaged to me and wishes to speak to my mother.'

'Shut up, Sameer!' Even though a faint smile involuntarily touched her lips, she still needed the answer. 'Just quit messing with me!'

'Okay, okay! As you know, your Abbu is back. Your Ammi wants me to come to your place. Your father wants to meet me.'

'When?'

'She said as soon as I can.'

'Then let's get moving, before something really disastrous strikes.'

'But, wait!' he insisted and then paused, locking his eyes into hers, 'I still want to know if you question my intentions, if you really feel that I am treating you as some trophy?'

'This is a conversation for some other day,' she got up smiling, her gaze never leaving Sameer's face.

'I need an answer now!' He held on to her wrist.

She kept staring at him as if trying to draw out his most intimate secret. Then, she lowered her head and after a brief pause, raised it again. She sighed, 'Sameer, if I doubted you, I would have never met you after our first date. But I needed answers. I guess I was just being stupid or plain curious.'

Sameer shook his head as a faint smile caressed his lips.

Two hours later, at Inara's house...

An emaciated Imtiaz Khan lay on his bed, his face supported by a plaster, his head, by two white soft pillows. It seemed that his face would just disintegrate without support. He wore a white kurta pyjama and he had grown a long salt-and-pepper beard unlike the trimmed French-cut he usually sported. He could barely speak and every word that he spoke came with a whiff of pain and Sameer who sat next to him on a wooden chair, had to strain his ears to hear what he was saying.

'You see that girl,' Imtiaz raised his trembling index finger and pointed towards Inara who stood next to her mother. Sameer turned as his reluctant eyes met Inara's. As a reflex, she bowed her head.

'You know who she is?' he spoke with a painful slur.

You bet I know who she is! And by God, if you knew how I know her, you would have had my liver for dinner!

Sameer moved his head sideways but then reluctantly nodded in the affirmative.

'She is the woman I have loved the most in my life, much more than my mother, much more than my wife. My daughter!

125

THE KAAFIR'S LOVE

That day, when I was shot, the only picture that scarred my mind and was more painful than the fresh bullet wound was the panic-stricken face of Inara and the tears in her eyes. The only thought haunting me as I kept gaining and losing control of my senses was, what will happen to her if I die? I am a rich man. Inara and her mother would not have to go to anyone and can lead a comfortable life. But the scary thought that I would not be a part of her life anymore... Ya Allah!'

Imtiaz Khan paused as a thin film of tears covered his eyes, 'So, I see your good deed of saving my life, in that light. At this moment, you can ask for anything you want. Anything at all. I am a Pathan! I give you my word!'

Sameer was so tempted to turn around and look at Inara, just to see the expression on her face but he also knew that the moment he did that, all hell would break loose. Even someone like her father, who had no clue about what was happening between his daughter and his saviour, could see the connection.

'I did what anyone would have done at that moment. It's embarrassing when I am credited with saving your life.'

'I detest modesty! And I know that you don't mean it when you say that you don't deserve the praise. Anyway, are you working somewhere?'

'Yes sir! I work with a multinational firm called...'

'Would you like to work with me?'

'What sir?'

'I shall pay you more amount than you can even dream of! No more night shifts! You shall have more time with your mother. And a better life; something you could have never imagined.'

The patronizing tone of Imtiaz Khan took away whatever sympathy Sameer had for him, but it did not matter at that

ABHISAR SHARMA

time. Nothing mattered when she was around, and the prospect was seductive. This would mean unfettered access to Inara's home. This would also mean that he would be in the inner circle of the Khans. What else could he ask for?

That evening as Sameer was about to leave for work, he got a call from Inara, who was on the rooftop of her home.

'Hmm, so you are going to work for Abbu, haan?'

'I am considering it. It's an offer I find hard to refuse.'

'I warn you, you will lose me if you even dare to respond to it. I like self-made men. Once you start working for my father, you will be expected to do a lot of things that will ultimately make you his slave.'

'Your Abbu indulges in a lot of shady business, I guess,' he teased.

'Careful! Only I have the right to criticize my Abbu! But please tell me that you are not taking up that offer. Please.'

Sameer paused and then smiled, 'The only reason I would take it up is because it will bring me closer to you. I have no other reason to take up his offer.'

'But...ufff!' Inara jerked the phone away from her ear and saw the call that was waiting. It was Zubeida's. Her ears turned crimson.

'What happened?'

'It's bloody Zubeida! Her call's waiting.'

'So speak to her! Why do you have to get irritated at everything?'

'I do not get irritated at everything but I am irritated with her. It's just that she has been acting very weird recently!'

'Weird? How?'

'Nothing! I will call you later. Let me speak to her.'

And before Sameer could respond, Inara had switched the calls.

'Hi Inara. Why haven't you been taking my calls?'

'Zubeida, I have been busy. You know that I have started working.'

'I am sure you won't have the same answer if that Kaafir asked you...'

'Zubeida! Now you are crossing the line. I...'

'I hope you realize that what you are doing is very dangerous and will cause many problems, Inara. Please...don't do this! Your Abbu will be so hurt.'

'What I do is my business! Please do not interfere. I am not answerable to you, Zubeida, so just don't...'

Zubeida interrupted, 'I am not doing anything. Your parents have plans for you. How can you go around roaming with that loafer! That bloody Hindu?'

'If this is all you have to say, then I will prefer to hang up because I have reached the edge of my patience with you. And not only during this call, but for life; forever! Get it?'

Zubeida paused and then took a deep breath, 'You have changed, Inara. And for that guy with whom you have no future whatsoever, you are insulting me? I have been your friend since childhood!'

'Oh please, Zubeida, I know why we are friends! I know how you treat girls who don't match your economic clout. Don't make me say it now.'

'Allah!' she gasped, her voice broke as she started sobbing.

'Oh God, Zubeida, please stop it. I think it's difficult for me to continue this call.'

'Why Inara?' she cried, 'You want to destroy everything for that Hindu boy without bothering about the pain it will bring to your parents? Forget about me, but your parents, Inara?'

'Let me make one thing clear to you. What exists between me and Sameer is something personal. It's only between me

128

and him. I am not answerable to you or to anyone.'

Zubeida stopped sobbing and asked, 'Are you in love with him, Inara?'

Inara could feel her blood rising. She suddenly felt an intense feeling of disgust for her former best friend.

'Tell me, Inara. Are you in love with him?'

And before she could stop herself, Inara blurted out, 'It's better than falling in love with you, Zubeida, because that's what you want, isn't it?'

And that was when Zubeida disconnected the call. It was at that precise moment when Inara knew that something was about to happen, something that would change things forever. She knew that things would never be the same. Hell hath no fury like a woman scorned and Zubeida was that woman.

A sudden gush of wind woke up Inara next morning, as she had slept with her window open. It looked like it was going to rain. Grey clouds were gathering above the Walled City. After the initial joy of the temperatures dropping dramatically, the gloominess of the dark skies made her heart sink. She looked at the skies with her eyes barely open and then closed the window, slamming it to the grilled apparatus of the frame. Inara heard her mother climbing the stairs and she curled back up inside her thin white sheet. The air had a chilly edge to it. She shivered a bit as her mother, the portly Rukhsar Begum, came and sat next to her bed, caressing her tousled hair, with a familiar fondness on her face.

'I think it's going to rain heavily, it's already gone dark outside. You stay at home today.'

Irritated, Inara turned her face away from her mother and said, 'I can't, Ammi! I have a godforsaken meeting. The proprietor of the company wishes to meet the staff and he is

129

here just for a day. He leaves for Jeddah tonight,' Inara yawned as she turned back to her mother, now burying her face in her lap.

Rukhsar gingerly ruffled Inara's hair as she mumbled in a muffled voice, 'I don't want to go, Ammi.'

'Today Abbu's car will drop you. You don't have to go by the metro.'

'I don't want to go,' she moaned.

'So don't!' Her mother replied.

Inara grunted and pushed herself up to sit on her bed, strands of her hair all over her sleepy face. Rukhsar pushed her hair back slowly, revealing the noor of her own morning flower.

'Someone, somewhere will be one hell of a lucky man; the man who will marry my princess.'

Inara looked intently at her mother as her lips stretched into a small smile. Something about what Ammi said, tickled her.

How would she, even in her wildest dreams, know that her little princess had already been taken by the Kaafir?

In an hour, Inara was all ready to go to office. She peeped out of the window. It was still dark as the clouds seemed to be hovering over the entire area. It still hadn't rained. But the atmosphere had an eerie feeling to it. Each time she looked at the skies, her heart sank. A storm was rising in the distance, like an ominous sign. She shut her eyes and murmured a few aayats her mother had taught her. Inara did that every time she was engulfed by panic. Only this time, it was unexplained.

A few blocks away, Nasir's Internet café

Sameer had just returned from his call centre, but decided to meet Nasir before he dozed off to sleep. Nasir had been

ABHISAR SHARMA

calling him for the past two days and wanted to meet him once. Not deliberately, but maybe subconsciously, Sameer had been avoiding meeting Nasir.

'You have been avoiding me, haven't you? But that's fine!' he winked, 'I would have done that too, had it been for a girl like Inara.'

'Don't be daft, Nasir.'

'Oh that's fine, Sameer. By the way, I saw the two of you in Connaught Place recently.'

Sameer's eyes widened as he looked at Nasir, 'So why didn't you meet us?'

'Really? Wasn't that supposed to be your secret rendezvous?'

'Hardly,' Sameer smiled wryly.

'There is still time.'

'For what?'

'Don't make me say it over and over again, Sameer.'

Irritation writ large on his face, Sameer looked outside the window of the Internet café overlooking the street and then strained his neck to raise his gaze to the skies. The Gods were gargling, but still no rain was forthcoming. Suddenly, he moved ahead and clasped the iron grills of the window with both his hands as he saw a black Maruti Esteem jumping on the bumpy road in front of the café. It was Inara. She was sitting on the back seat of the car with her eyes shut and head resting back on her seat.

'Sameer, her Abbu is back. Look, as long as you have a plan, and that leads you to happiness, I am fine with it.'

'I have no plans. Do I look like a man with a plan to you? I would like things to play out on their own.'

'At what cost?'

'The cost that I can bear.'

131

THE KAAFIR'S LOVE

'That's the problem my friend, the cost that would be inflicted upon you would be something you will not be able to bear. I hope that you soon realize that it isn't worth it! There is still a chance for a U-turn.'

Sameer's eyes were scarred with streaks of red and sleep was gradually drawing him in. He gestured to Nasir that it was time for him to crash. But as he walked towards his home, his mind kept replaying the scene with Inara sitting in the back of her car, being driven to work.

Why was she sleeping? Or maybe, she was thinking! But what? She seemed worried. Was she worried? I hope everything's fine at her place? Should I go to CP? Hmmm, let me give it a break today. And this Nasir is bugging me so much! What if he follows me home? Don't wish to be discovered by him again, walking my bum to the metro station.

With thoughts as myriad and restless as those, Sameer climbed the stairs to his house. The door was ajar and he could hear the sound of clanking vessels, and the angry burst of onions as they were tossed into boiling oil in the frying pan. Amma was there. He entered the house, slamming the door, just to tell his mother that he had reached, something that had become a daily routine. She called out his name to ensure if it was indeed him. Sameer mumbled and then lay down spreadeagled in the makeshift bed next to the sofa. Unable to keep his eyes open, he fixed them on a random black spot on the ceiling. His stomach was growling as hunger besieged him. The smell of the food was enticing yet torturous. He was trying to keep his eyes open and then drew his mobile phone out of his trousers and started looking at Inara's messages. Half a smile caressed his weary face as he scanned various messages and then opened the gallery of photos and videos.

Inara was vociferous in her disapproval of Sameer clicking

132

any photographs or making any videos of her, but Sameer would still do it surreptitiously. As he moved from one photo to the other, his eyes kept shutting. A part of his mind and his empty stomach wanted breakfast, but sleep, accompanied by the happiness he felt when looking at her pictures, was slowing him down, pushing him across the threshold, to the world of dreams.

By the time his mother came to the room, he was already snoring gently. The mobile phone, clasped in a loosening grip, rested on his chin. Prabha placed the plate of paranthas and omelette on the table. Then, she gently took the mobile phone from his hand and placed it next to the TV. But just as she was about to turn her head away, the screen light of the phone lit up, revealing the profile of Inara. Prabha turned around and looked at her son who was blissfully unaware that his mother was about to discover something dramatic. She picked up the phone and started scanning the photos.

Twenty-three photos of Inara and all of them taken from a very close distance. Her eyes widened with every photo. Pictures of Inara burying her face in the arc of her hand. Pictures of her hands. Pictures of her feet. Pictures of Inara talking to someone on the phone. Inara walking and a picture taken from behind. Pictures of Inara standing in a metro station and in the metro.

At first, she thought that Sameer was stalking her, but then some pictures could not have been taken unless he was sitting next to her. A swell of panic filled her emaciated bosom. It started travelling as a force right into her heart, as she clasped the handle of the chair next to the table and sat down.

Prabha shut her eyes and started chanting a mantra, moving back and forth. After a few minutes, she opened her eyes and looked at her son. She wanted to wake him up. Ask

THE KAAFIR'S LOVE

him questions. But she dare not. Not because she was scared of an angry response from her son. But what if it was indeed true. She looked out from the lone window. A storm was brewing in the horizon and it was about to smash everything in their perfect little lives, to smithereens.

That evening...

The skies had finally stopped rumbling. But the clouds still scarred the horizon, displaying a collage of orange, blue, speckles of dying white and a depressing dark grey. As Inara walked from the metro station to her house, she saw men sitting outside their houses fanning themselves with Japanese hand-held fans. The streets were unusually quiet and pensive as if something was smouldering under the cracked and pebble-strewn stretch to her house. The lights had just gone out, but that did not bother her. The noisy generator at home would be working. A cold glass of sherbet would be waiting for her. She licked her lips at the thought. As she took the left turn towards the road leading to her house, her gaze inexplicably—perhaps deliberately—skipped the Internet café which was a favourite hangout of Sameer's.

Sameer had been in her thoughts all through the day. She had been looking continuously at the two blank SMSs sent by him during the day. Sameer also did not push for a reply knowing the futility of such an effort, deciding to wait for her to respond.

At Inara's home

Everything seemed strange. The generator was emitting its usual rumble but it was dark inside. Abbu's noisy table fan

ABHISAR SHARMA

was running too, and she could hear it from the ground floor, but none of the lights in the house were on. She pressed the doorbell and that rang too.

Her Ammi opened the door for her. She could not see her face in the dark, but Inara could sense that her mother's usual warmth was missing. She just turned her face away from her and started walking without greeting her. Usually, it would be Ammi who would shut the door as she entered the house but not today.

'Why are the lights out, Ammi?' Inara asked, hesitatingly.

'Shut the door, Inara, and come to Abba's room upstairs.'

There was a frightening stillness in her voice that was cold and unfamiliar. Inara's heart sank as dizziness engulfed her. She shut the door and trailed her mother in the darkness, climbing the stairs, following the sound of her hostile footsteps.

In the darkness, she saw silhouettes of two people. Her Abbu was on the rocking chair and her mother had taken the sofa next to him. She stood like a petty criminal as the silence between them tore her apart. The sound of the massive blades of the fan swirling over her head was rather intimidating. It was the only sound in the room and it felt as if the blades were ruthlessly shredding the delicate bond between Inara and her parents. Between the sounds of the fan and the silence, she could also hear her father's erratic breathing.

'Your Abbu is too shocked to speak and I expect nothing but the truth from you. I don't want any explanations; I just want to know since when. Since when has this been going on between you and that Hindu?'

'Ammi, I don't know...'

Rukhsar Begum suddenly jumped from the sofa and howled, 'Inara, enough! I told you I will not tolerate lies! Zubeida was here and I hope this bit of information should

135

THE KAAFIR'S LOVE

put an end to your farce!'

'She is lying...' Inara protested defiantly.

'Don't!' Rukhsar raised her forefinger, pointing it at her rebellious daughter. 'You should be thankful to Allah that you have friends like Zubeida. I have heard everything.'

'What have you heard?' Inara's voice suddenly dropped, a cloud of nervousness engulfed her senses.

'You want me to replay the rubbish that Zubeida recorded on her cell phone?'

It was like a full-blooded slap on her face. She stood stunned as her throat went absolutely parched. Her tongue seemed glued to her mouth and her cheeks started quivering. Inara's hands were trembling as she felt sick to her stomach. It was not a contest now. She had been entrapped, by her best friend, who was a woman scorned. But her mother did not stop.

'What did you say? "What exists between me and Sameer is something personal. It's only between me and him. I am not answerable to you or to anyone." Really Inara? Is that so?' Her mother paused and took a deep breath to calm herself, 'You are my daughter and I will still take your word as the final truth, so tell me, is there something going on between you and him?'

Inara was too stunned to react. In the darkness, she looked at her father, who was quiet, his head slouched towards one side, not wanting to look at his daughter.

Inara's voice was barely a whisper as she said, 'Please switch on the lights. I can't talk like this. I am...'

'You know why the lights have been switched off, Inara? Because your father does not wish to see your face. He does not wish to see a liar instead of his daughter. You...his precious daughter, the woman he has loved the most, the one he trusted blindly. He is too shocked to even speak. More than anything,

136

he can't believe that his daughter could indulge in something as sinful as this...going around with a Kaafir, a two-penny, good-for-nothing Hindu?'

'Ammi...'

'What, Inara? What?' Her mother's voice boomed loud across the room as she sensed that Inara was about to offer a defence for her actions. She could sense her blood rise and she exhaled deeply.

'Rukhsar,' Imtiaz Khan's voice crumbled with a strain of melancholy. He slowly turned towards his wife and said, 'It's futile to talk further on this matter. You know what my problem is? It is true that the Hindu boy saved my life and I am indebted to him for the rest of my life, but...but...that Kaafir...he dared to...'

Imtiaz Khan's voice choked as a sting of pain rose across his still unhealed wound.

'Ask her Rukhsar, ask her! Did he touch her? Did she let herself be poisoned by the Kaafir's touch? Ask her!' he cried with all his might.

Inara clasped her ears with her hands and closed her eyes, tears flowing from her sealed eyelids.

Imtiaz Khan whispered slowly, 'My infinite trust in her has been breached, Rukhsar. My pride has been trampled upon. I shall not ask her any further questions because I can't take the sight of her lying through her teeth! I can't see her demeaning herself! If I can love her unconditionally, then I am also capable of extreme hatred. You know I can't ignore her but I can't punish my soul with a negative emotion for my daughter, my only daughter.'

The undercurrent of emotions crashed and rebounded, only to get violently entangled in knots. The three of them were mum. Each had their own reasons. Imtiaz Khan's head was slouched on one side as he gazed at the floor. Inara's

137

mother looked intently at her daughter, though she was not exactly looking at her. Memories of the immediate past kept replaying in her head, she kept thinking about the Hindu boy and how he had made a dramatic entry into their lives. Inara, on the other hand, stared into the darkness, her eyes soaked with her misery.

'You remember, Rukhsar, when the doctor said that you can't have babies after...' he paused, his voice expressing reluctance to even say her name, 'after she was born? No one could have stopped me from marrying again! But I saw her. I saw the noor in her eyes and I told myself that I shall love her and raise her like the son I would never have. I was a proud father. But today, look at me, this is what it looks like when your pride gets trampled. That's what...'

Her voice laden with turmoil, and her nose choked, Inara finally spoke, 'I have no words. I am so sorry that I have given you so much grief. I will not meet that boy again. I prom...'

Imtiaz raised his right hand, his eyes burning red. He mumbled something to his wife who got up and grabbed Inara's hand and asked her to leave the room. Before she could protest, her mother dragged her out and shut the door on her face. Tracing her way through the dark uncertainty, she could sense the shame drowning her as she realized what she had done. By apologizing, she had accepted that it was a sin. By apologizing, she had, in one stroke, unknowingly shifted the blame on Sameer.

The storm had now dawned upon the Walled City.

Outside Nasir's Internet café

'Don't hide anything from me! Remember, we are best friends, through thick and thin! I had warned you then, but I know

you were way beyond listening. I will support you, Sameer, come what may.'

Sameer smiled at Nasir, a playfulness in his eyes, and slapped his back. Nasir mocked a look of pain on his face and then clenched his fists like a boxer, trying to intimidate his adversary. The look on Sameer's face softened as he put his arm around Nasir's bony shoulder.

'Even if you had not supported me, I still would have dragged you down, bugger! Listen, Amma is not well, it seems. Just keep a watch on her. I know she has these mood swings, but I don't know why, she has gone quiet and speaks of a terrible headache, so just keep a watch on my old woman...will you?'

Nasir nodded as he kept looking intently at Sameer, worry evident on his face.

His emotions and his confidence were betraying him, but still Sameer said, 'Don't worry, everything is going to be fine; just meet my mother. Ask her if something is bothering her.'

Meanwhile, at the car park at Atos original campus, Noida

A group of executives and call centre employees stood at the car park, many of them carelessly holding a cigarette between their fingers, some raising their head and exhaling the smoke. Another group could be seen standing at the rear of an SUV, the back door open, plastic glasses of beer balanced precariously on the edge of the seat, along with an assortment of kebabs and peanuts thrown in. Girls and boys dressed in a mix of casuals and formals cracked jokes and laughed loudly as one of the street lights above them flickered. A swarm of mosquitoes and insects buzzed around the line of street lights and on the light above the billboard that announced, 'ATOS ORIGINAL' in bold letters.

THE KAAFIR'S LOVE

At a distance, a white SUV with thick, darkened glasses slowed down. The window at the driver's seat rolled down to reveal a clean-shaven man with short hair and kohl-lined eyes. He started to look for his mark amongst the crowd of boys and girls carelessly chatting outside the gate. Suddenly, his eyes widened as he saw his target right at the gate of Atos Original entering the building. He turned back and mumbled something to someone sitting in the back seat which was followed by someone opening the left door of the car. A well-built bearded man with glowing eyes and wearing a skullcap, stepped out. He seemed certain of what he wanted as he looked straight at the entrance of the firm. The other car doors also opened and half a dozen men followed him, a mix of both young and middle-aged salwar kameez-clad Muslim men. Stupefied, like a herd of deer, the boys and girls who were standing around, noticed the approaching pack. Like a prey stunned by the appearance of the predator, the conversations stopped mid-sentence, as they gaped at the advancing men.

The leader approached the security guard and mumbled something to him, who stared at them, mouth slightly open, overwhelmed by his intimidating company. He reached for the intercom and dialled a number. On getting a response from the other end, he said, 'Someone has come to meet Sameer saab.'

The wait...

The men waiting to meet Sameer stood at the gate at strategic locations, their eyes shifting from the entrance to the car park behind them, faking an air of nonchalance, but burying within them a rage that was about to be unleashed. The unsuspecting victim was on his way out, curious but hardly aware of what awaited him at the boundary of the secure confines of his office.

The leader of the pack beckoned one of his men who walked towards him with urgency in his steps. His gaze was fixed on the boys and girls looking at them. He whispered something to the man who turned around, looked at the baffled onlookers and shook his head.

Suddenly, the well-built man's ears pricked up as he heard someone speak and he turned his head towards the entrance with a sudden jerk.

'Guard, has someone come to meet me?'

The man walked towards Sameer menacingly as his eyes narrowed down to his target. The pack accompanying him started to converge on Sameer as well. His eyes darted from one man to the other, nervously, still unable to fathom the chain of events unfolding at a dramatic pace around him.

'Yes?' he mumbled.

'Sameer,' the leader of the pack growled, 'There are certain lines that are not meant to be crossed, but you crossed them, didn't you! Why?'

Before Sameer could respond, the man swung his swarthy and hairy right hand in a semi-horizontal arc and it loudly landed on the edge of Sameer's jaw.

Crack!

Sameer spun once and crashed on to the iron gate, the right side of his face landing on the grilled bars of the gate with a metallic echo. A gush of blood started to stream down from the deep gash on his right cheek. Sameer fell on the ground, his head hitting against the grill of the gate. Slowly, he raised his right hand and touched the cut on his cheek. Stunned and shocked, he was confused and found it difficult to decide which was more unnerving: The dark red on his fingertips or the buzzing sound inside his skull that blurred his sight. As he raised his head to face his nemesis, he got a hard kick from another guy who was clean-shaven and wearing a dark skullcap. The kick, which crashed straight into his abdomen, was a cracker. Sameer gasped and howled in terrible pain as a stream of saliva drooled from his mouth. He clasped his stomach and lay on the ground, writhing in agony as he mumbled, 'Ma.'

The leader turned around, his eyes burning, and glared at the shocked audience around him, 'Come on, scatter, all of you! You think this is a show? Move...move...move!'

The bunch of youngsters started running helter-skelter, as girls yelped and boys stumbled, some even falling in sheer panic. Meanwhile, the leader of the pack turned his gaze back at Sameer and gestured to another man who moved ahead and grabbed Sameer's hair, turning his face up, towards him. He looked back at the leader, who nodded. The man wore pointed shoes, and the edges of his shoes shone with the evil intent of its wearer. Groaning in pain and fuzzy in the head, Sameer tried to open his eyes as tears streamed down his face. It was at this moment when he had barely opened his eyes, the right eye to be precise, that he saw something approaching him, something shiny. The prelude was a whiff of dust smacked at his face and what followed was a forceful kick in the face. The metallic edge landed right under Sameer's right eye, piercing the skin underneath and cutting it in a jolt, gnawing at the cornea in its upward thrust.

Sameer felt like a beast that had just been beheaded. He writhed and jumped in pain on the uneven ground. He jerked and shrieked, holding his eye. At a distance, the onlookers saw the mayhem with horror writ large on their faces but none of them could muster the courage to walk up to him, leave alone rescue him. The guards just stood there, watching the hapless Sameer howling continuously. It was Sameer's moment in hell; the longest, most harrowing single moment in his life. The stinging pain in his eye was like a jolt of electric shock that tore across his face, rising from the point of impact. Even in that moment of unbearable pain, he could see the shock in the eyes of the security guard standing next to him. Even in that moment, he could feel something had been torn off his eye, like a shred of his skin or eyelid.

The leader gestured to his other men. They looked at the crumpled body on the floor for a moment and then pounced on him. It went on for another ten minutes as they continued to punch and kick Sameer. Within five minutes, Sameer had stopped moving and shouting. He had lost consciousness and the will to fight back and defend himself.

The corridor leading to the OT, Fatima Hospital

Prabha dragged herself across the corridors of the hospital in Noida. One end of her sari brushed the sanitized surface of the floor as she mumbled something incoherent. Even though her eyes were streaked red, she still did not have a single tear in them; just a lazy string of saliva dripping from one end of her mouth. She had not seen her son yet. In fact, she was dreading the sight of him. Standing at the end of the corridor in front of the operation theatre, Nasir turned his face towards her, and his eyes widened in alarm. As she reached him, she raised herself on her toes, trying to catch a glimpse of her son from the glass opening of the operation theatre.

Her voice barely a whisper and eyes still trying to see through the small glass opening of the operation theatre, she asked, softly, 'Is he going to live?'

Nasir immediately tried to console her, realizing how inadequate his vocabulary was to offer any form of comfort to the distraught mother.

'Tell me how bad it is, Nasir, and don't lie to me,' she insisted with firmness in her voice.

His voice shook with hesitation, and he spoke haltingly, 'The doctors...they say that he has lost some blood. There are a few cuts across his face and left armpit and there is a deep... uh...gash on his back.'

Without warning, tears rolled down from Prabha's eyes, moistening her wrinkled cheeks.

'And...?'

'They say and I am not sure about his, but they say he has suffered some internal bleeding too and they are trying to operate upon it as we speak.'

For the first time, she turned her face towards Nasir, locking her eyes with his, 'He is not going to live, is he? You are just trying to...'

'Why do you say so, aunty? He is fine, it's just that we need to wait for the doctors to give us a medical overview.'

After a moment of silence, Prabha whispered, 'This happened because of that trader's daughter, right? I should have stopped him when I saw those pictures on his mobile. I should have at least spoken to him.'

Nasir was stunned but he quickly got over his shock, 'You think I did not do that, aunty? I always had a bad feeling about this, but he would just not listen. If this would have been some random Muslim girl, I would not have bothered. But Inara? She is Imtiaz Khan's daughter and he is the most powerful man in the entire Walled City.'

'The second most powerful man,' she mumbled. 'Do you think Imam sahab will give us an audience? Only he can save my son,' the last sentence was uttered in a faint whisper, making it impossible for Nasir to hear.

Suddenly, a nurse appeared out of nowhere with an urgency in her voice, 'Who is the mother?' her eyes scanning the people standing in front of the operation theatre.

Prabha stepped ahead and mumbled hesitatingly, 'I am.'

'You can look at him, but don't speak to him or go near him. You will be separated by a glass door. He still runs the risk of getting an infection, get it?'

There was a glass door that still separated her from her son. Her face half covered by the pallu of her own faded sari, she looked through the separation, placing her trembling fingers on the spotless glass. Another stream of tears poured from her sunken eyes, dampening her lined cheeks, stopping at the threshold of the pallu of her sari which covered her desperation. Her heart had never cursed anyone, but seeing her only son in that condition, she felt a swell of anger for the girl who had brought this upon her perfectly normal and peaceful world. She wanted to question her. Like any other mother, she needed to blame the girl for wreaking havoc in the life of her son.

Meanwhile, at Raj Narain Pandey's residence

The Sanskari Party leader listened intently to his personal secretary, Gupta ji, as he gave him the dope on the incident that occurred outside the Noida campus of Atos Original. A shadow of a smile played upon his lips occasionally, as he toyed with the clump of hair sprouting above his ears.

'The men who were used to target Sameer were all outsiders, with the exception of Majid who had accompanied them to identify him. He is a local. Now, I am not sure, but either Sameer had teased Inara, Imtiaz's daughter, or there was something going on between them. Sameer had also saved Imtiaz's life, so there is another connection. It makes perfect

145

sense to assume that there was something going on between Sameer and Inara.'

'What's the buzz in the Walled City?' Pandey's probing eyes shone through the gold-rimmed glasses, as he uttered the words without any change of expression on his face.

'People are confused. There are murmurs across the streets. Conspiracy theories abound. Sameer was a local here and had catapulted to fame after he saved Imtiaz's life. He was recommended by none other than the Imam sahab himself.'

'What about Imam sahab?'

'No one knows yet. There is absolute silence from his side on the issue right now. But I am sure he is up to something.'

'Hmmm,' Pandey rested his head on the cushion of his chair and shut his eyes. Gupta ji stared at his master, waiting for a more pronounced response than the 'hmm' he had just mumbled.

'Let it brew, Gupta ji. It's the perfect setting for our future plan of action. But it is still the early days,' Pandey paused but then, as if struck by a sudden thought, he continued, 'What about the MNC employees working in the campus? I am told that a lot of these MNC employees are right wingers? Why can't we organize a sit-in dharna against the attackers in the campus supported by our students' wing?'

With a hint of reluctance in his tone, Gupta ji said, 'Sir, the problem is that these MNC kids can rant and abuse on social media, but when it comes to real action on the ground, their balls just drop off. They just don't have it in them. They are basically cowards who can attack people through the comforts of their laptops and social media, but that's it!'

Pandey took a deep breath and said, 'The Hindus are a coward race, and the educated middle class and upper middle class Hindu is nothing but a bag of gas. Imagine, had a Muslim

been attacked like that, they would have burned the place down. But still, I shall wait for the right moment, and something tells me that the moment is not very far.'

Imtiaz Khan's house

Imtiaz Khan stared pointedly at the static blades of the fan above his bed, never even blinking as the Imam, sitting next to him, fiddled with his prayer beads. There was a nervous energy in his fingers as his eyes moved sideways; his mind continuously replayed the mayhem in front of Sameer's office, as narrated to him by the other boys who worked with Sameer. The Imam had been sitting next to Imtiaz for the past five minutes and not a word had been spoken. Imtiaz's wife Rukhsar Begum sat across a black translucent curtain looking at the two men, as a cloud of unease loomed in the room, engulfing all of them.

'I am not a politician, Imam sahab, nor am I diplomatic. I don't pretend. No one can just violate my most precious possession and then walk away like that,' Imtiaz Khan spoke, his voice barely a mumble, but it was firm, his anger unmistakable. 'He saved my life and I put him on a pedestal, but what did he do? The parasite that he is, he cast an evil eye on my only daughter. My Inara!'

The Imam shook his head and turned his eyes away from Imtiaz.

'Did you even bother to speak to Inara about all of it?'

'How does it matter? How does it matter what she thinks?'

The Imam interrupted, 'Before beating him to a pulp, wasn't it fair to know his side of the story?'

'There are no sides, Imam sahab. It is easy for you to judge dispassionately, but this is my daughter we are talking about.

147

THE KAAFIR'S LOVE

Some lines are not meant to be crossed. Some boundaries are not meant to be breached. But that Kaafir did exactly that. He violated my trust, my faith in him.'

'Faith?' His voice loaded with sarcasm, the Imam hit back, 'Did he ever ask you to trust him? Did he not deserve some benefit of the doubt?'

'And why would I care what he deserved or not?'

'Because,' Imam sahab paused, 'because you have just brutalized the boy whom I had presented as the symbol of Hindu-Muslim amity! Of all the boys, you had to...'

'Everything does not always have to revolve around politics, Imam sahab!' Imtiaz Khan's retort was followed by a painful gasp as he could feel the pain rising across his still-bandaged, wounded jaw, 'With all due respect, I just finance politicians, I am not one myself. But you, Imam sahab, have become a hard-boiled one. You have become even better than the ones who seek your blessings.'

'But you don't mind seeking undue favours from them! You don't mind financing their dirty work, never bothering where and how your money is used. And then suddenly, you play the pious Muslim when it comes to your daughter? Some things are meant to be handled with caution, Imtiaz! You cannot act in isolation and then expect us to further your interests that have nothing to do with the community!'

'I saw something in Inara's eyes, something for him... I even hate the mention of his name! He should have known his place. He should not have entered my house. He dared, so he paid the price! But he is still alive. His mother should be thankful.'

'All I am saying is that you could have come to me first! Now look what a mess you have created!'

'I was angry. I needed retribution.'

'As I said, Imtiaz, you could have come to me.' Imam

Zulfiqar Khan started caressing the bridge of his nose. 'You don't even realize what a huge political mess you have drawn us into. We are now virtually sitting on a powder keg. A storm is rising...'

As usual, the Imam was right. It was exactly the political elixir that Sanskari Party leader Raj Narain Pandey was desperately looking for. The week that followed saw skirmishes at various points in the Walled City. Mysterious bottles of alcohol were hurled in front of the famous Bukhara eating joint. The Imam's son Imran Khan's car was hit by a stone as he drove out of the Walled City towards Meerut. There were attacks on Muslim call centre employees in Ghaziabad. It had not developed into a full-scale confrontation but it was brewing ominously. Zulfiqar Khan had warned his son not to react whatever the provocation, but Imran Khan was seething within.

It was the ultimate battle of nerves. Both sides were waiting for the other side to make the first move to escalate it further.

Ten days later...

Meanwhile, Sameer lay on the hospital bed, miserable, blankly staring at the gecko above his ceiling fan, with his left eye. His right eye was bandaged, as it had been punctured during the assault. The gecko slithered, waiting to pounce and feast on scattered insects splayed across the pale white cracked ceiling of his room. Even though his mind was fixed on his sole object of obsession—Inara—it had not paused on one single thought. It oscillated restlessly across myriad moments spent with her, sometimes many thoughts converging at an instant, like a collage. Her memory rose like a sting across his chest, painful, culminating into a drop of tear, stuck in his eyelashes, reluctant to cross the threshold of his misery.

THE KAAFIR'S LOVE

How much she relished my misery as she caught me following her for the first time in Connaught Place.

He smiled faintly, but it was instantly followed by a jolt of pain across his jaws which were held together by thick layers of bandages stained by blotches of his own blood. His chain of thought was broken by the creaking of the door. His mother entered the room. Her face pale, as if every small emotion and grain of energy had been sucked out of her. The past ten days had been harrowing for her and if Nasir and his family had not force-fed her, she would have collapsed and would be lying in a room next to Sameer. Without looking at him, she came and sat next to his bed on a dark wooden stool.

'It's all my fault,' she mumbled. Sameer looked at her with a hint of confusion in his eyes. 'I should have warned you; I mean, stopped you,' she fumbled for words, her eyes shifting sideways as if trying to assemble her scattered thoughts.

Dismissive of his mother's statement, he patted her hand, 'It's got nothing to do with you.'

'I had seen her photographs on your mobile phone. I should have...'

'You've been checking my mobile phone, Amma?' Sameer asked incredulously.

'No, I should have warned you, I should have...' she kept repeating her words, biting her lower lip, as if cursing herself. 'Promise me that you will never ever meet that girl, ever again!' As if struck by another thought, she said, 'In fact, we will shift from here. I am sure we can get a good accommodation in a far off place in Delhi or Noida, near your office.'

'We aren't moving anywhere, Amma! And stop cursing yourself. It's not your fault. I have no regrets.'

'That's what I am afraid of. You still have no regrets. You still crave for her, I know! You still yearn for her.'

150

Sameer replied, irritated, 'Be quiet, Amma...'

'No, you can't! You just can't! I have no one else but you. You can't do this to me.'

On the verge of losing his temper, Sameer spoke slowly but firmly, 'Nothing is going to happen to you, or me, just...' Sameer paused, his chest heaving, the warm air swirling within, accentuating his misery. His irritation was directed at his mother, but he knew he was being unfair. He was still thinking of Inara.

How can I still think of her, knowing the storm she has unleashed in my life; the pain that my mother is undergoing!

He realized that the feeling of guilt within him wasn't enough to erase her from his thoughts. The door made yet another creaking sound; this time it was Nasir.

'Nasir, take her away. I am in no mood to speak to anyone.'

'Don't avoid the question, Sameer. You cannot meet her, ever again. In fact, we can't stay here any more. There is just pain and suffering here and nothing else,' he begged too.

'Nasir!' Sameer now had an edge to his voice as he glared at a bewildered Nasir.

Nasir delicately held his mother's shoulders and pleaded her to accompany him. Prabha kept mumbling as she was taken away. She kept looking back at her son, pleading, her eyes bleary. Sameer shut his eyes as a drop of a tear squeezed through his eyelashes. His mother's voice was still echoing across the corridors.

Flashes of Inara went through his mind, like a sudden burst of pyrotechnics in a dark sky. His body shook as he remembered the times she had smiled back at him...from Connaught Place, from the terrace of her house while pretending to read, from the corner of the metro train bogie where she stood, holding her beige-coloured purse. The flashes stung him repeatedly and

THE KAAFIR'S LOVE

heightened the physical pain that throbbed across his body. He moaned in agony. He wanted to cry his lungs out but the stitches across his face and armpits made it difficult for him to even smile.

He promised himself, and this time, with a note of finality.

I will never meet her. I will never meet the girl who caused so much agony to my mother. I shall never desire her. How could I be so selfish? What did I even do to deserve this brutality? Here I am, battered and broken, lying in this wretched hospital with the stench of phenyl and medicine overwhelming my senses! What did I ever do to deserve this? No person, however cruel, would let his mother go through all this again. She was right. We don't belong to this place. Never again. Never, ever...

The door creaked again. Without even looking at the door, he said, irritated, 'I said, leave me alone for some time!'

The black burkha and the hijab concealed her identity perfectly. No one would have recognized her, but Sameer did, instantly. How could he not identify those immaculate feet, though not perfectly pedicured this time, but still encased in her signature beige-coloured sandals. As she drew closer, the smell of lavender musk filled his senses. She lifted her hijab and revealed a pale face, haunted and violated by the cataclysmic events of the past. The kohl applied in her eyes was uneven. The lipstick was done in a hurry. The blush on her cheeks needed a bit of blending. It was as if she was confused: should she look beautiful or should she go as she felt—miserable? As she neared him, he could feel the crumbling of the feeble frontiers he had just built around him. It was a vow to the self that was never meant to be.

'I know that we don't have much time,' her voice trembled. He had never ever seen her so nervous.

152

'I just want to know, how far are you ready to go?' She was not seeking an answer but throwing a challenge at him. She was daring him, which became clear as she further confided in him.

'My father wants to marry me off to some fat slob in London. That is not happening. I would rather run away than fulfil his whims and fancies just because he thinks I have hurt him. He believes that because I am involved with you, it gives him a right over my life. He is delusional.'

Then she stared deep into his eyes, 'I want to know, do you have the guts to stand with me? To stand up against my father's might?'

Sameer studied her expressions closely and spoke slowly, 'Is it about standing with *me*? Or is it just about standing up to the might of your father? What about standing together? What about answering the question I had asked you the last time we met?'

With a hint of irritation, she retorted, 'What is that supposed to mean?'

'I mean, it's not about you. I mean, it's not about only you! Why do I still yearn to listen to those three words from you?'

'Oh! Just because I never said 'I love you' means I don't? You think it's because of some high, or some bloody impulse, that I am challenging my father?'

She paused and turned her face away. Her eyes turned watery.

'If there is one man with whom I wish to spend my life, cribbing and complaining against, it's you! In matters big or small, I have given that solemn right to you and no one else. I can't think of any man touching my body and soul as intimately as you do. How does it matter if I haven't spoken those three corny words to you?'

153

THE KAAFIR'S LOVE

He knew that every word she spoke was straight from her heart.

'Why are you guys so linear? Why are you so superficial? Why?'

Sameer looked hard at her, 'So why bother if I am superficial? Why bother if I am like the rest of them?'

A smile caressed her lips as she whispered, 'Because you are not...you will never be...like one of them.'

She paused as she stepped closer, 'Because beyond all the struggle and all the loathing, I see a future for ourselves. I believe that as we come together, we shall resurrect trust and faith between two communities living in fear and hatred for each other. I am an optimist, Sameer! Our love goes beyond us. I am sure there will come a day when Abbu and Imam sahab, with their preconceived notions, shall see reason through our love. I believe that our children shall be the model citizens of a progressive society that we strive for, that this nation ought to be.'

Sameer raised his right hand to caress the single strand of unfettered hair through her hijab and he felt a sting in his armpit. It felt as if a stitch just came undone. But her words were comforting. Her words might not have meant anything for the merchants of hate and Sameer knew that ultimately nothing would ever change. After all, he had seen life bare and raw enough to realize that. There were no fairy tales for him; none narrated to him in his childhood and none available for him now. But still, her words were comforting, her words were the only source that could calm the pain that ran through his wounds. Her words were unbound, her words meant freedom.

154

A month later...

Sameer and his mother had shifted to Noida.

Inara was counting days till her wedding to the fat British slob named Tariq.

Ten days to go.

On the other hand, Sameer was calm. Initially, Nasir had tried hard but eventually he had given up on convincing Sameer to abandon his plan. Sameer and Inara were going to board a flight to Varanasi on the approaching Tuesday. The real challenge was to stay undetected for the days that were to follow. They planned to get married and then escape to Nepal and stay there until things calmed down. Sameer and Inara knew that Imam Zulfiqar Khan would ultimately see reason. They believed that he would be able to convince Inara's father too.

First things first, Sameer and Inara had to reach the Dashashwamedh Ghat after landing in Varanasi. Nasir's uncle Faizu Miyan was a tailor working at one of the many cloth shops facing the Ghat. His employers had also given him a two-bedroom shelter above the shop. But the only problem was that Faizu Miyan could not be made a confidant in their plan. So, how were they to present themselves in front of the old Faizu Miyan? Telling him the *truth* was a proposition that was too unorthodox for a peace-loving Faizu. In addition, there would be questions from other shopkeepers and from his own employer. After much deliberation, it was decided that Sameer and Inara would disguise themselves as a newly-married Hindu couple who had come to visit Varanasi. And to look like one, another plan was etched out. Before reaching the Dashashwamedh Ghat, they had to go to the famous shopping paradise in Lahurabir. This is where Inara would dress up to look like a newly-married Hindu woman and don the customary henna, red sari, bracelets and bangles right up to her elbow, along with bindi, sindoor, etc.

But that was hardly an issue. They had bigger problems at hand. They were not just any normal runaway couple. It was a Muslim girl running away with a Hindu boy. This meant major consequences would follow and none of them was ready to face them. They were nervous but remained optimistic. Of the two, it was Inara's positive attitude that kept the hope alive. Sameer was more cautious, considering that he had to do most of the planning.

Is there going to be a happy ending to all this?

Sameer was apprehensive, but Inara was unusually confident.

That Tuesday...

Inara usually left home at 9 a.m. to reach office by 10. But that day, she left at 8.30 a.m. Her destination was the domestic airport, where she had to board an 11.00 a.m. flight to Varanasi. She took a metro to Connaught Place and another one to the airport where Sameer was waiting for her. Both of them knew that unless they came across one of Inara's relatives at the airport, everything would go smoothly—according to plan. And that was precisely what happened. The tickets were procured from different sources, hence both entered the airport separately and checked-in individually. Clearly, there was another plan behind checking-in independently. After the security check, there was hardly any time left for boarding the flight. It was in the women's restroom that Inara changed into a traditional sari which was neither too flashy nor too casual. As they made their way to the boarding gates, their

ABHISAR SHARMA

eyes searched for familiar faces around, but thankfully, they could spot none. Before boarding and during the flight, their eyes would often meet. Half a smile and a look of reassurance would be exchanged. They were sure that they had nearly made it. Just a few steps more, some odd hurdles to cross, and everything would be all right. That is how they wanted to convince themselves...that in the end, everything was going to be all right.

They landed at the Lal Bahadur Shastri airport at Babatpur, Varanasi, and Sameer hired a car which took them straight to the bazaar in Lahurabir.

At Lahurabir

Inara sat on an elevated stool as the man with somewhat effeminate fingers applied henna on her hands. Sameer stood and gazed at her as a gentle smile caressed his lips. Fascinated and excited as the man applied the henna on her palms, Inara looked up and caught Sameer gazing at her fondly. Her lips stretched into a shy smile. Sameer noticed that there was a thin line of perspiration just above her lips. He looked at it intently and then licked his own lips.

Then, he whispered softly, 'Thirsty?'

She nodded.

Sameer turned around and headed to the mad swell of people as his shoulders brushed with sweaty bodies. Varying odours of spices, fried foods, bad breath and sewer water besieged his senses. His eyes glanced through the crumbling walls of the market that were sprayed with paan spits and appeals to vote for promising candidates in the upcoming state elections. He had nearly missed the shop, but the corner of his eye caught the billboard: Banaras ki Mashhoor Mishrambu

157

ki lassi'. Sameer turned around and walked back to the shop. A man with a large belly and a red vermillion mark on his forehead sat on the counter, chewing paan, unmindful of the people around him. He raised his head and nodded at Sameer.

'Lassi?' Sameer asked with a hint of hesitation in his voice.

'Would you like to have it along with Bholenath ka Prasad?' As the man mumbled the words, a spray of paan peek also came out of his mouth.

'Excuse me?'

The man spat out the paan, nearly missing Sameer's trousers and spoke with a little more clarity, 'Would you like to have it with bhang?'

Sameer retorted, 'No, why would I...' But he stopped mid-sentence.

A little bhang would not hurt her. In fact, it might soothe her nerves and she could sleep a little longer, undisturbed by any thoughts that beleaguered her after the adventure of a lifetime that we have just embarked upon.

He smiled and then looked at the man at the counter. The man raised his head and mumbled, waiting for his permission, but Sameer nodded in the negative and said, 'Forget it, please make two sweet lemonades only.'

As Sameer headed back, he realized that the man at the henna shop had started applying henna on Inara's other hand too. Sameer stood before her, admiring the concentric circles on her palm, with rose petals criss-crossing them in a neat and immaculate pattern. Inara looked up and saw Sameer holding the two glasses in his hands.

'Sorry,' she gestured towards her hands, implying he would have to hold the glass and feed her. Sameer bent down and sat on his haunches, balancing his derrière on the heel of his shoes, which stood raised above the ground. Even though

uncomfortable in that posture, he raised a glass of lemonade to her lips. As she sipped gingerly, their eyes locked onto each other and a combination of desire, nervousness and hope enamoured their senses. The henna guy, who was pretending not to watch them, smiled.

At 8.30 p.m., The Walled City

Even though they were talking in murmurs, the anger simmering within was palpable in their stance. Groups of young Muslim men stood huddled in front of Imtiaz Khan's house. Their heads were bowed as Imtiaz Khan's voice boomed from inside the house. Women stood at the terraces gaping at the house with the children holding their mothers' arms. Imtiaz was on the phone, shouting at somebody. His mouth was frothing and his eyes were bloodshot. He was surrounded by a group of men in his drawing room. His wife stood at a corner, mouth covered with her dupatta, her face streaked with unstoppable tears.

'I want that bastard alive because I want to have the pleasure of tearing him open!' he was barking on the phone as the men in the room looked pensive. One of them held prayer beads in his hands, fingers rolling them nervously, his mind trying hard to focus on the prayer. Another man continuously whispered curses at Sameer, with a tightened jaw, but his eyes were fixed at the father whose antics were now bordering on hysterical.

Still on the phone, Imtiaz turned around and looked at his wife. 'No need to cry for that girl. She is as good as dead for us. She will be buried in an unmarked grave! I don't wish to see her again! Never, never ever!'

Inara was the apple of her husband's eye and never in a million years could Rukhsar Begum have imagined him spewing such vitriol, such venom, for her. She tried to reason with him, even tried to convince him that Sameer must have kidnapped Inara, that their daughter was innocent, that she deserved another chance, but Imtiaz Khan would hear none of it. He had crossed the threshold of hate, and there was no turning back now, even if he wanted to.

At 8.45 p.m., the Imam's lair

'This is how emboldened they get! You trusted this man, Abba, he was your mascot for peace, wasn't he? Now look what he has done!' Imran spoke with controlled rage, and his father listened solemnly, his cataract eyes shifting nervously as if trying to hold on to a thought, to a solution. He knew that this time matters had gone out of his control. He knew that this time it would be impossible to contain the fallout. He knew that this time they will not listen to his voice of reason.

But more than reason, his mind was on politics. He knew for sure that this event will give a window of opportunity to the right wingers to find a stronghold in the Walled City and around. Flashes of a smiling Raj Narain Pandey haunted him. He feared that if his son or the men who shared his belief, had their way, it would result in such a fearsome polarization that it would obliterate the centrist and the leftist parties from the Delhi-UP region.

'We want retribution, Abba, and even I can't stop the youth this time. They are fuming with rage. These Hindu imbeciles have to be taught a lesson, so that no one dares to raise an eye on our women,' he fumed.

Zulfiqar Khan shut his eyes and tilted his head back. He murmured an aayat of the Quran faintly but it was audible to his restless son. 'Bismillaha ir Rehman ir Rahim...Inallahe Ma-a Saabreen. Allah is with those who have patience, Imran.'

After a brief pause, with his eyes still shut, the Imam said, 'Do you know Imran, Allah mentioned patience 90 times in the Quran? I advise you, son, to retire into the prayer room or retreat in isolation for some time. It will...'

Imran stood up with such force that the chair toppled backwards. He said firmly, without raising his voice, 'Abba, you continue to patronize me, but I shall not be held responsible for my boys getting caught unawares. You have to understand that we are under attack. Either we let them enter our houses or we let them know that it is time they guard theirs.'

At 9.07 p.m., Dashashwamedh Ghat, Varanasi

The gust of cool breeze sweeping across the dark Ganges struck her bosom as Inara held on to Sameer's arm tightly. The stone steps of the Ghat were wet and littered with prayer material. Animal waste also lay strewn around, but it did not matter to them, as the echoes of 'Har Har Gange' rose from an adjoining ghat. Inara was in awe of her surroundings, though they made her nervous too. She was continuously thinking about what her father must be doing at the moment. She was aware that things must be tense back home, though she was still oblivious of the storm they had unleashed. Nevertheless, she was optimistic. She knew that her Abbu would forgive her. But she also knew that there would be a price to pay.

She rested her head on his shoulder and whispered, 'If acceptance by Abbu means embracing Islam...will you?'

Sameer turned his head around as Inara lifted her head to face him. He looked at her intently and caressed her cheek with his thumb, 'Haven't I already?'

161

THE KAAFIR'S LOVE

'Here I am, dressed as a Hindu bride and he says that *he* has embraced Islam, huh!'

'So you would have preferred that we disguised ourselves as a Muslim couple and became the object of interrogation by Faizu Miyan? At least this way he hasn't asked us any uncomfortable questions since we checked in at his place.'

With a long shadow of worry on her face, she said, 'That may be so, but we need to find a closure. They will have to accept us. How far can we run and for how long?'

'You amaze me, Inara! Yesterday, you were the optimistic one, and now, look at you!'

'I am still optimistic! I just wonder if our story will have a happy ending, with my father accepting you as his son-in-law...'

'Then what? You think we will be able to rest and shut our eyes to the struggle after that? There will be more eyes on us than on any other normal couple. The scrutiny on our marriage will be intense. Will you be able to withstand that pressure? Knowing how the media has been interested in the happenings within the Walled City, I wonder how they would portray our situation.'

Sameer paused as if struck by a thought, but was wary to speak his mind.

'What?' she asked, 'What are you thinking?'

'I'm worried about my Amma,' he spoke with a hint of anxiety in his voice. 'She must be thinking that I am on a night shift or something. She does not even watch TV and God forbid if this spins out of control, she won't come to know, even if they buried me.' He paused again as the shadow of anxiety on his face got darker, 'I'm worried about Nasir too! I'm worried they will hound him to reveal our whereabouts!'

ABHISAR SHARMA

Midnight, Jamia, Delhi

As he ran down the narrow alley, he knew that he had no chance. He had already twisted his left foot while jumping from the first floor of his cousin's house and escaping to the backstreet. As his shoulders brushed and hit the walls of the alley, he mumbled an incoherent prayer as saliva streaked from his mouth. He kept running, trying not to trip over small rocks lying on the cracked street of the back lane. He could hear the footsteps of the men behind him and realized that they were catching up with him.

Nasir kept looking back every now and then, oblivious to his fate that lay ahead. His eyes saw the end of the lane that opened up to a road, a few metres ahead. He could see cars and trucks whizzing across. He held on to the hope that he would find an auto and escape to safety. As he turned back to see how close his pursuers were, a shadow emerged at the end of the lane.

Crash!

Nasir slammed straight into a muscular man wearing a skullcap. As he crumpled into a heap on the broken street, he looked up at the huge man, first with confusion, and then with sheer terror. Fear engulfed his thin face and he broke out in a sweat. The man headed straight for his thin neck and grabbed it with ferocity. Nasir immediately started choking; his eyeballs started to turn red. The men who were chasing him also caught up and one of them swung his right leg that rammed straight into Nasir's frail back. His body jolted in agony. It was the single most brutal and painful force Nasir had felt in his entire life. He yelped 'Allah!' as tears began to streak down his cheeks. The man's grip started tightening as Nasir bloodshot eyes started bulging out. He struggled hard to extricate himself from the powerful hands of the monster, but in vain. Suddenly, one of the men intervened and pushed back the man choking Nasir, saying 'Majid bhai, Imtiaz sahab wants him alive! Please control your rage.'

The man spat right on Nasir's face, 'You have just bought yourself some more time. But I promise you that it shall be my honour to wring your miserable life out of you, you traitor!'

He kicked Nasir hard in his groin and Nasir simply passed out.

A few minutes later, a girl from a nearby rooftop saw a man being bundled into the back seat of a black SUV.

At the Imam's lair

The Imam's close confidant of many years had an urgency in his step as he walked towards the Imam's room. His footsteps echoed sharply in the long corridor as he neared the Imam's room.

'Imam sahab, I am sorry to wake you up, but I have some news.'

The Imam was already awake and he responded immediately in the dark, 'It's okay. I am glad you came. Time is precious. Tell me.'

'They have found Nasir. He was hiding at his cousin's house in Jamia. They are bringing him to Imtiaz's storage facility house in Ballimaran. I am afraid we shall have to act fast.'

The Imam grimaced as he got up. He could hear his bones creak. He searched for his footwear. The confidant moved ahead, grabbed the Imam's shoes and placed them under his feet.

As he stood up, the Imam looked straight into the confidant's eyes and said, 'Let's go!'

164

Nasir's hell in Ballimaran

The torture was meticulous. They knew that he would not survive continuous pummelling, so he was given a break at regular intervals. There were times when he gave them a break too, the times when he would simply pass out. In fact, he was doing that too often.

The frail and delicate Nasir could not withstand their torture. He was continuously crying and pleading, but no amount of begging softened his tormentors to give him some respite. He wanted to tell them everything he knew but Imtiaz's men were not interested. They just wanted to give him hell.

Two hours later, Nasir had a fractured arm, his frontal teeth had been dislodged from the roots and there was blood gushing from his mouth. The undertakers were careful not to hit him on his chest or stomach, so that there were no internal injuries. They had planned it to the minutest detail, as per the orders. The final blow was to be delivered by Imtiaz Khan himself.

He blabbered incomprehensibly, 'Khan sahab, I beg... spare me, I...tell you everything... I... sorry. Can't take the... pain...'

Unfazed and unmoved, Imtiaz Khan responded coldly, 'I am afraid I shall have to reject both your requests. Firstly, I am not interested to know what you know, because I shall know it soon enough any way. Secondly, I can't stop this because seeing you cry with agony and begging for mercy is the only way the fire within me has got some respite.'

Suddenly, Majid, the leader of the pack, grabbed Nasir by the hair and started tearing it from the roots. Nasir howled, and listening to his screams, no one could have figured out whether this howl of pain came from a man or an animal.

Imtiaz Khan wobbled towards Nasir who was tied to the

THE KAAFIR'S LOVE

base of a cement pillar, spreadeagled on the dusty, grimy broken floor of the storage room. Nasir's bleary eyes briefly scanned his surroundings. Broken furniture, large portraits covered in dirty cloth, haphazard steel trunks with inscriptions in Arabic and broken wooden boxes used for packing of mangoes lay strewn around. The musty smell in the air was making his ordeal even more unbearable.

A man grabbed a chair and placed it in front of Nasir.

Imtiaz Khan sat on the chair and started caressing Nasir's face. He paused briefly as he saw dark red blood on his fingers which was oozing from Nasir's injuries.

He spoke softly, as if to a child, 'You know, Nasir, when you were small, like three to five years old, your father would often ask me, "How do I cure Nasir? He is always so ill. He is so thin; he does not eat; he is so irritable. What should I do?" And I would tell him, "I know the best doctors in the city." I had promised him that you would grow up into a fine young man,' Imtiaz paused and sighed deeply. Then, he spoke again, with intense hatred seeping into his words, 'But look at you now! You are pathetic. There is no gravity in your character. You are hardly a Muslim. Too much time spent with that Hindu has made you a bloody coward.'

He paused again, as if trying to calm himself down.

'So I feel as if I have failed in my responsibility. I have broken my promise to your father. And now, I will rectify my mistake.' Imtiaz stretched his right hand out. A man standing behind him drew out a long knife with a jagged edge. Nasir's eyes widened with horror and he started screaming, shaking his head violently. His entire body shook with whatever strength he had left, most of which had already seeped out. A few men stepped back, cupping their mouths, as Majid's eyes widened in anticipation. Nasir started to howl louder.

166

His agony was just a feeble whisper outside the storage facility as at the same time, a pack of dogs started howling in the distance. Fireflies jumped and danced around the singular lit lamp post of the deserted road in front of the facility. The rumble of a vehicle and its screeching tyres echoed from a distance. It seemed that the driver of the SUV was driving fast, manoeuvring the sharp bends and turns of the locality. The men inside the SUV had hopeless prayers on their lips. They were running out of time.

Back in the storage facility, Imtiaz Khan bent down and moved his face closer towards a hysterical Nasir and spoke softly, 'The struggle shall make your ordeal even more torturous. I advise you to calm down. Shushhhh,' he placed his bloodstained finger on Nasir's lips, as he started to plead harder. But suddenly, he stopped howling, though tears were incessantly streaking from his eyes. He saw a glimmer of hope in Imtiaz Khan's eyes. A drop of tear lay entangled in his long eyelashes.

'Close your eyes now... It will be easier, my son.'

Imtiaz gripped the knife harder.

The SUV stopped and its tyres squealed in front of the storage facility. Zulfiqar Khan and his confidant emerged out of the car and headed towards the door.

Imtiaz placed the knife on Nasir's neck and shut his eyes. He mumbled something, as if asking for His forgiveness.

'I know, Nasir, there is place for me in Hell for what I am about to do. But I am ready.'

Suddenly, there was furious banging on the door. Imtiaz Khan looked at his men in alarm. His men started to look at each other in confusion as Majid, the most ruthless of them, drew out his knife and started moving towards the door.

'Open the door!' The voice sounded familiar to Imtiaz

167

Khan. His heart started to pound as he feared who the person might be. He looked at Nasir and then at Majid, who was now near the door and was about to open it. The banging at the door increased as a second person started pounding at the pre-independence style door that looked as if it might crumble anytime now.

Majid opened the door and Imam sahab entered, his eyes burning, his wrinkled face covered by a thick layer of sweat. His eyes scanned the room and then paused at Imtiaz who wearily got up from the chair. Nasir started blabbering something incoherently, trying to raise his arms towards the Imam, as he knew that his saviour was there.

The Imam came in and stood right in front of Imtiaz Khan, but his gaze was continuously on Nasir. He bent down and started caressing Nasir's tousled hair. Then, he spoke without even looking at Imtiaz Khan, 'You trade in people's miseries, Imtiaz! You are a merchant of hate. All I asked was for you to be a little patient, but you continue to disrespect me. There are bigger things to be taken care of. I repeat, you cannot act in isolation. There are issues related to the whole community.'

Imtiaz Khan lowered his head, his jaws tightened, clearly not liking the reprimand. The Imam breathed out gently, exhaling the anger within, knowing that admonishment won't work with the irrepressible father. The man was on the highway of retribution and he won't stop unless he had got it.

'We need to talk. We have to sort this out, and we will. Now! Let's go to my place.'

Few hours later...

The sound of chirping birds had started permeating the Imam's prayer room, cushioned in a corner of the huge sprawling

ABHISAR SHARMA

residential complex which was an extended part of the mosque. The Imam and Imtiaz Khan were now joined by Imran, who looked at Imtiaz with empathy. Majid, Imtiaz's henchman, sat in a corner, listening intently. They had been talking for some time now and the Imam was running out of options that he could offer Imtiaz. The Imam got up and moved towards the window and pushed it open gently. The startled pigeon sitting on the windowsill fluttered away as the Imam looked at the rising sun and closed his eyes. The warm and golden rays of the sun caressed his face which was lined by worry, anticipating the storm that was about to strike the city.

'You don't want them to lead a life away from all of us, in peace, because you seek revenge. You don't agree even to the possibility of the boy embracing Islam—which to my mind, is the most practical solution—because, somehow, you think it will be shortchanging your daughter. You are so hell-bent on revenge that you can't even read the contradiction here! On one hand, you say you don't care about your daughter, but on the other hand, it bothers you who she gets married to!'

Imtiaz was a wily old man. He knew when to press the raw nerve that would put the Imam on the defensive, 'You are spared from this misery I am undergoing because you don't have a daughter!' He then looked at Imran, 'What if Imran had a sister, and what if she had run away with an infidel! Would Imran be satisfied merely by having the bastard embrace Islam?'

Imran turned his gaze away from Imtiaz as his jaws tightened. Imtiaz's parched lips stretched into a smile as his sleep-deprived eyes revealed some shine for the first time during that conversation. Zulfiqar Khan moved ahead and placed his right hand on Imtiaz's shoulder.

'It's all about pride, isn't it, Imtiaz? Well, here is my final solution.'

169

THE KAAFIR'S LOVE

Imtiaz gaped at the Imam in anticipation.

The Imam raised his right hand and pointed it in a direction. Imtiaz's gaze followed his raised finger.

4.12 a.m., Varanasi

They had returned from the Dashashwamedh Ghat around midnight and were lying still on the bed, facing each other, still maintaining a respectable distance from each other. They deliberately did not broach any topic that would veer them towards intimacy. They had decided to not touch each other, not to cross that thin line before their wedding.

It had been four hours since then. Sameer was wide awake, thanks to his call centre training but Inara's eyes were blinking rapidly as she mumbled one incident after the other about her friends and family, yawning occasionally. Sameer extended his hand and entangled his finger with a strand of her hair. Sameer could see that she was gradually sinking into slumber as the words from her mouth started disintegrating gradually and then, she went quiet altogether. A flash of a distant light from the ghats kissed her face as a mesmerizing reflection of dark blue and golden courted her eyelashes. The occasional vehicle passing by would create a sudden burst of light on her face which glowed for a while and then faded into blue, teasing and tantalizing his desires. The sound of ringing bells from the ghats rose as another swell of devotees chanted 'Har Har Mahadev', invoking the God of fertility.

Sameer dug his fingernails deep into his palms, in an effort to inflict pain and bury his desires deep within. But his heart fluttered and head spun, the soft and pleasant sensation rose and tempted him to cross the invisible boundaries. He became restless, exhaled deeply, tossed around gently, careful not to

ABHISAR SHARMA

disturb her. Finally, when nothing seemed to help, he decided to take a walk down the ghat. But he could not leave her alone, so he rose from the bed to move towards the balcony, but a faint whisper stunned him.

'I am scared. Can you hug me?' Her words pushed him across the threshold of self-control. Sameer's hands shook as he moved back to the bed. Inara gazed at him as he drew closer, his face moving from the darkness to the faint light from outside. As he lay next to her, his upper body supported by his elbow, she raised her hand and started to fiddle with his shirt, her fingers tracing the button line. She gently removed his first button and started tracing the warm bronze skin of his chest. Her tender palm lay still on his chest as his heartbeat rose like an unfettered crest. Her hands trembled, because she knew that she was breaching limits. She closed her eyes and nervously licked her upper lip. He placed his hand on her cheeks, the little finger caressing her warm neck. His thumb was now relishing her moist and soft lips that quivered slightly. Sameer drew closer and pressed his lips to hers. How many times had he kissed her, but this moment was unparalleled. It had the adrenaline rush of penetrating the walls they themselves had erected, coupled with the purity of their first ever kiss. As their bodies entwined with each other, the bangles and jewellery around her neck shook and made a lyrical sound. They paused and looked at each other for a moment and smiled, clearly tickled by the sound and the thought that it may be carrying to the neighbourhood.

'I think you need to remove them,' whispered Sameer.

'I agree,' Inara's voice had an urgency to it. As Sameer held her, Inara gazed at him longingly, her eyes following each and every motion on his face as he bit his lower lip trying to disentangle the reluctant bangles from her henna-stained

171

hands. She moved ahead and gently kissed his lips.

'You are criminally distracting me, Inara,' he pleaded as she smiled playfully, poking her tongue to her cheek. Sameer looked at her for a moment as his chest rose and fell, unable to control the rush in his heart. He shook his head sideways and mumbled, 'You are incorrigible and I don't care about the sound your bangles are going to make!' He pushed her down on the bed and dug his mouth deep in her neck as she moaned feebly. Sameer breached the first limit as he unbuttoned her blouse. As a reflex, Inara placed her arms on her chest. Sameer removed them gently and started teasing her cleavage with his nose and lower lip. Inara gasped and dug her nails deep into the warm flesh of his back, pressing him further to her immaculate breasts still cushioned in her pink bra. She felt his hand moving on her back as he opened the bra hooks. An involuntarily gasp escaped her. With the tip of his nose, he nudged the lining of her bra and explored further, relishing the smoothness of her breasts. She begged him feebly to stop. He started nibbling them now, teasing her, but Inara was not prepared for what was about to happen next. Sameer paused and then gently took off her bra and threw it on the ground. Then, he started to relish her breasts gently, licking and tasting them, pressing them. Inara moaned loudly and grabbed the pillow to put it on her mouth. She was in a trance of intense desire. She felt dizzy as undiscovered fragrances emanated from their pores and a burst of ecstasy rose from her heart and travelled down, drenching everything else in its path. Though controlled, Sameer was stuck somewhere between consciousness and delirium. His eyes were shut as he explored her body, licking and inhaling the scent of every crevice, every curve and every pore of her body. As he neared her navel, Inara grabbed his hair and mumbled, 'Stop...please!'

ABHISAR SHARMA

Sameer raised his head and his eyes met hers, 'I have been waiting for this moment to know how you taste. Trust me.' He slowly moved down, and Inara cupped her mouth with one hand and clawed the bed sheet with the other. The ceiling in front of her eyes danced and swayed as lights emanating from outside struck the darkness of the room like arrows and disintegrated its fragile calm. As Sameer drew each and every drop of nectar from her and teased her pleasure spots, Inara sank further into the throes of ecstasy. The tip of his nose on her clitoris and his lips continuously savouring the sweet moistness within, he would occasionally nibble and lick her warm thighs. As his tongue explored her depths, Inara clutched his hair with both her hands and drew him further, burying him deeper within, unleashing passions that fissured forbidden walls, as they kept crashing one threshold after the other.

One hour later...

As the lone tear rolled down from the corner of her left eye, he whispered, 'Look into my eyes as I love you, as I lose myself in you, as I unravel your deepest desires like never before.'

Inara held him tighter as the first rays of light from the rising sun revealed the new day, the first day of her life that shall never be the same as before.

Noon, the Imam's lair, The Walled City

Zulfiqar Khan hardly had a couple of hours' sleep, that too was ruined by continuous phone calls. A visibly shaken Nasir sat in front of him, his eyes blinking continuously. The Imam's eyes were tinged with red, not because of lack of sleep, but because of the patience which was running out at an alarming pace.

'I could have called you last night too, but I wanted you to recuperate, have a good night's sleep. I know that they are in Varanasi, Nasir, but tracing them would be like finding a needle in a haystack,' he continued, almost in a whisper, 'Look, Imtiaz is like a man possessed. In fact, without mincing my words, it would not be incorrect if I called him a madman. I have reigned him in for the time being, but I can't put him on a leash forever. He has assured me that there will be no further bloodshed, but I don't trust him. We need a permanent solution and I have offered him one.'

Nasir gaped at the Imam with deference. He had the look of a man who had been rescued from certain death, whose life had been saved at the last moment. But deep down, he also knew that in no way could he betray his best friend.

'As a devout Muslim, I understand the concept of loyalty, of Imaan, and I know that Sameer is your best friend and you can never abandon him. All I ask of you is to connect me with him on the phone! For his own safety and for Inara's safety. As I said, I can't keep a madman on a leash. I am also worried about the impact this incident may have on the city and beyond. I hope you realize that a Hindu boy running away with a Muslim girl is a sensitive matter. The boys are getting restless. We are sitting on a powder keg... There will be retribution.'

Eleven hours later...

The Imam was not wrong. His ominously prophetic words rang true in a locality not far from the Imam's house. Praveen Gupta had just shut his retail shop in Chandni Chowk as his 19-year-old daughter waited for him in the car parked outside the shop. Devika was getting restless. She was repeatedly looking

174

at her watch every now and then, because after a long time, the family had decided to watch a Shahrukh Khan movie in a nearby multiplex. It was the last show for the day that was about to begin in fifteen minutes. Devika was incessantly asking her father, who was on the phone while shutting the shop, to hurry up. Suddenly, Devika's phone rang as well and she answered, saying, 'Mumma, Papa has finally shut the shop. We shall be there in ten minutes. No, I promise we will be there...'

Wrong choice of words and a promise she could never keep. Two men on a motorbike zoomed straight to Praveen Gupta and placed a countrymade pistol on his forehead. A Zen came from the other side and stopped in front of their car. Devika stared in horror as three men deboarded the car. From a distance, one could hear the echo of Devika's agonizing howl as the men dragged her out and pushed her in their car with tinted glasses. The two men who had pointed a gun at Gupta drove away as soon as the three men had got their target. Speechless at the mayhem unfolding in front of his eyes, Gupta gaped at the Zen carrying his beloved daughter. He grimaced, his facial muscles contorted as he slowly raised his left hand and started scratching his chest. He kept mumbling on the phone as a strain of lazy saliva drooled from his half-open mouth and then, with a sudden jerk, he clasped his chest tighter. The next moment he crashed first on his knees and then collapsed, never to get up again. His blank and open eyes watched the car driving away with the painful shrieks of his daughter now a mere muffle in a dark starless night.

The following day...

While women in white howled in front of a body wrapped in a shroud, men dressed in white kurta pyjamas restlessly

THE KAAFIR'S LOVE

paced, talking on the phone, still trying to trace the daughter of the family. Sanskari Party leader Raj Narain Pandey had arrived an hour ago and was sitting in a corner surrounded by male members of the bereaved family. They spoke in whispers as Pandey nodded his head feigning pain and shock at the incident which, in reality, was his best shot at political revival. What else could he have asked for? A Hindu boy who was beaten up mercilessly by Muslim thugs bravely escaped with the love of his life—a Muslim girl. A Hindu girl kidnapped by men in skullcaps and beards. He knew that this was the right moment to make the political pitch that would catapult him to a sure-shot victory in the Lok Sabha elections. As the women continued howling, Pandey emerged out of the house. His eyes shone at the sight of the long line of TV cameras waiting for a sound byte. He cleared his throat, folded his hands, and smiled involuntarily; suddenly, realization dawned and he quickly buried the smile and replaced it with pain and shock. Then, he walked towards the sound byte hunters who jostled for space in the narrow alley.

'We will not tolerate this terrorism of the Imam and his son. We will not be mute witnesses to the centre's inaction on the thuggery of Imran Khan. A daughter has been kidnapped. I demand she be brought back to her home with her honour intact. Enough of this! Our silence should not be construed as our weakness. We know that any response from our side will have consequences for the whole country, but this government dare not test our patience.'

His eyes shut, the Imam's chin was locked to his neck as the TV splashed images of an angry Raj Narain Pandey on screen. Unable to sleep properly over the past few days, he had dozed off again as the tea placed on the table next to him went cold. Suddenly, his confidant entered the room and gently

176

whispered something in his ear. The Imam slowly opened his eyes and raised his head to face the TV. The confidant switched the channel and tuned it to another one. The reporter on this channel stood on a rooftop, looked excited, and the pitch of his voice bordered on the hysterical.

'Gargi, we are in the middle of a precarious situation. On one hand is Imran Khan who is leading his supporters, and marching in from the other end is Gullu Pandey, who is a close confidant of Sanskari Party leader Raj Narain Pandey, shouting slogans. As you can see, this street is surrounded by many houses but this has not deterred petrified onlookers to scale their rooftops and watch the situation unfolding from their houses. It is as if both the marches have been synchronized to lead to this confrontation...'

'Well, let us cross over to our reporter, Sunil, who is at the scene where the situation is rapidly deteriorating. Sunil, what's the latest?' asked the news anchor, Gargi.

'Gargi, I have had a word with Imran Khan who is leading this march from one end. He has said that he is leading a non-violent protest and that he is demanding that the government increase security in Muslim-dominated areas where Muslim girls are routinely kidnapped by Hindu boys. I also had a word with Gullu Pandey who has demanded the safe return of Devika Gupta to her house and that the culprits, who he alleges are being sheltered by Imran Khan, be arrested soon,' replied Sunil.

The protestors from both ends neared each other and as they grew closer, they slowed down, but the pitch of their respective slogans rose. Soon, both came to a halt but their tempo rose, testing the patience of the other side. Imran stood surrounded in an arc. The men around Gullu Pandey raised their sleeves up and closely watched each and every expression of their adversaries. A woman standing right above

177

the convergence cupped her mouth in tension as her child held her arm and badgered her with a demand, the sound of which was buried in a crescendo of slogans. At a nearby street, the car of Yashwant Mohite, the police officer who had the famous confrontation with Imran Khan, screeched at a curve as a truckload of constables followed him. Yashwant Mohite was continuously on the phone, barking orders to the local SHO, 'Bastard, why did you let them enter that street? Why did you not divert them elsewhere? I don't care if you got orders from some fucking politician! If the situation gets out of hand, I shall slice off your balls with a blunt knife!' Mohite's eyes were burning with anger. The man whom he hated from the depths of his heart, Imran Khan, was there too. He yelled as the driver and the constables seated behind him listened pensively, 'This fucking government has just lost its balls. Bloody cowards! Now, the bloody press will be after the police if this goes out of hand!'

As the police neared, the sloganeering became almost deafening. The people who had scaled their terraces now rushed inside their houses, shutting their windows and doors as shopkeepers scrambled to safety by shutting down the metallic shutters, creating an apocalyptic feeling to the situation which was about to explode.

No one knew where that first rock came from or which side threw it. But it was large and landed in the empty but threatened space between Imran and Gullu Pandey. The second rock was hurled from Imran Khan's side as it landed straight on Gullu Pandey's shoulder. The hefty man standing next to Gullu retorted by charging and swinging the baton in his hand as one of the human shields of Imran Khan came ahead and took the blow. Suddenly, men from both sides converged and jumped at each other. The human shields of both the leaders dragged them away as the foot soldiers pounced on one another. Whistles, catcalls, inflammatory slogans rent the air as sticks crashed against each other. Skulls and bones cracked as blows rained from both sides. Knives were drawn and brandished as the stakes of the confrontation got higher.

Suddenly, from one end, the sound of police siren startled the men engaged in mayhem. Some turned around and started running through nooks and crevices of the area, others enmeshed in rage, charged with ferocity at the common enemy, the police. Policemen in helmets, holding shields, came from behind Imran's men, ruthlessly raining batons and cracking skulls as they charged. In the middle, a bloodfest had erupted as metal was ruthlessly thrust into flesh. Blood splattered and gushed out like a fountain, as men dropped on the ground, wailing in agony. Some who had probably seen their own blood spilled for the first time, howled as their attackers mercilessly stabbed them. Men from both groups started to pounce on individuals from either sides, as bodies started piling up on the ground. Yashwant Mohite looked at the mayhem and knew that his options were limited. All he could hope for was that the warring men would disperse at the sight of the marauding police. He nodded to one of his men who ran and whispered something to one of the constables.

Suddenly, like a well-synchronized act, tear gas shells were lobbed in the air, some of which hit the protestors straight on their heads, other shells crashed on the ground as smoke rose and the warriors cupped their mouth and nose and started to run. The strength of both sides had been dramatically breached by the tear gas attack.

Suddenly, someone fired three shots. No one knew who. A man dropped on the ground, clasping his abdomen. He was the first one to die on the spot. Thirty minutes later, as the

179

THE KAAFIR'S LOVE

police cleared the mess, twenty-five men were taken to the hospital, ten of them serious, having lost a lot of blood. Six men, including the man who was shot, had died on the spot. Of the ten seriously injured, three would die in the next ten days, tossing their families into darkness, and none of them would be able to recover for a long time.

Section 144 was imposed in Matia Mahal, Ballimaran and certain areas of Chandni Chowk. Police presence was increased on the periphery of the Jama Masjid area. A protest march at the Jamia Millia Islamia University was curtailed at the intervention of the local MLA who was contacted by the Delhi Police Commissioner himself. The Imam put his foot down as Imran Khan was confined to his house in Jama Masjid and Gullu Pandey was put under house arrest. But the damage had been done and the politics of the entire constituency had changed as a result of the clash.

Meanwhile, in Varanasi

Face smothered by panic, his hands shook as he held the crumpled newspaper in his hand. Sameer dashed into the room, jolting Inara who uttered a surprised, muffled shriek. He came and sat on the bed next to Inara and tried to reign in his uncontrollable breath. His eyes shifted sideways as Inara looked at him in apprehension.

'What happened?' She moved closer and placed her hand on his shoulder.

Sameer raised the crumpled Hindi newspaper to Inara, 'Page 4,' he mumbled. Inara took the newspaper from him, ironed it out with her hand and then turned to page 4. She scrolled down and then sideways, till she spotted the detailed news item. Her eyes grew wider as she started reading the report.

'I think it is a much bigger story than what has been reported. Newspapers tend to underplay communal clashes. I think we need to act fast now. I don't think we can stay in Varanasi anymore. They will hunt us down and then...' he couldn't bear to finish the sentence.

'They will hunt us down anywhere we go. This is not going to stop unless they...' she paused, fearing the inevitable.

'I hope Nasir is safe. I hope Amma is...'

A wave of guilt overwhelmed him as he realized the futility of his thoughts, knowing that it was he who had brought this upon them. He undertook this journey, aware of the perils it posed to the two people he loved the most, and now six innocent people had died because of them. He looked at Inara, who had buried her face in the bend of her arm. He continued looking at her intently as her shoulders started shaking rhythmically.

'Six...pe...people d...d...dead?' Her voice broke as she struggled to speak. She raised her head to reveal eyes full of tears.

'This is the life we chose for ourselves, Inara. There is going to be a special place for me in Hell, if the people I love suffer because of me.'

Suddenly, Sameer's phone started to ring. This was a number that Sameer had procured just before departing for Varanasi. It was meant only for Nasir to convey any important bit of news but the number that was flashing on the screen alarmed Sameer.

'Why is Amma calling me?'

Hesitatingly, he pressed the green button. The voice on the other end was indeed his mother's. The pain and sense of betrayal in her voice was palpable.

'She came and met you the same day that I had begged

181

THE KAAFIR'S LOVE

you not to meet her, didn't she? And now...now, you have run away with her, tossing our lives into Hell.'

'Amma, who gave you this number? Where is Nasir?'

'Do you even realize how many lives are in peril because of you and that girl? Do you, Sameer? How many more people do you want beheaded on the altar of your love?' Her voice started breaking and her words started coming out in gasps and sobs, 'Since when did you start pretending that I don't exist any more in your life? What am *I* being punished for and why?' Every grain of moisture was sucked out of her scorched throat, as she struggled to speak, 'I want you to come back. Come back home... But you have shut that option forever! However hard I try to run, I will never be able to reach you. I feel so helpless...'

'What do you want me to say, Amma? I know I am on a path of no return. But this was not only my decision! It was a choice I made along with another person. I feel sad at the loss of lives and the pain it has caused you...and there shall come a day when I will pay the price for it, but I still don't regret it. I don't! I can't lie to you. I still feel that this was the right thing to do!'

Prabha's knees wobbled and she struggled to hold the mobile phone in her hand. Her heart raced as panic overwhelmed her. Breathless, she opened her mouth to suck in as much air as possible. A stinging pain rose up her spine as she held onto a chair for support. Her grip loosened and the phone began to slip from her hand. Nasir, who was standing next to her, grabbed the phone before it dropped on the ground.

'Sameer! It's me, Nasir.'

'Why did you have to involve Amma! Why?'

'Why did I have to involve Amma? Do you even realize how illogical you sound? You haven't come home for the past

three nights! How was I, your best friend, supposed to explain that to your mother? How?'

Nasir paused as he wiped the sweat from his forehead, 'Being your mother, she deserves to know where her son is. Not telling her was cruel and unfair! She has no one but you! I still would not have come here, had it not been for Imam sahab!'

'What about Imam sahab?'

'He is here.'

'What do you mean he is here?'

'I mean, he is here with me, at your home.'

Home. The word from Nasir echoed in his mind. At first, it puzzled him and then it struck him as a bolt of lightning. His head felt dizzy as the room around him spun, his mind still unable to grasp the impossibility of the situation. The Imam had landed in his house!

'The next voice you will hear is his,' said Nasir.

Disbelief.

Shock.

The old man first held the mobile phone to his ear, listened in for a few seconds and then gently cleared his throat.

'It is the Imam.'

He paused, giving Sameer a chance to say something, anything. But when no sound came from the other side, the Imam continued,

'I can't watch the city burn and descend into Hell. I am a man of God, they say. Some expect miracles out of me, but all I do is convey His message to His followers. I don't think what you did is immoral or even a crime, but as I said in the beginning, I can't watch this city descend into Hell. There are other interests involved here, serious political interests that want the situation to deteriorate so badly that it engulfs the entire country. All I want now for you is to come back.'

183

THE KAAFIR'S LOVE

'Come back to what, Imam sahab?' Sameer countered, 'I love this girl.' Even though he knew that the Imam couldn't see him, he raised his hand and pointed at Inara. She watched him, tears rolling down her grief-stricken face.

'I have made this choice and have even abandoned the woman who raised me. You say this city's sinking into Hell? I have already hurled my mother into the Devil's domain. I know these are the questions I shall have to answer on Judgement Day and I am prepared to answer them then. Even as I see my mother suffer because of my actions, I feel no remorse. This is the life I have chosen to live. You ask me to come back? But even if I do come back, then what? You think Imtiaz and his men would leave me alive? Is it going to be a happily ever after? For Inara and for me? For my mother?'

'But what if there is a way out?'

'How can there be one?' Sameer retorted.

'You have to learn patience, my son. I am a man of my word, I am a man of God, you have to believe me. I do agree, there will be a price to pay. The question here is: Are you ready to pay that price?'

'What price?' A doubt shadowed Sameer's mind.

'This is what has been agreed upon. You will let Inara go. She will come back. You will then proceed straight to me at Jama Masjid and embrace Islam. For a month, you will work as a helper in the mosque, serving the devotees and doing other chores. As we complete a month and if you still feel comfortable and don't have any doubts, you will start working with Imtiaz, helping him in his business. After six months, if the father feels comfortable and thinks that you are worthy enough, your marriage with Inara shall be solemnized in the traditional Muslim way.'

'And what if her father does not like me and considers

184

me unworthy of his daughter at the end of six months? What happens then?' Shadows of doubt crept across Sameer's face. Inara, who could listen to only one side of the conversation, became restless.

What is this deal the Imam is talking about?

'You forget one thing, Sameer. The deal is solemnized on my assurance. I shall be the guardian of this deal. I know you and there is no way Imtiaz can shortchange you, cheat you or deliberately fail you, as you fear! I won't lie to you. Imtiaz does have issues with you embracing Islam. It took a lot of convincing and cajoling for us to reach this compromise. Now it's a consensus. There is no turning back. So, what do you say?'

Sameer looked at Inara's anxious face. She raised her head and mouthed, 'What is the Imam saying?'

Sameer mumbled, 'Imam sahab, I can't take this call on my own. I have to consult Inara.'

'Fine. I can wait, but don't take too much time. And I think it is my duty to tell you that any alternative you might be thinking of will only lead you to your doom. It only means running around for the rest of your lives and someday finally getting caught. I am waiting in your house for another hour. I need your response before I leave.'

And with that last remark, the line went dead.

Fifteen minutes later...

Inara stared at Sameer with an expression of inevitability as he started narrating the Imam's deal. She knew where this was headed. She knew that the only way to end this matter would be if her father had his way. She was not convinced that Imtiaz Khan had agreed to a scenario where Sameer would embrace Islam leading to her nikah with him.

There has to be a catch somewhere; a sting to this tail.

Her father knew how to extract his pound of flesh in any deal and this 'deal' seemed like a losing proposition for him. There had to be something for Imtiaz Khan in this matter.

'Do you trust the Imam?'

Inara's question was disconcerting. His options stood diminished if he questioned the Imam's motives. Sameer was looking for a messiah and the Imam had just presented himself to be one. He didn't want to answer the question and the irritability on his face was obvious.

'What do you mean? Shouldn't I?'

'You know that's not the answer to my question, Sameer! Should we trust the Imam?'

'He calls himself the man of Allah, Inara! Whom do I trust if not him? I guess I do have another reason to trust him. He has raised me like a guardian angel. Even though he has never interfered directly, but it can't be denied that he single-handedly sponsored my education and made me the man I am. Whom do I trust if not him?'

A long shadow of helplessness besieged Inara's face as she tried to extricate herself from the feeling of mistrust in the options open before her. Her faculties stood sapped as she felt every grain of energy being sucked out of her body. She was tired and nervous, overwhelmed by what stood in store for them.

'I am ready to run with you for the rest of my life, Inara, and I promise you that I won't let their filthy hands reach our world. That is a promise I can make, but to go back home is a call that we have to take together. Once we decide to take that path, there will be no turning back. We can't abandon home and run again. So now tell me, what...'

'Oh, how convenient! The burden to take a call and the

186

consequences are mine to bear, so that if it all goes wrong, you can always convince your conscience that it was I who wanted to go back home! How easy it is for you to console yourself that you are ready to run with me for the rest of our lives and keep their filthy hands away from our world!'

'I said we would take the call together, goddammit! I don't expect people to take my decisions. I don't shirk my responsibilities. That's what I am, if you still haven't fucking figured it out, Inara Khan!'

'Careful...'

This was what the Imam's proposition was doing to them, it was creating doubts and gradually usurping the fragile confidence they had in each other because now there was an option, the wretched alternative.

As they bickered, a nagging thought haunted both of them.

Could they outsmart them, outwit them, every time? Could they outrun them all their lives?

The ground beneath them was getting deceptive and smaller. Motives of people around them were suspicious.

Could they spend the rest of their lives watching their backs, fearing for the unknown, dreading that someone was always watching them, stalking them, like a crouching predator about to make the lunge?

The burden of taking a call was wearing them down. They stopped speaking and stood at two corners of the small room with their backs to each other. Everything that existed between them suddenly seemed so brittle.

Finally, an unspoken consensus was reached, because none of them wanted to give words to the thought that their relationship was as good as over if they had to lead their lives constantly badgered by fear and suspicion. Neither of them wanted to accept that the relationship had an expiry date, and that too, so soon. Shadows of the bustling world outside their small room scarred his face as Sameer stood at the window, clasping its rusted grill tightly. Mutilated thoughts and vague scenarios bounced and crashed on the shores of his vulnerable mind. As she walked towards him, her presence manifested itself as a dark reflection on the wall. He turned his gaze away, knowing that ultimately it will be his burden to bear. She was not comfortable at the thought of returning home but she also knew that they could not run forever.

His jaw tightened and with tears in his eyes, he said, 'Home it is then! Let's go back. I have no reasons to doubt the Imam's motives. I trust him. Let's go back and see what's in store for us.'

She nodded feebly, clearly unconvinced, but helpless at the same time.

'What could go wrong, Inara? If it is your father you fear, then he will get me sooner or later. But now, we have the grand old man's word.'

The Imam's word was like gospel for many. It was the brightest hope for the two lovers. In exactly forty-five minutes since they spoke last, Sameer dialled his home number. The reluctant decision was conveyed, so was the mistrust in Imtiaz Khan.

The Imam proposed a plan to bring them back to Delhi. He told them that police officers in civilian clothes would reach their house in Varanasi and then take them to the Babatpur airport. Nasir, along with a couple of trusted aides of Imtiaz, would be waiting for them at the airport. The two would take a flight to Delhi and then would be taken to their respective destinations. It was also agreed upon that Inara would not stay with her parents, rather, with the Imam himself. This, Sameer felt, was the clincher and strengthened his belief in the Imam. It was also agreed upon that Imtiaz Khan would have to prove,

by his actions, that he had indeed forgiven the two and was ready to approach the matter with an open mind. The next day was fixed as the day for their journey back home. Tonight was their last night in Varanasi.

Midnight, Raj Narain Pandey's house

The news about the clincher had *mysteriously* reached Pandey. He was huddled with his confidant Gupta ji and henchman Gullu Pandey. The trader's abducted daughter too had reached her home, *unscathed*. The reactions to the action were dying down. They needed desperate measures to ignite the matter again.

'How is Sameer heading back home?' Pandey's eyes were fixed on the paperweight as he stirred the hot piping tomato soup with a silver stirrer.

'He is flying back,' said Gupta.

'Pity he isn't travelling by road. Things would have been easier. It would have been so easy to intercept him.'

Pandey continued to stare at the paperweight through his gold-rimmed glasses, 'Revolution requires desperate measures. We have to upset the status quo. Sacrifices have to be made.'

The meeting went on till 2 in the morning. It was around 2.30 a.m., when an SUV with tinted black windows left Pandey's house for its destination.

3.30 a.m., Varanasi

Sleep had eluded both of them. The ghat was just a few yards from their house. The crescendo of the morning bells rose as Inara cuddled up to Sameer in bed. There was calmness on her face.

189

THE KAAFIR'S LOVE

'For the first time, I don't feel intimidated by the sounds of the bells, and the echoes of the morning aarti. I have to confess, when I went there for the first time, I felt nervous. The religiosity of the moment against the symbolism of my own religious beliefs, it was so intimidating. It's not that I see hope, but the inevitability has suddenly enthused a sense of peace in me.'

'And why aren't you hopeful?'

'No, I don't mean to say that I don't see *any* hope. I am happy that I spent this time with you. When we get married and look back on these days, it will be such a rush, wouldn't it?' A smile caressed her sleep-kissed face. Sameer smiled and nodded gently.

'We could tell tales of our adventure to our children...' She left the last word hanging as she went quiet. This was the first time she had spoken about children.

Our children, the voice in her heart spoke.

She bowed her head and then slowly raised her eyes. Sameer moved towards her and kissed her forehead. Inara closed her eyes as Sameer traced the tenderness and warmth of her skin with his lips. Soon their lips were locked together in a lyrical symphony. The lilting sound of the bells from the Dashashwamedh Ghat caressed their ears as their lips moved gently, savouring each drop of the emotion-laden moisture.

'Shall we make love?' he whispered in her ear.

'No, it was painful,' she moaned.

'But I was so gentle.'

'You were, but...' she said reluctantly.

'I promise to be gentler,' he smiled.

'Promise!' She looked at him with trust in her eyes.

He caressed her hair and pushed the single strand back across her forehead.

190

ABHISAR SHARMA

'And promise me that you will not come inside me.'

Sameer giggled.

'What? We are not getting married yet. Do you want another storm in our life?' she feigned outrage as he started nibbling her ears and kissing her neck. She moaned again, shutting her eyes, letting him explore the curves and crevices of her body.

Then, they made love again...

7.12 a.m., the alley behind Jama Masjid

A boy in skullcap climbed the cemented edifice in front of a house and craned his neck. Still, he could not see the view ahead as it was obstructed by a large group of people whose eyes were glazed with horror. The boy moved his head sideways, restless, wondering what they were looking at. As he raised his head further up, he reached the edge of the edifice and slipped. It was at that precise moment that he caught a glimpse of what was lying on the ground... The bloodied spreadeagled body of a man with a gaping wound in his abdomen surrounded by petrified men and women who stood huddled together. A commotion ensued on one end of the gathering as the police forced its way through the crowd. The men in khaki started to disperse the surge of people around the body apologetically and nervously, knowing that the matter was sensitive. The air was thick with tension.

Suddenly, there was a sound of a woman wailing bitterly. Then, an old woman in salwar kurta pushed her way through the crowd as her dupatta dragged across the broken dusty by-lane behind the mosque. The police let the silver-haired woman near the body as she started to wail louder. She stood in front of the corpse, flung her hands in the air and crashed

191

THE KAAFIR'S LOVE

on her knees. She knelt down and grabbed the corpse with both her hands and shook it. Her cry was that of a woman violated by the Devil a thousand times over and it sent a shiver down the spines of even the most hardened bystanders. She kept shaking the lifeless corpse as a policewoman bent down and tried to console the mother whose spirit had broken at the sight of the dead body of her only son.

Who would kill a noble soul like him? What had he ever done to anybody? Whom could my son harm?

She shook his body again and again, pleading him to get up. Even though she knew that now he would never get up again.

Nasir had crossed over.

8.12 a.m., Inara and Sameer's hideout, Varanasi

The knock on the door was gentle but firm and as soon as Sameer opened the door, the man introduced himself as Prakash Yadav from the local police station. Even in plain clothes, the look was unmistakable—the unkempt moustache, the scumbag-entitlement-to-something look on the face, the short hair, the desperate effort to hide the protrusion of his pot belly. As Inara nervously watched the conversation, Yadav produced an identity card and gestured, implying that a vehicle was waiting outside to take them to Babatpur airport. Sameer shut the door as Inara, a little uneasy, kept looking at him for reassurance. Sameer nodded his head and hugged her. She hugged him back and dug her fingernails deep in his back, trying desperately to bury her anxiety as well.

'It's going to be fine,' he mumbled, his voice unable to hide his own apprehension.

'I know,' she spoke, her voice barely a whisper, knowing

192

the assurances weren't enough to suppress the storm rising within their hearts.

Sameer thanked Faizu Miyan who looked bewildered, glancing surreptitiously at the two vehicles, an Indica and a Sumo, that waited for them outside. Curious shopkeepers also stared at them, wondering what it was all about as they saw the low-profile couple boarding the Indica. The police officer Yadav sat in the Indica along with the driver and gestured him to hit the accelerator.

'Imam sahab in Delhi has personally asked the state home minister to see that you are safely escorted to the airport. I am aware of the sensitivity of the matter and the ruckus it has created. I was told to assure you. It is just a matter of time,' Yadav's lips stretched into a half-smile which meant half an assurance, but both of them were ready to latch on to that too.

As the two vehicles cut through the narrow alleys of the bazaars of Varanasi, Inara held Sameer's hand and he grasped it back tighter. The two vehicles jumped and fretted across the dilapidated lanes, as sadhus cloaked in ash refused to give way, glaring back at the drivers who honked in anger. Inara gazed at a man making paan in his small shop, his own mouth swollen with betel juice. A group of men sat at a table in front of the shop, reading the local newspaper. One of them raised his head and looked at the two vehicles. The others curiously looked at the couple sitting inside the car with a man who clearly looked like policeman in plain clothes. The paanwala spat out the red juice which landed just a few inches from the moving cars. Meanwhile, the sadhus hurled expletives at the drivers, pointing their trishuls at them menacingly. Their haunting, angry red eyes stood out in faces covered with white ash. One of them locked his eyes with Inara's as he smiled lecherously, slithering out his

THE KAAFIR'S LOVE

tongue which was forked like a snake's. Inara jerked her head back, shocked at what she had just seen. The sadhu bared his teeth and pointed his trishul at her. Inara couldn't stop herself from looking back as a curious Sameer nudged her. 'What?' he whispered.

'Nothing.' She shook her head and gently placed it on his shoulder.

Did he really have a forked tongue, or have I started imagining things?

The image came back again to her, this time like a slow-motion replay of a creature baring its diseased teeth and slowly slithering out its tongue. She wanted to bury her face in Sameer's chest as fear and nervousness engulfed her heart, but the wretched policeman kept looking back and staring at them. He was probably trying to reassure them, but this gesture was making them uncomfortable instead. The cars manoeuvred and cut through Varanasi, and after 30 minutes, they were on a straight road leading to the Babatpur airport.

Sameer gazed at the bare-bodied farmers, with merely a dirty cloth strapped around their torsos, sweating it out on the fields, as reluctant and dazed bullocks dragged the plough, brutalizing the parched land, and staring at the merciless skies. Inara kept her eyes closed, she wanted to shut the sounds of the world as they permeated her fragile and vulnerable state of mind. Sameer could feel her restlessness, which compounded his own. His mind was on the tarmac of the Delhi airport. He hoped that his mother would be there to receive them. He imagined Imam sahab pacing in his room at Jama Masjid waiting for their news. He imagined that Nasir would be landing in Banaras airport any time now as they were going to board the same flight back to Delhi. Nasir's mobile phone was switched off since morning.

He must be in the early morning flight.

Stung by myriad thoughts and immense possibilities, all enmeshed in ambiguity, Sameer shut his eyes and murmured a faint prayer that he had learnt in school. As he closed his eyes, a pleasant dizziness overcame him, he felt dragged down to the depths of sleep. The gentle and rhythmic jolt of the moving car also acted as a sleep inducer. They had hardly slept for a couple of hours last night and weariness was pulling them down further in a state of semi-consciousness. The sounds of the outside world grew fainter, melting into a fading echo, though they were occasionally awakened from their slumber by a rogue sound or unexpected bump on the road.

A few moments later, it was dark and silent. Suddenly, the car jolted again. Sameer opened his eyes for a moment and then shut it back, not before realizing that the surroundings had changed. It was greener and the road was narrower. From the corner of his left eye, he saw long sugar cane plants converging on them. The drive too suddenly got bumpier and rough, as if they were driving through a field, which indeed they were. They had changed course and were not driving towards the airport anymore. Sameer opened his eyes wider and gaped in bewilderment. They were driving right through a sugar cane field and were no more on the way to the Babatpur airport. He nudged Inara who opened her eyes and looked around, disoriented. She raised her eyes to look at Sameer who mumbled, 'We have changed course,' and then he raised his voice, 'We have changed course?' When no one answered him, he moved forward, tapping gently at the policeman's shoulder, 'Why have we changed course?'

This time panic had set in his voice as Inara looked around wildly, clearly unsettled. Her eyes, already groggy with lack of sleep, reflected a tale of horror, as she held Sameer tighter. In that state of panic, it dawned upon them that they had been betrayed.

Sameer looked back and saw that instead of the Sumo, another Scorpio van was following them now. This one had tinted dark glasses and it looked oddly familiar. It did not take him long to realize that this was the same vehicle that had descended upon his office, the day he was attacked by Majid and his men. Suddenly, their car stopped. The policeman opened the door and jumped out, drawing his revolver, pointing it at them, all in one fluid motion. Inara gasped in horror and buried her face in Sameer's arms, as he grabbed and pulled her head down reflexively.

'Don't worry, I will not shoot you. Just let the girl out,' the policeman said calmly. Sameer turned around and noticed that the Scorpio was parked behind them. He saw its doors open and men in skullcaps and white clothes emerged with urgency in their bearing. Sameer's hunch was right. The last man to exit the Scorpio was Majid. He had a small smile on his lips, though his eyes were bloodshot and his jaws were clenched. It was a smile with no cheer, it was dripping with the sadism of a ruthless predator.

The policeman gestured to Sameer, 'The girl...slowly, so that no one gets hurt.'

Inara raised her head and clasped Sameer tighter as he held her back. Her eyes widened in horror as she saw her father's undertaker. Majid was now standing in front of them, his head tilted to his left and the arc of his smile fading gradually. Suddenly, a man emerged from the other side and tried to open Sameer's door only to discover it was shut from inside. He tried to unlock it violently, his mouth frothing with anger. Inara howled and grabbed Sameer with both her arms. The driver sitting in front turned around and unlocked the door from Sameer's side as well, throwing it open. The man flung it open further and moved menacingly towards Sameer who raised his right leg and kicked him hard. The sole of his shoe landed straight on the man's nose as he stumbled back. A fountain of blood gushed out of his nose as he moaned. Sameer knew he had no chance but he knew that he still had to try, for Inara's sake. He grabbed her arm and tried to run from the other end of the car.

Majid growled, 'How I wish I could kill you with my bare hands, but that is not my brief. I have been asked to spare you, much against my personal wish. Just let Inara go. Else, I shall have to exercise my last option and pretend that I tried to save your lives but you gave me no chance.'

Majid now gestured to his men who pounced upon them as they exited the car and caught hold of both of them. Inara started to shriek loudly as tears streaked from Sameer's eyes with a dreadful acceptance of where this was finally leading. Still howling, Inara tried to hold on to Sameer but the half a dozen men were too powerful for them, pulling them apart from both sides. Suddenly, a full-blooded punch landed on Sameer's face, disorienting him for a moment as his head fell back. He swung his arm but missed his nemesis. Then, in sheer desperation, he moved his legs which landed straight on the man's groin. The man fell backwards, further enraging him and his men. Sameer started blindly pulling his punches and kicks, hitting in all directions, surprising the attackers. As he swung around, he saw their faces. These were the men who had attacked him in front of his office. This time, he would not let them go unchallenged. He would not go down without a fight.

Meanwhile, Majid watched calmly, his gaze fixed on Sameer. The policeman watched helplessly as the other SUV

197

emerged behind the Scorpio. The policemen in plain clothes jumped out rushing towards Sameer and Inara. Something glinted in the sunlight and Sameer noticed the iron rod lying in the foot of the seat. He turned back and picked it up. He now had a weapon. Majid's men got more excited, like a pack of hyenas challenged by a lone lion fighting a last brave battle as their adversary. This was getting out of hand now. From the looks on the faces of these men, it was clear that they were now going in for the kill. If there was indeed a deal to spare Sameer's life, it was off. Their faces were contorted as hatred glazed their eyes. Their fists were clenched and some gripped their knives harder, baring their teeth. They jumped around him, their shoes enmeshed in the muddy slush of the field, banging on the window and bonnet of the car. Sameer swung the iron rod at the man who had held Inara. The man ducked but fell back, releasing Inara immediately. The policeman watched the mayhem and knew that time was running out and he had to intervene if this had to be a bloodless encounter. He roared and ordered his men as they drew out their revolvers. The policeman pointed his gun at Majid now.

'This has to stop, Majid bhai. I was asked to hand over the girl to you and make sure that the boy reached Delhi unhurt.' The policeman shifted his gaze to Inara, 'I have my own limitations. I can't control them,' he said nodding his head in Majid's direction. 'You know that the price will be too heavy to pay. They will let the boy live, if you go with Majid and his men. Sameer's life depends on your decision.' He knew that he had now touched a raw nerve. Suddenly, it got quieter. Inara and Sameer stopped struggling as men around them backed off, threatened by guns.

It was now time for Majid to speak again, 'I have been asked to get you back to Delhi. We board the flight in an hour. This was bound to happen. Sooner or later, we would have caught up with you, but we never knew that the Imam would help us in this...'

The Imam would help us in this...

The last sentence hit Sameer like a ton of bricks. Every word that Imam had said, came back to him like a mutilated echo.

You forget one thing, Sameer. The deal is solemnized on my assurance. I shall be the guardian of this deal. I know you and there is no way Imtiaz can shortchange you, cheat you or deliberately fail you, as you fear!

Majid started to move around the car as he spoke, 'I was there, Sameer, when the deal was struck. I was there sitting amongst the men where the plan to murder your pathetic love story was hatched,' he smiled, his face laden with sarcasm as he still kept circling the car. 'Since the deal has been struck, I have been waiting for this moment to see this look on your face, the look of losing the last straw as you sink. That night... still so vivid, that eventful night.'

It came back to Majid as he narrated the deal that was struck...

Imtiaz said, 'You are spared from this misery I am undergoing because you don't have a daughter! What if Imran had a sister, and what if she had run away with an infidel! Would Imran be satisfied merely by having the bastard embraced Islam?' Zulfiqar Khan replied, 'It's all about pride, isn't it, Imtiaz? Well, here is my final solution. But you, Imtiaz, will have to promise me that nothing untoward will happen to Sameer.'

'That depends on what deal you have to offer,' retorted Imtiaz.

The Imam pointed at his son.

'I offer you my own son, the noor of my life as the suitor for your daughter. I had a long chat with him and he has agreed

THE KAAFIR'S LOVE

*to marry your daughter. She shall be the pride of my house
and in return, you will spare Sameer.'*

*The Imam paused and said, 'The death of the boy is a
heavy political price that I can't afford to pay.'*

*Everything around them went quiet. Stunned, Imtiaz
kept gaping at the Imam. This was an unexpected surprise
that Imtiaz had not imagined even in his wildest dreams. He
mumbled, 'But my daughter, she is stubborn. How will we even
trace them? What if they get married before that?'*

*'I pray that they will not and if we do speak to them in
time, I promise you, I will convince them to come back. The
boy trusts me. Once Inara is in Delhi, I will personally speak
to her. I hope this assuages your hurt pride.'*

'But my daughter...you think...'

*'Leave your daughter to me. She will shift to my house as
soon as she arrives in Delhi and the marriage will be solemnized
as soon as possible. But remember, you will not touch Sameer.'*

'Why, Imam sahab? Why so much empathy for the Kaafir?'

*The Imam's face hardened, 'There are lines that are not
meant to be breached. Ideally, I should have reported you to
the police as your behaviour is nothing short of a criminal
offence. But there are other lives involved. This is the best possible
solution I could offer, even if it means swallowing my own pride,
even if it means that my son accepts this...this shame. Because,
I think you would agree with me Imtiaz, when I say that men
of your stature will not be lining up anymore to marry your
daughter after she ran away with...'*

*The Imam was quiet. He slowly walked towards his chair
and sat down with a feeble grunt.*

*'I believe that Inara is a virtuous child. She is a good girl.
I don't blame people for their personal choices. She fell in love
with a Hindu. Do I hold it against her as a crime? I don't.*

ABHISAR SHARMA

But that is just me! I know for a fact that had that boy been a Muslim but a poor Muslim, you would have still opposed it. You are a mercenary, Imtiaz, a parasite, a blot on the community, but that is just me!'

Imtiaz smiled. His question had still not been answered. But the prospect of Inara marrying Imran was stranger than fiction. How he wished Sameer to rot in Hell! But he could tackle him another day.

As Majid narrated that eventful night, Sameer's grip on Inara loosened. His knees felt weak as panic started to set in. His heart fluttered as warm air filled his stomach. Inara stared at him in shock as he let go of her hand. Everything around him was a blur. Inara was trying to say something to him, but every sound was just a buzz. Suddenly, the policeman grabbed Inara and pulled her away. She howled, calling out Sameer's name. Sameer slowly turned his face towards Inara as she stretched her hand out, pleading her captors to let her go. She stretched her hand towards Sameer, who kept sitting on the ground. She kept calling out his name as they dragged her towards the Scorpio, but Sameer just kept staring at her, not moving. Majid threatened her that they would kill Sameer if she did not come along quietly, but the crying continued unabated. Every man standing there was shocked and shaken by her cry. It could melt the heart of even the most hardened. Majid gestured to one of his men who drew out a revolver and pointed it at Sameer. Inara cried louder as she pleaded with Majid not to hurt Sameer. Her cries were incoherent, but she kept on blabbering. The policemen trained all their revolvers at Majid's man who immediately raised his hand and kept the gun on the ground. The policeman accompanying them moved ahead, slapped the young man and took away his gun.

He thundered, 'You have the girl. Now go! Enough of this lunacy!'

As they dragged Inara inside the SUV, her cries faded and then everything went absolutely quiet. Inara had fainted inside the car.

But Majid was not done. He walked towards Sameer, smiled and said, 'How I would have loved killing you but let me tell you, I enjoyed breaking your friend Nasir's neck too while he begged me to spare him. Ah! The high of thrusting metal in his emaciated body, as the knife cut through his weak bones...'

Majid walked away, taking away everything that Sameer ever loved in his life... His best friend and his lover. He wanted to cry out loud, but the overwhelming guilt of what he had done was wearing him down. Did he not tell Inara that there would be a special place for him in Hell for letting the people he loved the most fall into a bottomless abyss created by him? Every word of Nasir came back to him, all the times when he had pleaded with Sameer to not think about Inara, all his warnings about some things forbidden. He wondered if Nasir had foreseen that some day, because of Sameer, his own life would be cut short, so brutally.

Nasir words echoed.

I can't talk to anyone except for you and Ammi and Abbu. This is my world...

Nasir's world was Sameer, his Ammi and Abbu, in that order. And now because of him, Nasir was no longer in his own world.

Meanwhile, The Walled City

As Nasir's parents mourned over his corpse, curious onlookers descended from all sides, like scavenging vultures moving in

202

on the kill. They provoked the grieving couple, trampled over their dignity, intruded on their sorrow of losing their only son. They said, 'See! We told you so! This is what happens when you hang out with a *Kaafir*. It is the Hindu boy who has brought this upon you!'

Stereotypes were reinforced and vulnerable minds, already staring at death, embraced them without a shred of doubt.

As Nasir's parents buried each memory of their time spent with Sameer one-by-one—followed by a deluge of curses—a different drama was being played out across the Walled City and beyond.

Both sides were billing the murder of an innocent Muslim by a faceless Hindu as yet another communal incident. Nasir's death had brought the city on the edge again. Section 144 was imposed across Chandni Chowk with curfew in and around the Jama Masjid. The police had a major problem in their backyard, hence the police commissioner called a meeting with leaders of both the communities. It was the first step from the administration that went beyond policing. They were now thinking in terms of building trust too. It was a tall order but a beginning had to be made. Out-of-the-box thinking was required so that this did not spread beyond the Walled City.

The government at the centre and the state of Delhi was worried. Their credibility had already gone down to an all-time low and the communal twist was the last thing they wanted, but the reverberations were already being felt. Thanks to the national and social media, people were discussing it and were outraged about it, depending on which side you belonged to.

Some ominous and worrying signals were emerging from Uttar Pradesh and Bihar, where an effort was made to stir the communal pot, the dynamics of which would emerge soon.

203

THE KAAFIR'S LOVE

Meanwhile

They had drugged Inara so that she would not create a ruckus in the plane or even before that, at Babatpur airport. Sameer was just too stunned to react as the contours of the great betrayal became clear to him. It did not matter to him whether the UP police threw him in a ditch after killing him in an encounter or left it to their Delhi counterparts to do the honours. As it happens, the Imam had, for some unknown reason, asked them to spare him. Inara reached the Walled City by noon and Sameer entered Delhi as it grew darker. Inara was taken to a room deep in the mosque where she had a female attendant to monitor her. The effect of the drug kept her dazed throughout the day.

As for Sameer, he was driven to ACP Yashwant Mohite's house. Mohite was waiting for him since Sameer had left Varanasi. The same Mohite; the man who had an axe to grind with the Imam and his son.

At Yashwant Mohite's house

'My sources in UP police tell me that Imtiaz Khan had bribed them to eliminate you.'

Sameer continued to stare blankly at the paperweight on his table.

'I am also told that the Imam was against it. Tell me, what's the matter? I can help you! If you go public, I can provide you protection, but it is a call you have to take.'

Sameer blinked, but still kept staring at the paperweight.

'I empathize with what you've been through, but you have to help me so I can help you!'

Sameer slowly raised his eyes and looked at Mohite,

ABHISAR SHARMA

'I just need to get back home! That's it! I am indebted to you for saving my life, but I have to get back home now because my mother will not be able to survive without me.'

Mohite looked at him and knew what he was dealing with. Through Sameer, he could get even with Imran and his father. However, he also knew that he had to tread carefully. Mohite gestured to one of his men and asked him to drop Sameer at his home. He walked up to Sameer and patted his back.

'You know where to come. I am like your elder brother and I am always here to help.'

In a few minutes, he was off to his house in Noida in a police van. As he entered his house, he did not even look at his mother, who had promised herself that she would not ask him any questions. He dragged himself straight to his room and as he lay on his bed, he closed his eyes.

Prabha came and sat by his bedside, caressing her son's hair and murmuring something, nothing of which was audible to Sameer. Like so many 22-year-olds, he had also learnt to shut himself off from his mother. Like others of his age, he had learnt to ignore the single most important woman of his life who would never judge him. His mind seemed like a beatbox, as sounds, echoes and words thumped and reverberated through his body. The image of Inara being dragged away that morning kept haunting him and her pleas to the undertakers to let her go and spare him, echoed in his ears. His chosen act of cowardice at that moment by not rising to save her, further wore him down.

But what could he have done? It was a choice between letting her go and certain death.

As random musings went through his troubled mind, he was dimly aware of his mother's voice coming from far away, intruding into the ebb and tide of his thoughts. She was saying something. At first, he decided to ignore her, but then he realized that she might have some answers to the questions he sought.

'Did you know they would betray me?'

His sudden question stunned her as she asked, 'Wh...what?'

His voice rose dramatically, 'I said, did you know that the Imam was lying from the beginning; that it was all one big trap? Were you a party to all this, Amma?'

Taken aback by his intimidating question, tears welled up in her tired eyes as she mumbled, 'The only thing I begged him for was that your life be spared. The Imam and Nasir were talking about your marriage with the girl, but what happened? What are you trying to drive at, Sameer?'

Prabha had no clue of what had transpired, this much was clear to him now. The Imam had kept her in the dark and possibly Nasir too. His shoulders rose and fell as rage filled his heart. Restlessness, coupled with anger, swelled up in his chest as he realized with a stab in his heart that the Imam must have been responsible for Nasir's death too.

The Imam—the object of his hatred.

In a sudden burst of anger, his right hand rose in a semi-horizontal arc and struck the steel glass filled with water. As the glass flew and struck the brick wall of the room, Prabha clasped her heart. She looked nervously at her son whose eyes held revulsion for the Imam.

'Why did they kill Nasir, Amma? Why?'

Prabha gasped in horror as tears started streaming down her pale and tired eyes.

'Did they kill Nasir just because they wanted to teach me a lesson? They have left me alive because they want me to endure the pain of losing my best friend for the rest of my life... And to think that the Imam, the so-called man of God, my guardian angel, was behind all of this?'

She murmured, 'It can't be...'

'Why did he lie to me? Why did he snatch away the love of my life? Why did he not leave us alone? Why did he not let us live our lives as we wanted? I trusted him and this is what he did to me?'

Like a woman in trance, she kept uttering those words, 'How can this be? He can't do this! He can't do this to you!'

'What do you he mean he can't? He has! Can't you see?' Disbelief scarred her eyes.

Why wasn't she convinced? Was it because she saw the promise being made right in front of her eyes? Or was there something more to it?

She mumbled again, 'It can't be...

Simultaneously, in a room at the living quarters of the Imam, Jama Masjid

Her face bore testimony to the most tumultuous forty-eight hours of her life. It seemed that the glow in her eyes had been extinguished.

Inara stared at the Imam. Her cheeks bore streak marks of dried-up tears. Her spirit was broken, but she still had a thousand questions in her eyes. She was weak, but her face was flushed red because of the simmering rage within her bosom. The Imam's head was bowed, unable to look back into her eyes as he struggled with his own thoughts. Imran stood at the door, his eyes slowly moving from his father to Inara, the girl who would be his bride. Inara sat with tremendous discomfort on the edge of her bed as the Imam settled on a chair across her.

'I know what you are thinking. I know that you accuse me of betrayal, but...'

'You are no different from my father who would sell a life for a bit of profit,' Inara croaked, fighting back tears.

Imran, enraged at the insult hurled at his father, moved ahead menacingly and said, 'Careful what you say. Don't forget that we are in this soup because of you and your father! One more word against Imam sahab and I will bury you right here, right now!'

Clearly irritated at his son's intervention, the Imam raised his hand, gesturing him to keep quiet as Inara stared back defiantly at Imran.

She trained her eyes back on the Imam and said, 'You are a man of Allah! You lied! How could you lie? You were Sameer's last hope. He buried our plans because he thought that you will be just! Is this the price he has to pay because he trusted you? Is this your justice?'

A small pause followed her tirade, as Inara stared at him.

Then, the Imam spoke, 'Justice is just a one-dimensional word for you, Inara. I couldn't have sacrificed the peace of the community for your adrenaline rush. My choice was crystal clear. It was either saving your lives or digging an unknown grave for the both of you. Because, trust me, your father would have caught up with you sooner or later. I was dragged into this mess and I was forced to seek a solution which I did.'

Her voice rose as she retorted, 'But what about us? Did you ever stop to think about *us*? Do our lives mean anything at all? Do we have a right to choose the way we want to live? Do we?'

The Imam was getting restless and a shadow of discomfort crossed his face. He wasn't ready to get into an argument with this feisty girl and answer any of her questions.

'Peace is a bigger issue for me than your love story. Sacrifices have to be made. I can't let the world burn because the two of you are having a hormonal episode.'

'A hormonal episode? Is this what our love means to you? What about the filth that some of your peers preach? What of the hatred that leaders of our community propagate? The lunacy practised by your gullible followers is fine, but our harmless love becomes a threat to peace, isn't it?'

The Imam's ears had turned beetroot-red. He had no answers. His chest heaved as a heavy sigh escaped him. He rose and started walking towards the exit. He paused and said, 'I am not answerable to you.'

'You are answerable to the truth!' Inara shouted.

He gave her a small, wry smile, and slowly walked towards her. He stood at the edge of her bed and said, 'Maybe you are right. But this is how it works. In a week, you will get married to Imran. If you refuse, Sameer's mother will have to lead the rest of her life alone, wondering whether her son will ever return.'

Sameer's house

Prabha was inconsolable. Sameer saw his mother slowly disintegrating, her eyes wide with shocked disbelief. She kept mumbling incoherently, her voice smothered by her own sobs. All he could hear was, 'How could he? How could he?'

Prabha was burdened by a secret that she could not bear any more. Then, amidst the sobs and the tears, Sameer heard her mumble, 'Justice by the Imam is a right that you deserved without question.'

Sameer thought she had a right to feel outraged as he was her son. But there seemed to be more to this than met the eye. He placed his hand on her shoulder and said, 'What justice, Amma? They are Muslims, we are Hindus! He will think about

209

his own kind. We were just showpieces that he could parade to uphold his charade of charity, his secular facade. He used me when it suited him, but now, he has shown what his true colours are. What is shocking is that he is a man of God and he lied. He lied shamelessly! He betrayed us.'

'Why, Sameer, why? This was not what he had promised me,' she cried inconsolably.

'He broke the promise, Amma. Why are you so shocked? Because he made that promise in front of you?'

'No!' This time her voice rose dramatically, silencing everything around them, 'I am not talking about that promise. I am talking about the promise he made to me and to me alone.'

The twitch in her left eye was alien to him. Her eyes had widened in rebellion. It was an unfamiliar expression on his mother's otherwise linear face. He never thought that he could ever see his simple mother outraged in this manner at the Imam. Her life revolved around him and it never crossed Sameer's mind that she could have a secret world of her own. The rage in her eyes and her clenched fist belied that impression. It revealed a hitherto unknown layer to her persona beneath the benign exterior. Something had been simmering inside her all these years, something that he had ignored and could not comprehend looking from the prism of his own selfish existence.

'He had promised me that even if he would not be there for us, he would look over us, like a guiding angel, and that...'

Sameer's head felt dizzy as he retorted with a hint of anger in his voice, 'But why would he be there for us? I admit that I owe my existence to him and that he sponsored my education, but...'

'You think he did that out of charity? He owed it to you!' she paused, 'He dare not club you with the crowd of those

210

ABHISAR SHARMA

derelicts and vagabonds he feeds and proudly raises, he dare not!' Her breath was getting out of control as words came out of her mouth in spurts coupled by fits of rage.

'What are you trying to say? Why would he owe me anything? What are you trying to say?' His heart sank further. Silence.

Prabha stopped sobbing. His eyes were bloodshot as she fixed her gaze at a random point on the floor. She finally decided to speak and she knew that this was the right moment.

'What?' He was not completely sure that he wanted to hear what she was about to reveal. He somehow knew that things would never be the same again afterwards.

'For the past twenty two-years of your existence, I have kept this secret buried in my heart.'

Her story...

It started when my father could not pay off his debts and died. My maternal uncle lured me to Delhi, promising me work so that I could pay off my father's debts. I was just 22, waiting to be married off. Instead, I was about to be betrayed and interred in the flesh market of Delhi. I took the journey to Delhi along with my brother, accompanied by our maternal uncle. As we reached Delhi, we were taken to the notorious G.B Road by some suspicious-looking people. My brother Raju could make out that something was not right. He protested and insisted that he and his sister be taken back to the railway station. He was beaten black and blue by them and thrown into a gutter, left to die. But he survived and called up our paternal uncle back in Azamgarh from a phone booth. Time was running out as they were getting ready to either sell me off to some sheikh from Dubai or even worse, force me into prostitution.

My paternal uncle asked him to get in touch with Imam sahab, Zulfiqar Khan, who had just been crowned the religious head after his father's death. As Raju got in touch with the Imam, he immediately spoke to the local police station and the M.P of that area. The rescue was swift and low-key. No one, not even the media came to know about it. I still remember when I was taken to the Ambassador car that was waiting at the edge of the road as the Imam sahab had personally come to rescue me. From G.B Road, I was taken to a room in the recesses of the Jama Masjid. My brother Raju was waiting for me there. We kept waiting for our relatives from Azamgarh, but nobody came. I was a liability, and now due to my tryst with the flesh market, a notorious one at that. My brother could not wait endlessly, so he left, promising he would come back. I still remember watching him leave, with tears in my eyes. He kept looking back at me as I saw him fade away from the terrace of the mosque.

He never came back.

That is the last memory I have of Raju, my brother. I know, you would want to know why I did not go with my brother! My relatives had bluntly refused to accept me even as Imam sahab was continuously trying to convince them. Their behaviour had hurt me and I had decided that I will not go, unless they came to fetch me. What else could they have asked for? They washed their hands off me and said good riddance! I was alone in the room and an old maid called Rubiya was my only company. I would cry for hours, waiting and hoping that someday my mother would turn up along with my uncle, and beg me to come with them, but no one ever came.

Imam sahab started visiting me quite often. He would talk to me for hours and while he did, Rubiya would disappear.

At that time, I did not know where this was leading to. He would visit me more than once a day, at times, sitting for hours, talking randomly, as I bowed my head and listened to his voice. But one night changed it all.

I was crying endlessly, as Rubiya kept knocking at the door, asking me to stop and assuring me that everything will be fine. I buried my face in the pillow to stifle my cries. I was shocked by the pain that was breaking my heart. I thought I would die. Rubiya stopped knocking and all I could hear was the echo of my turmoil rebounding across the cracked walls of my existence. I could have missed the gentle knock on the door after a few minutes, but what I could not miss was his voice, his gentle soothing voice as he called out my name. Suddenly, as if in a trance, I was jolted out of my misery and I lunged towards the door. As I opened it, I saw him standing there, looking at me affectionately. I felt like embracing him but instead, I kept gazing at him. He walked in as I saw Rubiya retreating, her footsteps melting away in the corridor. I was vulnerable and he sensed it. His hands started to shiver as he moved towards me and then sat on my bed. He kept looking at me as I stood across from him.

I don't when or how it happened, we capitulated at our first physical contact and everything, after he touched me for the first time, became a blur...

'Stop!' Sameer recoiled as the vivid imagery of that night struck him with immense force. He got up and walked towards the window, his eyes now fixed on the random traffic outside. He felt dizzy as the view around him blurred, but his mother's voice was still echoing in his fragile mind. He turned around to face his mother, his chest heaving with rage.

'You never protested? Not even once?'

She kept quiet.

213

THE KAAFIR'S LOVE

'How can you expect things to be normal between us after you reveal this to me?'

She still kept quiet, her head bowed, her fingers wrapped around the pallu of her sari.

'How did you meet my father? The father who raised me?'

She kept quiet.

'I am asking you a question. Just answer me, goddammit!'

The lone tear crossed the threshold of her eyelashes as it moistened her wrinkled cheek and stopped at the crevice above her lips, but she did not break down and regained her composure. She gazed steadily at her son as he looked back at her in anger.

'It became a regular feature after that night and I could not even figure out if it was with my consent or against my will, until one day his wife found out.

She barged in and hurled the filthiest and the vilest of abuses at me. She grabbed my hand and wanted to throw me out. It was at this time that Imam sahab walked in. His eyes were lowered with shame. His wife angrily issued him a warning that she will leave with her son unless I left immediately.

Imam sahab could not just throw me out, so he did what he thought was best for me. He spoke to Sukesh Verma, the fruit seller and his confidant of many years. Just like Imam sahab, he was double my age, but impotent. I think that's why he was chosen. I was married off to him within the next few days, as the world applauded Imam sahab for his humaneness in rehabilitating me, a destitute whose own family had turned their backs on her. Your father, rather, your chosen father and I have had a silent existence. We hardly spoke to each other, but it was a good deal for him. The Imam sponsored our wretched lives and yours too. From that day onwards, we did not have to earn a single penny and that was what caused your father's

214

dramatic downfall. He started gambling and lost interest in his fruit selling business. He was not even around when you were born. Why would he? After all, you were not his flesh and blood. But surprisingly, as you grew up, he started liking you, until he became so fond of you that you both became inseparable. I decided to consciously keep a distance from you so that the father and son could come together, you and your chosen father that is.'

'Stop saying that!' Sameer crashed down on the chair, tearing at his hair in distress. His eyes were shut, but a collage of images kept flashing through his troubled mind. The chosen father, the real father, Inara…each image was more painful than the previous one.

The story of his life flashed in front of his eyes like brushstrokes against a canvas by a man in a drunken stupor.

'Is it not possible that Sukesh Verma could be my father?'

'You have not been listening to me, have you? He was impotent. We never had any physical contact in our entire life. I was married off to him so that the Imam could still visit me whenever he wanted and keep me as his secret mistress.'

'Did he?' Sameer's eyes welled up with tears of rage.

'I did not let him. I know he was gradually getting obsessed with me, but I drew the line. I told him that his faith allowed him to have a second wife and even if he married me, no one would question him. But his wife did not want me inside the mosque so I would not have him in my life. He was burdened by shame more than me. I was someone who had exposed him and shown him his true colours. I was a living example of his vulnerability, his weakness, his dark side that the world could not see. He could not have abandoned you, his son, his flesh and blood, so he kept a watchful eye over you, like a guardian angel. You are alive only because of him. That day when you

215

and Inara were in Varanasi, that day when he called you in that act of betrayal, he told me that Inara's father would not listen to him and wanted you dead at any cost. He had tears in his eyes as he spoke to me. He said he was helpless that he could not do anything for you, his own son. Too much was at stake. All he could do was save your life.'

'Why are you still defending that, that...man...that bastard! Why?' Sameer's voice rose dramatically as his mother shuddered by the sudden eruption. 'He is the one solely responsible for the mess we find ourselves in. Don't you get it?'

'But you are alive because of him,' she whispered with a hint of guilt in her voice. 'We owe our existence to him, even my own existence. If it were not for him, I would have been rotting in a gutter at G.B road.'

She was right. Every word she uttered was true. But he could not rid himself of the heart-wrenching feeling, his thoughts coloured by extreme hatred, his breath erratic as he exhaled deeply, his mind cracking with pain as if ready to explode and all because of the volcano of pain and anger erupting within him.

He trained his unforgiving gaze at his mother and said, 'Am I to believe that just because he got you out of the hellhole, he had the right to throw us into another? Does he have the moral right to crush my life, just because he rescued my mother from a brothel? What am I supposed to do now? I have lost the girl who loved me, my friend has been murdered because he stood by me, though he did not have to. I am burdened by the guilt of his death and the fact that Inara has been thrust into a life against her wishes! Do you realize what that means, Amma?'

'It won't matter. All of this won't matter in the years to come,' she spoke with almost deadpan calm, as if she knew where this would lead to. 'I thought that I could never live

216

without my family. I cried and I cried when they left me to rot in that brothel, but within a few weeks, as I was rescued, they were the ones I despised the most. I never wanted to see their faces, and I never have!'

He stood silently, staring blankly at a random point in the small room, mulling over his mother's revelation. The path ahead looked blurred and gloomy. In the past fifteen minutes of his life, he had suddenly assumed a new identity.

I have a new father, but technically, I am also a bastard. I am the Imam's illegitimate son.

The last thought struck his heart with immense force and the broth of emotions simmered within him. He rose from his chair, banging his hand on the armrest. His face was contorted with hatred, his ears red as he felt the discomfort rising within his chest. He suddenly felt claustrophobic. Even the presence of his mother was making him uneasy. He knew he was unjustified in directing his misery towards her, but he was helpless and weak and that just made him feel worse. He started looking around for his shoes but could not find them, his mind too unhinged to search for them. So he exited his house barefoot.

The Imam's lair

The Imam's wife sat next to Inara whose gaze was fixed on the floor. The fondness in Afshan Begum's eyes spoke volumes. She liked Inara and was not uncomfortable at the prospect of having this young and beautiful lady as her daughter-in-law. She slowly raised her hand and started caressing her hair.

'I have always liked you. In fact, there have been so many instances when I told Imam sahab that Inara is the only girl in the whole Walled City who could be Imran's bride. Try to forget this chapter as soon as you can. All it will give you is

217

pain. You have to realize that we have been so magnanimous in accepting you in spite of what you have done.'

Inara clasped the rug beneath her, clawing at it with suppressed rage as her jaws tightened. She hated the patronizing tone in Afshan Begum's voice. She had little appetite for rubbish and the woman caressing her hair with her henna-dyed hand was irritating her no end. The Imam had sent her because he thought that a motherly presence would soothe Inara's feisty nerves, but it only served to exacerbate her misery. Afshan Begum kept speaking, but Inara shut her ears to her voice and instead began to picture Sameer in her mind. Tears engulfed her eyes as his image started blurring. Sameer was at a place far away from her. Her flow of thoughts was rudely interrupted by a knock on the door.

It was the last man she wanted to see—Imtiaz Khan, her father, her Abbu. The man who had destroyed her life stood at the door, limping, supported by Majid, his henchman, the man who had killed Nasir. She was surrounded by the people who were responsible for the turmoil in her life. Intense hatred welled up inside her for all of them. She sensed that she was in a bottomless abyss of intrigue and betrayal which was sucking her further. She felt as if she was going to explode and wished that they would all burn with her. She had never felt hatred this strongly for anyone in her entire life. But it was these people only who had taught her to hate—something she thought she wasn't capable of.

'I am thankful Afshan Bi that you have taken Inara under your wing. Your blessings shall wash off all her sins,' he spoke softly, his voice devoid of all emotion. Supported by Majid who glared at Inara, he sat on a chair with a grunt.

How much Inara hated him now! The sight of Imtiaz's tired, wrinkled face, with the unkempt beard filled her with

intense hatred. The smell of tobacco mingled with the scent of rose itar which hung from his crumpled kurta, left her nauseated.

'Allah is merciful. He knows and he forgives. I am a mother and a woman too. Inara's behaviour shocked me, but now she is back. Though that boy will have to atone for his sins for betraying our trust before the Almighty. But then, what else could you expect out of an ungrateful wretch.' Her face and ears turned red, her emotions surging at the mention of her husband's illegitimate son. Any talk about Sameer had always made Afshan Begum uncomfortable and now he was the focal point of their lives. He was like a curse on her, the spell which could not be broken.

Inara's head began to pound, sending powerful shock waves of intense pain through her, like powerful waves on a rocky shore. The scene around her started spinning and everything became a blur. She closed her eyes as a single drop of tear paused on her eyelashes. As darkness surrounded her, the hostile voices around her became muted and were now mere echoes. Even in that darkness, she could imagine Sameer smiling at her. She felt his face close to hers and opened her eyes to him, smiling back. She stretched out her hand to reach for his face, her fingers caressing his unshaven cheeks, his lips. He gently nibbled her fingers as he looked at her intensely with a hint of playfulness. Suddenly he started drifting away as the echoes from the corridor started coming back to her, striking her heart with another jolt of pain. She heard her father speaking:

'I am honoured that Inara shall be the noor of your house. I hope that she will not disappoint you. She better not. Allah has given her another chance.'

Suddenly, Inara got up and said, 'I have to go to the toilet!'

219

'Can you wait? The help has gone to have lunch!' Afshan Begum retorted with no empathy on her face.

'I can't wait! Can you?' she retorted harder with an edge to her voice now.

Imtiaz Khan said, 'Don't worry Afshan Bi, she will not run! She can't do that to us now or to herself, for the sake of her own pride!'

Inara walked out of the room, her eyes fixed on the cemented surface. Imtiaz gestured to Majid to be alert. He was not one to take any chances. Majid stood up and walked slowly towards the door as he saw her walking across the corridor. As she neared the toilet at the end of the stretch, her mind was seized by a sudden thought. She was thinking of a window that was like an artery which opened up in the market behind the mosque. She pushed at the toilet door which loudly scraped against the floor and opened with a groan of protest. Inara banged it shut forcefully against the outside world, and the sound of it echoed sharply as Majid looked across the corridor with disdain in his eyes. He hated the Kaafir, but he was not fond of Inara either.

As Inara stood near the window, she reasoned with herself calmly.

If I escape, there will be no turning back. I will not be condemned to spend the rest of my life cursing myself that I did not try that one last time when I had the chance. But what if he doesn't want to meet me? What then?

She sat on the commode, staring blankly into space. She lowered her head and gently exhaled, the warm air caressing her chest.

Across the corridor, Majid stood outside the room, keeping an eye on the door of the toilet. Inside the room, Imtiaz Khan looked at Afshan Begum with gratitude in his eyes as she kept

ABHISAR SHARMA

mumbling something inane about wedding arrangements and how important people across the country would be attending the wedding of the Imam's only son. Outside, Majid's gaze towards the door was unwavering as he shuffled uncomfortably in his posture; maybe he had an intuition of what Inara was thinking and planning to attempt.

Meanwhile, Inara knew that if she wanted to escape, she did not have a single moment to lose. This was it. She stood up and inspected the window. It opened to the back alley and was tied by a string. Her mind now raced, weighing her options. Her eyes scanned the toilet for a sharp-edged object or a pair of scissors. She found a badly rusted one in the dressing cupboard behind the mirror. It was a useless piece of junk, but it would have to suffice. She thrust the rusted piece of metal through the small crack in the window and opened the mouth of the scissors, wrapping it around the strings. It was a struggle as the rusted edge tried to cut through the strings. Inara's mind was on Majid too as she knew that she could not attract his attention by making any sound. After a few attempts, the strings yielded and the window opened with a slight creak. Her hands shaking in panic, Inara gently pushed the window and looked down. It wasn't a big leap. She just had to climb down on the cemented top of the window and then jump into the alley. Her cheeks and eyes were flushed red, her breathing was uncontrollable from the exertion, and then, without thinking twice, Inara took the leap. As she landed in the alley, she strained her eyes to look at the market that opened at the end of the narrow walk. She started running as her chappals started slapping on the pebble-strewn ground. She emerged out and her eyes searched for an auto. Voila! There it was!

'I don't have money, but I have these gold bangles. I need

you to drop me to this place on the banks of the Yamuna. I also need your phone, please.' She was desperate and he could sense this. He wanted to go for the kill further.

'Not just one bangle. I want more. How do I know it is made of gold?'

'Here, you can have all of them. Just take me to the place I am asking you to.'

The deal done, she sat behind and grabbed his phone. With trembling fingers, she dialled Sameer's number.

As the unknown number flashed on Sameer's phone, he first glanced at it hard and then ignored it eventually. He was sipping coffee in his office canteen. He was unshaven and his eyes were swollen. Inara dialled again, her lips murmuring a silent prayer that he pick up this time. Sameer's eyes were fixed on an indefinite object, and his mind was occupied with a collage of moments he had spent with Inara, as his phone rang again, breaking his reverie. A colleague sitting at the next desk looked curiously at Sameer as his cell phone rang persistently. Sameer caught the guy staring at him as he gestured to his mobile. Sameer mumbled, 'It's nothing!'

Meanwhile, Inara was fuming, her jaw tense as she cursed him silently. The auto driver looked at her with a hint of amusement. She dialled again.

His face flushed with anger, Sameer looked at his ringing phone irritably. At first, he reached for the red button to switch it off, but he did not want to miss the kick of abusing the unknown number.

'If I am not picking up the phone it means...'

'Why the fuck are you not picking up the phone?' she growled as the sharp sounds of the traffic around the auto permeated through her phone to his.

'Inara! Is that you? What...where...where are you?'

'I am on my way to Noida. I have escaped again.'

'Inara...,' his voice rose as he stood up, people around him turned, staring at him in shock.

'I can't...and if you can't or don't wish to...I will still go ahead... But I can't marry that Imran, or anyone else... I just can't, Sameer...' Her voice broke and she sobbed into the phone, tears streaming down her face.

Sameer had already started walking towards the exit gate, his eyes now searching for an auto as he decided that he wanted to meet her halfway.

'Inara, I don't know what to say.'

'You don't have to say anything, Sameer. I have taken the step. I can't go back. I just can't!'

Suddenly, the auto stopped with a jerk. Inara cursed reflexively as her head banged into the bar in front of her.

'What the... What happened, bhaiya?'

'I don't know, madam, the auto seemed to have just stopped.' He tried to restart it, but the vehicle protested, making a loud sound. A large bus and some cars behind it blared noisily as the bus driver gestured in anger, raising his middle finger, and spewed out the choicest of expletives at the auto driver. Shaking his head, the auto driver, with a lot of difficulty, dragged the dead auto, trying to navigate through the angry traffic. The auto driver managed to park the auto at one side of the road, bordering the gate of a yard on the banks of the Yamuna.

'What?' she screamed in frustration.

'Madam, it's not my fault! The auto has just stopped working. I need to take it to the repair shop.'

'How will I go to Noida now?' she howled. The auto driver just raised his shoulders in helplessness.

Sameer who was listening to this conversation intently,

said, 'Inara, baby, I am on my way. It will not take me more than an hour. Just give me an idea about your location.'

'I don't know what place this is... It's some yard, and it is on the Yamuna bank,' she said, with a hint of panic in her voice.

'Take it easy, Inara, I will be there soon. Just get inside, don't stand on the road. They may be looking for you.'

'This is a bad omen, Sameer,' she cried.

'It doesn't matter! I am in an auto now. I will be there soon. Don't panic.'

A few minutes later, the auto driver took his phone back and dragged his auto away, abandoning her at the sidewalk. Inara sat there, staring blankly at the passing traffic, her eyes welling up with tears. Sameer's voice echoed in her ears, '*Just get inside, don't stand on the road. They may be looking for you.*'

Inara got up reluctantly and started walking towards the yard. It was getting dark and even from the entrance she could see the Yamuna, which like the rest of the world, seemed angry and hostile to her. She walked further. There was no sound except that of the traffic outside. She placed every step carefully, her heart laden with fear, as dusk descended and darkness approached. She felt as if someone was following her and looked around furtively. The thought that the yard could be a den of drug addicts crossed her mind, spooking her further. As she walked towards the bank, she paused and stood there in the dark, wondering if she should turn back, but Sameer's voice kept echoing in her mind, '*Just get inside, don't stand on the road. They may be looking for you.*'

Finally, she found a spot to sit on, a large rock on the riverbank. It was not hidden from the outside world, but she needed space to escape in case she had any unwanted guests from the yard itself. She started to wait for Sameer to come and get her.

224

The sound of the traffic reduced in the background and was now merely a lazy echo from a distance. She strained her eyes to look at the entrance of the yard, expecting Sameer to walk in at any moment now. Her eyes started hurting so she closed them, murmuring a faint prayer. She bowed her head as darkness around her started to converge in, engulfing her further. The fury of the Yamuna enhanced the fear in her heart. She opened her eyes and tilted her head towards the river. Huge logs and broken trunks of trees floated in the waters. Haryana had just released extra water and had hence flooded the low-lying areas of Delhi. The flow was also sucking up the bank bit-by-bit, as Inara could see the water surging towards her stealthily. She curled her toes as a reflex. She wanted this to get over as soon as possible but she knew that she had just started it all over again.

She trained her eyes back at the yard's entrance. A cool, reassuring breeze swayed across, cooling her. An unexpected smile caressed her face, but her gaze did not waver from the yard's entrance. Suddenly, she heard footsteps.

Her eyes strained to pierce through the darkness to see who it could be. She stood up seeing the faint silhouette of a man and the smile on her face grew wide. She started to walk towards him although the fear in her heart still unnerved her. And then she saw him...

The arc of her smile receded, her tired eyes froze and she stepped back in horror when she realized who it was.

Majid!

His face flushed with rage and jaws tightened, Majid walked inside, his burning eyes never leaving the sight of her. Inara yelped feebly, 'Allah!' She clasped her chest as her heart thundered with fear. Her head suddenly turned warm, as sweat beads glistened across her forehead.

225

THE KAAFIR'S LOVE

Majid was alone. He was usually never alone, but this time, he was. He had come with a purpose. Inara turned back and looked around wildly for a means to escape, but the river stared back, angry and unforgiving. She wanted to run, but the only way she could was across Majid, towards the entrance. So, she just stood there as he advanced towards her menacingly.

'You know you can't run,' his voice was cold and his eyes dark. His mannerisms were clearly unfamiliar as he stared hard at her, scarring her delicate body with his gaze.

'Go away, or I will jump in the river!' her voice trembled as she stepped back.

'You know you won't. I am assuming that he is on his way. How will you warn him of my presence? If you jump into the river, won't you miss out on knowing how I kill him?'

Suddenly, he lunged forward and grabbed her hand. Inara screamed but her voice was drowned in the torrent of the Yamuna waters and the traffic.

❧

He kept asking the auto driver to drive faster, as he shifted restlessly in the back seat. His hands trembled as he fidgeted with his mobile phone. The number from which Inara had called was now switched off. He was still some distance away from the yard. Time was running out.

'Faster! Faster!' he roared.

'Can't fly, boss. This is peak traffic time!' the auto driver replied sarcastically.

He wildly looked at the traffic around him. He felt as if everyone was staring at him. He craned his neck to his right, looking out for the yard that Inara had mentioned. It took him another fifteen minutes to reach his destination.

ABHISAR SHARMA

He asked the auto to stop, just opposite the yard, but he was on the other side of the road. The traffic was streaming relentlessly. He jumped out of the auto, slapped a hundred-rupee note in the hands of the paan-chewing driver, who gave him a strange look. Sameer scanned the entrance of the yard and then looked to his right. The traffic was menacing. No one would stop for him. He raised his hand gesturing them so that he could cross, but the men behind the wheels honked in anger. And then his eyes widened in fear of what he saw next.

Majid emerged from the yard. It was dark, but Sameer could identify him by his bulk and his swagger. Majid walked to his right and boarded the SUV that was parked outside the gate. Sameer's heartbeat quickened. Something wasn't right. Where was Inara? He panicked at the thought that something bad had happened to her. He looked at the incoming traffic and then ran across the road. The cars honked hard but he didn't stop. He jumped across the divider between the two-way thoroughfare and then ran again, unperturbed by the approaching traffic. The SUV had left by the time Sameer landed before the yard's entrance. His heart was still beating frantically. He dashed inside the yard as darkness engulfed him too. He looked around, but all he could see was the harsh fierce waters of the Yamuna waiting to swallow the banks that struck against it. He ran towards the bank and stood there, looking around wildly. He flashed the small torch on his cell phone to see where he was going in the dark. With every passing moment, the panic in his heart compounded. His hands started to tremble uncontrollably as tears started streaking down his unshaven cheeks. He walked back and then stopped in the dark. A searing pain rose up from his spine and his shoulders started to shake rhythmically as a wheezing sound rose from his throat. He felt no shame as he cried out.

227

THE KAAFIR'S LOVE

'Inara!'

His feet numb, his hands dangling either side, palms open wide, Sameer started to call out her name, knowing that something terrible had befallen her. He dragged his feet towards a dark corner. The light on the phone screen kept going off as he kept shaking it and pointing it towards the darkness ahead. It did not take him much time to reach the edge of the bank. As he flashed the light on the ground, he saw signs of struggle. He bent down, his muffled sobs now an agonizing cry. Then he saw it.

Sameer stretched out his trembling hand. It was her earring that lay on the ground. His mind kept replaying Majid's hurried exit from the yard and his chest rose and fell with fury. He stood up and walked further deep towards the angry water, now calling out her name hysterically.

He remembered her words...

'Because beyond all the struggle and all the loathing, I see a future for ourselves. I believe that as we come together, we shall resurrect trust and faith between two communities living in fear and hatred for each other. I am an optimist, Sameer! Our love goes beyond us. I am sure there will come a day when Abbu and Imam sahab, with their pre-conceived notions shall see reason through our love...'

He cried her name aloud again.

❧

It wasn't difficult for Majid to trace Inara. By the time, she had escaped from the back alley of the mosque and boarded the auto, Imtiaz had already figured out that something was wrong since she was taking an unusually long time in the toilet. They had broken open the door and discovered that

she was gone. They followed her trail and reached the spot where she had boarded the auto. Luck favoured them as there was a CCTV camera installed by an Internet cafe owner, right in front of the auto stand. Majid had immediately asked the owner to replay the recording of the footage and the auto was identified. Armed with the auto's number plate, Majid had rushed to make inquiries. It was only after an hour of frantic questioning that one auto driver finally identified the auto driver and gave Majid his mobile number.

Majid dialled the number and enquired about the place where he had dropped Inara. This was it. He then called up Imtiaz Khan.

Imtiaz had no doubt in his mind. He had coldly instructed his confidant to do the unthinkable. He had told him clearly that his daughter was now dead for him and he wanted it to remain that way. Majid had smiled as he heard Imtiaz Khan utter those words, but he did not want Inara to die so easily. So, he decided to fulfil his deepest fantasy that he had harboured since the first time he had set his eyes on her.

Two hours later, The Walled City

Sameer cried for one hour in the dark and when he realized that his tears won't stop, he stood up. He focused. He focused his rage on Majid and his illegitimate father. He walked out, clasping Inara's earring in his right hand and took an auto to his next destination.

As he reached Chandni Chowk, he walked straight towards Majid's house which was on the first floor of a dilapidated Old Delhi, pre-Independence-style building. He could see from a distance that he had guests over for dinner. Sameer's cheeks were streaked with black patches and his eyes were bloodshot.

But he knew no one would notice or even bother. He waited in the darkness until he saw Majid coming down to drop his guests. He waited some more. He raised his head as he saw snake-like wires crossing each other above his head. Telephone wires, illegal electricity wires hanging precariously, but the people had been living in this condition for years and it had become a part of their wretched existence. He filled his senses with memories of the brutal assault that Majid carried out on him earlier and the violation that Inara had suffered. He kept playing an imagined sequence of Inara being raped by Majid over and over again in his mind. It was painful as hell, but it was filling him with rage. He needed to fill himself with enough anger to do what he had come to do. He was not capable of killing someone, but that is what he intended to do. That is what he had come for.

When the lights went out, Sameer advanced towards Majid's house. He was armed with an iron rod for the first strike. He climbed the broken and treacherous stairs carefully. His eyes were locked on Majid's door. He could hear him moving inside his house.

As he stood in front of the door, he glanced at the space between the door and the ground. He could see Majid's shadow. He was moving around. He stepped back and gripped the iron rod tighter. It was time to strike. He knocked at the door gently. The shadow stopped moving.

'Who is it?'

Majid opened the door without waiting for a response. At the creaking sound of the door opening, Sameer lifted the rod, ready to strike. His eyes heavy with sleep, Majid yawned as he opened the door. Sameer rammed the rod straight into his mouth with full force. The burly man fell back with a loud thud as the end of the rod hit his larynx. He clasped his throat

as he looked at his nemesis. Jaws tightened, Sameer swung the rod in a 45-degree arc and bam! The metal landed straight on Majid's kneecap as he yelped in pain. Sameer did not stop. He raised the rod and brought it down repeatedly with greater force, landing it all across his body.

The jab of the rod inside his throat had caused temporary damage to Majid's voice as he cried out in a hoarse, guttural voice. Sameer now flung the rod aside and raised Majid, his face facing his.

'What did you do to her?'

Without waiting for a response, Sameer rammed a full-blooded fist on his cheek.

Crack!

He raised him again.

'All we wanted was to live peacefully! Why did you do it?'

He rammed again. This time the punch was harder as Majid fell back, his skull hitting the cemented surface.

He raised him again and punched him harder. This time, the impact hurt Sameer too as he grimaced, flexing his fingers. Majid was now bleeding profusely, his eyes now moving sideways, on the verge of losing consciousness. Sameer got up and kicked him hard in his groin repeatedly.

For the next ten minutes, Sameer kept on kicking Majid all over, till he started losing his breath. With his half-open eyes, Majid was now begging him for mercy.

Sameer paused and walked towards the fridge and grabbed a bottle of water, as he crashed down on his knees. Gulping it down, his eyes grazed past the only opening in the dark room, redeemed by bursts of lights from the bazaar below. Lying on the ground on all his fours, he raised his right hand as he struggled to get up, supported by the wall, its peeling paint much like the raw burnt skin of his tormented soul. Faint

231

sounds from the colossal market down below permeated the room through a rectangular opening barred by rusty iron rods. He closed his eyes, out of habit from his twenty-two years of existence, when he heard the Azaan from the adjacent Jama Masjid. He heard a faint rustle behind him as he stood up and raised his head, soaking in the hint of breeze and sunlight from the only opening in the room. He felt the blood rising in him once again. He heaved as he exhaled the hot air that burned his chest. His eyeballs struggled to focus on the room—a walnut-wood desk stacked with half a dozen Urdu books; the wall adorned by framed Quranic verses. He remembered what Nasir called them—tughre. The first frame read, *Haza min Fazle Rabbi* (May Allah Be With You). The next frame was bigger and it read *Bismillah e Rehman ur Rahim* (In the Name of Allah, the Magnificent and Merciful). Then, he saw the biggest frame. Nasir once taught him that they were called Yasin, meaning, to ward off evil spirits.

Nasir… He felt a faint stab in his heart as he remembered Nasir. His bond with this world. Then, he heard it again… the faint mumble, almost like a moan, from a corner of the 400 square feet rectangular room. He jerked himself around to face the sound, his eyes shifting to his left, espying the rusty but powerful two feet iron rod. He wobbled towards the weapon, making his way through the scattered stuff on the ground. The edge of his toe struck the steel wall decoration as he grimaced and cursed under his breath. His rage only multiplied as he held the iron rod in his hand with finality. He looked at the corner again. The crumbled and broken body in the corner moved, attempting to revive itself one last time. His tall figure moved towards the mass of flesh and raised the weapon.

This is the last chance. There is no turning back after this.

If I don't swing the rod, he might survive. But if I swing it, I turn things forever, to a point of no return.

He paused and heaved. His eyes burning, his breath swirling in his chest with an intense emotion unmatched by any that he had known in his life. His grip on the rod was unyielding yet he tightened it further. Shutting his eyes, he turned his head towards the small window as the lights from the market shone on his face one last time. It seemed as if they were trying to reason with him and dissuade him from carrying out that single swing of anger. His eyes welled up with tears and his nostrils flared as hot air gushed in and out. The moment had come. There was no turning back. Sameer raised the weapon above his head, preparing to strike.

Sameer brought the iron rod down, crashing it on Majid's skull with full force. A fountain of blood spurted out of the crack in the skull. As he saw the blood gushing out, Sameer felt better. He raised the rod again, this time higher, and brought it down again and again and again.

As Sameer hit him, the sound of Majid's grunt echoed down the stairs of the house. Each grunt was followed by the sound of the skull cracking. Sameer kept on hitting until Majid's skull disintegrated.

A few minutes later, Sameer fell back, flinging the rod away. He felt like crying but he did not. His mind was now on his illegitimate father. He looked at himself. His shirt was all but soaked in Majid's blood. He touched his face, which felt like fleshy grime; perhaps they were tiny fragments of Majid's skull. He spat. He felt like vomiting.

With a painful grunt, he got up and walked towards the bathroom. He started tearing off his clothes as he entered the smelly bathroom. The plastic bucket held some water. Sameer opened the rusty tap. Water gushed out, reluctantly

233

at first and then spurted forth in anger. Sameer lifted the bucket and poured the entire water on himself in one go. He waited for another three minutes for the bucket to fill again. He repeated the same action—thrice.

As he emerged out drenched and naked, his eyes searched for his victim's cupboard. Majid was bulkier but of the same height. It did not take much time for Sameer to find a kurta pyjama for himself. He put his torn, bloodstained clothes in a black polythene bag and walked out of the door.

As he emerged from the house, his bloodshot eyes were fixed at the dome of the mosque. The sounds of the market around him seemed deafening and everything was spinning, but his gaze was unrelenting. He walked with a slight limp. He had pulled a muscle as he was raining blows over the skull of the hapless Majid who lay dead in a bloody mess back at his house. Sameer walked on. He was now nearing the residential quarters of the Imam and his family.

~

'I want to meet Imam sahab,' Sameer informed the guard.

'It's late!' the guard said.

'It's a matter of life and death. You have to let me meet him.'

'Are you fucking drunk? I told you it's late!'

The voice was loud and it carried inside as half a dozen security guards walked out to see what the commotion was all about.

One of them was able to identify Sameer.

'Aren't you that boy Sameer? What are you doing here?'

Sameer said calmly, 'You have to let me meet Imam sahab. It's urgent! You know, he knows me.'

The security guard looked at Sameer for a few moments

and then whispered something in the fellow guard's ear. The other guard too looked hard at Sameer and started walking inside the house.

As the man disappeared, the men at the gate threw baleful looks at Sameer, whose hair was still damp, and he was shivering slightly too. He ran his hands across his wet hair and lowered his eyes, as if hiding the crime that he had committed a few minutes ago.

The main security guard moved ahead and placed his hand on Sameer's shoulder.

'Are you all right?'

Sameer said, 'My mother is unwell. She is dying. I have to meet Imam sahab. I need his help.'

Suddenly apologetic, the guard said, 'Oh, you should have said that earlier! Why don't you sit down?'

'No, I am fine.'

Suddenly, the guard who had just gone inside emerged and said, 'Imam sahab will meet you now.'

After a brief pat-down, Sameer was escorted inside the house. The long walk across the corridor evoked memories from his childhood, and they flashed across his eyes like a painful bolt. He remembered how these corridors were left open for some kids of the locality. He now realized that it was all by design. The Imam could never own him, so he let him into his world on his own terms. It was all so subtle. As memories engulfed his mind, his chain of thought was broken by the voice of the escort.

'Here, they are waiting for you.'

'They?'

He soon understood what the guard meant, as 'they' came into the picture—Imam Zulfiqar Khan and his son, Imran Khan. The Imam was sitting on a single sofa as his son sat in the

235

one next to his father, glaring at him, oblivious to the bond he shared with Sameer. The Imam gestured to Sameer as he walked towards him. Sameer kissed his hand and sat in the bamboo chair next to him. The hierarchy was apparent: The father, the son and the illegitimate son.

'Where is Inara, Sameer? I am fed up of all this now, though I am indeed surprised to see you, because this is the last place I was expecting you to come to.'

'Let me ask the questions for a change, Imam sahib,' Sameer retorted coldly.

Imran clasped the chair, shocked by Sameer's sharp retort, but he did not display any sudden change of expression.

'Let me ask some questions, Imam sahab. You owe me a few answers, don't you?'

The Imam looked at Sameer hard, trying to read his mind through his cataract-afflicted eyes. His heartbeat quickened as he dreaded that the past was about to rear its head. Sameer's gaze was intense, fixed on the old man. In those few seconds, he had probably conveyed what he wanted to.

'Can I call you Abbu, now that I am among my family?'

'How dare you!' Imran stood up, advancing menacingly towards Sameer.

'Imran!' the Imam raised his voice but his gaze was steadily on Sameer, 'Control yourself and sit down! Do not speak unless I ask you to.'

Unperturbed by Imran's sudden response, Sameer said, 'I should be grateful to you. If it weren't for you, I would still be wallowing in the filth and squalor of the Walled City. After all, why would a pious man of Allah be condemned to abandon a woman whom he saved from hell?'

Imran was now totally unsettled, his eyes shifting from his father to Sameer.

'But doesn't Islam allow you to marry a second time? Why did you have to abandon her?'

The Imam closed his eyes and then slowly opened them. His eyes filmed over with tears.

'Ah, I know. You are a man of God. The one who is incapable of any sin, leave alone falling for the temptations of the flesh. If you had to accept my mother, the cloak of invincibility and piousness would have come off, wouldn't it... Abbu?' He uttered the last word after a small pause, his voice heavy with sarcasm.

'You rescued my mother from hell, you gave her shelter and she couldn't have had a better life than that...but then? What did you do after that? I don't judge people, Imam sahab, but I judge you! You may not have forced yourself on her, but deep down, you felt that she was indebted to you so you extorted the price of saving her. You exploited her misery, didn't you? You call yourself a man of God? Did she not deserve better?'

His eyes soaked with grief, the Imam exhaled, the warm air swirling in his chest like a storm.

'You could have left us alone, but no! You kept on following us like an obsessed man.'

His voice disintegrating, the Imam replied, 'So what else did you expect me to do? You think I should have abandoned her and abandoned my son? You tell me, what was I supposed to do? I have to answer for my sins when I meet my Maker, but I could not just abandon you! No!'

'You are wrong, Abbu,' Sameer spoke calmly, his gaze unwavering of his father. 'You could have left us alone, but like an obsessive stalker, you destroyed my life!'

'Rubbish!' The Imam lowered his eyes, clearly uncomfortable with Sameer's questions.

'You could have let us live in peace; you could have let

237

THE KAAFIR'S LOVE

us be. Instead, you betrayed me! You betrayed your own son. I trusted you and this is what you did?'

'There are far more pressing matters in this world than your love affair! Your relationship with Inara would have torn this city apart!'

'Really, Abbu? Are you even listening to what you are saying? My relationship with Inara would have torn this city apart? You really believe in that rubbish? Your men follow you around like zombies. They don't even question you! They blindly follow the path you herd them towards and you think that my love affair would have torn this city apart?'

The Imam felt irritation, and a shadow of guilt swam across his face, but he responded calmly, 'You will never understand the ways of this world. All you are bothered about is your love, but...'

'Now what, Abbu? Now what? Is there a happily ever after for anyone of us now? As I entered this room, you asked me where is Inara?' Tears started streaming down Sameer's eyes as his hands started trembling, 'Do you know where she is? They buried her! They buried her in the waters of the Yamuna! She was raped and then she was buried.'

Shocked, the Imam and his son gaped at Sameer. Then, the Imam asked hesitatingly, 'Who buried her? What are you saying?'

'Still pretending, are we? Or is this also one of your brilliant master strokes?'

There was silence.

'And look what you did to me too! You made me a murderer, your own son! I killed him with my bare hands.' Sameer spread out his right palm and revealed Inara's earring.

The Imam looked at Imran and said, 'Call Imtiaz! Rather, call Majid right away! I want to know what happened.'

ABHISAR SHARMA

Sameer gave a small smile, 'You don't have to call Majid, Abbu. I have rid him of his misery. He lies brutalized in his own house. See! You have turned me into a crazed killer. I have lost my love and now I am a murderer too. So much for your plan...'

The Imam got up with a painful grunt and walked up to Imran who looked shocked, with a thousand questions in his eyes.

'I know you want to know the truth. All I can say is that everything he has said is correct! He is indeed my son. As I said earlier, I will have to answer for my sins when I meet my Maker, but today I have to set a few things right. I want you and a few trusted men to go to Majid's house and check. I want you to clean up that mess.'

Imran kept staring at the Imam. The obedient son would still not question his father because he did not wish to see his hero falter, the only man in this world he deemed fit to idolize. Today, everything around him was falling apart. A single tear rolled down his eye and moistened his cheek. The Imam patted his shoulder as a lump of pain formed in his throat. Imran slowly walked out of the room, the echo of his footsteps fading away gradually.

The Imam then turned to his illegitimate son.

'You know, Sameer,' he said, as he walked slowly towards him, 'the day I had a press conference with Imran and you sitting next to me, it was the proudest day of my life. That night, that entire night, I could not stop my tears from flowing. It was so therapeutic. I had never felt that peaceful for a long time.'

Sameer retorted, 'Will you accept me as your son in public?'

'You don't understand Sameer. I am not an individual. I represent the entire community.'

239

'I don't care! Will you accept me now?' Sameer's eyes were bloodshot and his face was hardening.

'I have to sort out this mess. I have to get you out of this quagmire first. I can't let my son...'

'Fuck this! Just answer me! Will you or not?'

The Imam crashed down on his knees and started sobbing, covering his face with his trembling, wrinkled fingers.

'Please don't test me, Sameer. I agree I have sinned. I know I have. But please, just give me one last chance.' The Imam raised his head, his tearful eyes meeting Sameer's bloodshot gaze.

The Imam raised his hands towards Sameer, begging for absolution as Sameer stared at him. Reluctantly, Sameer held out his hand and pulled him up as the Imam buried his face in Sameer's chest and started sobbing uncontrollably. Sameer stared into vacuum as a thin film of tears covered his eyes too, but he would not break down. Not yet. He kept stroking the old man's head gently, but he felt no pity for his misery.

'Please tell me,' his voice a deathly whisper, 'will you own up my mother and me?'

The Imam kept sobbing and caressing his son's back. He did not have answers. Sameer's questions were tearing him apart as he kept mumbling a faint prayer, hoping for this too to pass, requesting Allah to give him an answer to the toughest question of his life. He prayed hard. He wanted this to end. He wanted peace for his son, for himself. He clasped his son, never wanting to let him go.

Sameer hugged him back tighter.

His grip unyielding, he pressed the Imam tighter into his chest, his powerful grip now suffocating the old man. Sameer's jaws tightened as he applied further pressure on the old man's fragile frame. The tears in Sameer's eyes spilled over as the Imam struggled to extricate himself from his deathly grip. He even tried to scratch Sameer, his face contorted and twisted, shocked, as life ebbed out of him slowly and mercilessly.

In a few minutes, the struggle was over...

Sameer carried his father to his chair and placed him gently, caressing his forehead as the Imam's blank eyes stared back at him. Sameer gently shut them as a lump choked his throat. He bowed his head before the Imam's feet and started walking towards the exit. The corridors were empty as the security was concentrated at the main gate.

As he neared the entrance, the guards turned around to look at him. His expression was cold and forbidding. There was no trace of his crimes on his face. His pulse was steady, his hands were not trembling, and his heartbeat was normal too.

'Imam sahab has gone off to sleep. He has asked not to be disturbed,' Sameer walked out, uttering those words. The security guards were puzzled as the Imam usually never sent out such messages through random people. The guards stared hard at Sameer who walked towards the auto stand. He knew where he had to go.

Two hours later...

Disbelief was writ large on Yashwant Mohite's face as Sameer narrated the entire events of the evening to him, his expression calm and stoic, his eyes unblinking. Mohite had no reasons to disbelieve his story. His mind was now thinking about the repercussions of the Imam's death and how the Walled City would react to this news. The Imam was, after all, the most important leader that it had known. His death would have national repercussions too, he knew.

As Sameer spoke, he would often go quiet for a minute or so and Mohite would offer him water and pat him

241

gently on his back. Mohite had no sympathy for him, but through Sameer, he saw an opportunity to get even with the Imam's son and avenge the humiliation he had suffered not long ago.

'...and then I walked out, took an auto and I thought I should meet you. I don't know why, but I thought I should come here.' His voice was now barely a whisper.

'You did the right thing, Sameer, but as you said, you have murdered two people, one of them being the Imam himself. I am afraid you are now at the point of no return. I wish you had come to me after you discovered that Inara may have been murdered.'

Sameer did not respond. His eyes were dry, not a drop of moisture, not a strain of melancholy, just the stillness and deathly quietness of the insanity that was ravaging him from within.

'Are you sure she is dead?'

He kept quiet. Mohite's words did not matter to him anymore. His mind was a landmine of memories, exploding within, painful, and sinking him further. Mohite kept looking at him.

'I will be away for a few minutes. I have to speak to a few people. Are you hungry?'

No response.

Mohite shook his head and stood up, patted Sameer's back and started walking towards the door, looking back at him as he exited the room.

2.32 a.m., the Delhi Police Commissioner's residence

It was a late night panic call. It could not have been something normal. With eyes scarred with sleep, Commissioner Asthana

ABHISAR SHARMA

took the call on his mobile and started listening to Yashwant Mohite.

'Sir...disaster has struck! The Imam has been murdered!'

That was enough to wipe off any sleep or irritation on his face as he jerked himself up.

'What the...?'

Mohite started narrating the entire incident as the commissioner listened to every word he spoke, the saga unfolding before the wide and baffled eyes of his mind. The narration lasted for half an hour with Asthana throwing in an occasional question. As Mohite stopped, Asthana started caressing the bridge of his nose as a searing pain rose across his spine and struck the back of his head.

With a painful grunt, Asthana said, 'This city is going to burn Mohite! Be prepared.'

'With men like Imran, we were always sitting on a powder keg, sir,' retorted Mohite, his chest heaving with disdain for Khan.

'Now, now Mohite, I know you have an axe to grind against Imran Khan, but the tranquillity of this city is way above your personal angst and retribution.' Asthana paused as he started to think about something.

'I think both you and me need to pay a visit to the next Imam of the Jama Masjid, right now! I want you to be at my place in half an hour and we need to meet him as soon as possible. Leave Sameer under strict and watchful eyes of your men. Don't let him escape. Get it, Mohite?'

3.34 a.m.

The two of them were in the commissioner's Ambassador car as Asthana reluctantly started scrolling the contact list in his

243

mobile phone. The Ambassador was accompanied by another vehicle with armed men sitting inside. As he reached the name 'Imran Khan', he paused. He kept staring at the number and reluctantly dialled.

'I was waiting for your call, commissioner. Please walk into my residence. I shall tell my security to escort you to my room.'

The commissioner's heart started beating fiercely. Imran's voice was calm but had a slight nasal twang to it, like he had just cried. He knew that Imran was reckless but he was also the heir to Zulfiqar Khan. The successor to the throne.

The security at the gate was aware of the high-profile visit but oblivious to what had happened to the Imam who lay in his room covered in a white shroud till his neck. His face was calm, but the glow was slowly melting. Afshan Begum sat next to her husband's corpse and kept sobbing quietly. She was woken up after her son discovered what had happened to his father. As the Commissioner Asthana and Mohite walked across the long corridor towards the room, they could hear the faint sobs of Afshan Begum echoing. As the duo reached the room, they saw her sitting next to the Imam's body, weeping gently as the son stared at his father, eyes scarred red. The two of them stepped inside the room. Imran slowly turned his head towards them and nodded as Asthana folded his hands and greeted him. Then, they gently walked towards the body and touched its feet, one by one. Imran turned his head towards the Imam's confidant and whispered something in his ear. The man then looked at Asthana and Mohite and gestured them politely to follow him.

The two were led into another room, the living room, where the father and son used to meet and brainstorm with people who would come to meet them, political and religious. As they waited for the son to arrive, they kept staring around. The room was decorated in a traditional Islamic way with breathtaking pictures of the Mecca and the Jama Masjid adorning the walls. There were a lot of inscriptions from the Quran in medium-sized and small photo frames. The air was heavy with the fragrance of ittar. The silence between the two was awkward and Mohite was feeling even more miserable as he was now in the house of the man he detested from the core of his heart.

First, there was the sound of the footsteps and then the man himself entered. The two got up simultaneously as a mark of sympathy and the sensitivity of the moment. Imran Khan came inside and sat in front of them. But he did not look at them, rather he kept looking at a photo frame of his father with former PM Indira Gandhi in Amethi.

'I am sorry, Imran. I know no words can assuage your pain, but as the commissioner of Delhi Police, I would like to assure you that I shall do everything that I can to get to the bottom of this matter. In fact, let me inform you that Sameer Verma is now in our custody. He walked into Mohite's house last night...'

Imran suddenly raised his head and locked his eyes with Mohite's. 'You have Sameer?'

Mohite nodded in the affirmative.

Imran then slowly lowered his head, his eyes moving sideways as a thousand thoughts struck his vulnerable and feeble mental balance.

'Why do you have Sameer in your custody, commissioner?'

Stunned, the two first looked at each other and then, the commissioner spoke slowly and reluctantly, 'The boy has confessed! He said that he had...'

Imran calmly cut the commissioner, 'My father died in his sleep peacefully last night. What are you trying to drive at, Asthana sahab?'

245

Bemused, Asthana looked at Mohite as his lips started to quiver in panic.

'Calm down, commissioner! I know why you are here. I am sure you must have told Mohite that this city will burn. And I also remember the conversation I had with Mohite sometime ago on the footsteps of the mosque, remember Mohite?'

'If any one of my men dies, this entire locality will burn. If half a dozen of my men die, this city will burn. If a dozen of my men die, your country will burn.'

'So just let it be. Dont try to dig deeper. It's calm out here. That's how it should be. 'In the other room, commissioner... the leader of the faithful sleeps peacefully.'

Asthana spoke with a lot of hesitation in his voice, 'Uh, the boy Sameer has confessed that he killed Imam sahab and Majid and as I said, he is in our custody.'

'I don't get it, Asthana sahab! Why would I be interested in Sameer or anyone for that matter? As I told you, my father died peacefully in his sleep last night. That's what my mother knows. That's what this locality will know when they rise tomorrow and that's what the world shall know...unless you want things to become complicated?'

Asthana was stunned. He was clearly not prepared for this.

'Zulfiqar Khan was not just an individual, commissioner! He was a legacy. He epitomized faith for many who had no hope in this world. He was the bridge between men of faith and politicians. I can't let that legacy die. If the word goes out about the circumstances of his death and his relationship with the man who killed him...everything that he had built over the years, and his forefathers, in the years before that, will be buried and gone.'

Imran got up and started walking towards one of the walls of the living room and stood in front of the photo of his father.

ABHISAR SHARMA

'I never believed that my father was just a man of God. He was as much a political animal that one could be. I had my objections to his hobnobbing with the rich and powerful, but that was his high. The fact that the powerful politicians would be at his doorstep seeking advice on various matters was his elixir. I can't let all that die with him. He sleeps peacefully. Let his legacy continue.'

With a hint of hesitation in his voice, Mohite said, 'What about Majid?'

'He was an orphan, Mohite. No one will miss him. He has been buried deep enough so that no one find him, ever!'

The commissioner asked him, 'So, now what, Imran?'

Imran said, 'You have two options. Either you go by my way or you open the Pandora's box and let all hell break lose. I think my way is better. Everyone goes back to their lives pretending nothing happened... But yes! I would like to meet Sameer. Once! One last time.'

Asthana looked at Mohite again.

6.01 a.m., two hours later...

They were alone in the room. The morning rays had just started seeping from the glass of the windows which had many aayats of the Quran scribbled on it in a haphazard fashion. Sameer had a cold expression on his face, as if nothing could affect him anymore. Imran's eyes were bloodshot as he looked intently at the reflection of the aayats of the Quran on the carpeted floor of the room.

'I loved my father. He was the centre of my universe, so much so that in front of him, even my mother did not exist. The worst fear that has haunted me for as long as I can remember is what if someday, someone killed him, considering the sensitive

247

THE KAAFIR'S LOVE

job he had on his hands. I always told myself that may Allah save the man, who would kill my father, from my wrath. I always thought I would make him die a thousand deaths and each one would be worse than the previous. But that night...'

He paused, and trained his eyes at Sameer who was looking at him blankly.

'...that night when I came back and discovered Abbu and realized that he had been...that you had murdered him, the only thought that came to my mind was how to save the legacy that has been bestowed to me. What if this entire matter gets out in the public domain? What then? I did not, and I repeat, I did not feel any animosity towards you, you, the man who killed my father, my blood, my brother...'

He left the last word hanging as a pall of discomfort engulfed the spaces between the two.

'I don't know why I wanted to meet you. I don't know why I wanted to speak to you. I don't feel anything for or against you. I have reasoned with myself the entire night. I guess maybe because this is what I would have done if I were you.'

'But I did not want to murder him, I did not.' The suddenness in Sameer's voice shocked Imran as he fixed his gaze back on him.

'I just wanted him to own me. I just wanted him to... have the courage to own up my mother and...accord her the dignity she deserves, that's it! I don't know what overcame me. As I was smothering him, I felt no hatred for him, just the tearing melancholy that was stabbing at my heart. A pain I could not bear anymore.'

'As I said, Sameer, I don't care and it does not matter. He is gone. I guess we should all move on... Which means that you will not let this matter out in the public domain. You will leave this city and, if possible, this country, with your mother,

248

so that we never cross each other's paths even by chance. And, another thing, Majid did not exist. No one will miss him. Abbu died a natural death, peacefully, in his sleep. This is the only truth that I shall let the world know after an hour.'

Sameer gaped at Imran who slumped back in his chair and then gently shut his eyes.

'You can leave now. There is nothing else to talk about. It's not as if everything is over for you, you still have your mother and she still has you, free, not in prison or in some unmarked grave. You can look after her in her old age. I hope you understand that the alternative is disastrous for you, for me and for all of us.'

Sameer got up as a stinging pain rose across his spine. The morbid feeling was so overpowering that merely walking out of the mosque was draining him. He walked slowly to the exit of the mosque as images of the night gone by struck his feeble mind.

The ride in the auto was the longest in his life. As the auto dragged itself towards Noida, spewing sporadic black fumes, Sameer shut his eyes, but images of the past twenty-four hours of his life struck him repeatedly. He shut his eyes harder but the images came back stronger, each time. He wanted to go back to the yard where Majid had killed and flung Inara in the Yamuna, his mind restless, to search for clues, to reassure himself that she may be alive. But his knees shook at the very thought of revisiting the horror. A sudden panic engulfed his heart as he clasped his chest feebly, his fingers shaking. Sameer slumped further in the auto as it jumped a road divider.

He said feebly, 'Stop the auto.'

249

His voice did not carry over to the betel-chewing auto driver.

This time Sameer shouted as the auto screeched to a sudden halt. Sameer rushed to the footpath and threw up, making a loud gagging sound. This went on for fifteen minutes as the auto driver looked at him with disgust, murmuring, 'Why do people drink so much when they can't handle it?'

As Sameer gained composure, he boarded the auto again as it drove towards his home.

Slapping a five-hundred rupee note on the autowallah's hand, Sameer reluctantly climbed the stairs of his house. He stood in front of the door of his house and wondered what he would do next. His mind was too vulnerable to process any thought as he pressed the doorbell. He could hear an unusual urgency in the footsteps of his mother, as she stumbled upon something which made a loud clanking noise as it crashed. She cursed under her breath and then stood in front of the door, still not opening it.

'Amma?'

'Are you alone or...'

'Amma open the door!' Sameer retorted in anger, his patience running out.

His mother opened the door glancing behind her son. Then, she raised her frail hand and gently dragged her son inside by his shirt.

'Is everything fine?'

'Nothing is fine.'

He had left behind him a trail of fire that had changed so many lives forever.

'I have killed the Imam...'

Prabha gaped at her son and crashed on the sofa behind her. She wanted to shrug it off in disbelief but something in

ABHISAR SHARMA

his eyes said that he had indeed killed the Imam. A sudden pain rose across her heart, the repercussions of what her son had done. She had nothing left for the Imam in her heart. It was over, a long time ago. But the immediate impact was still horrifying.

'They raped and killed Inara, Amma.' Sameer broke down burying his face in his mother's lap, his shoulders shaking as if in a convulsion.

'But...,' she said feebly and turned her head towards the door leading to their bedroom.

'Inara!' she called out, as Sameer raised his head with a jerk, looking around and then fixing his gaze at the door of the bedroom. The door opened gently as Sameer rose and started walking towards it.

Inara emerged from the door, dressed in Sameer's T-shirt and misfit trousers. A mix of fear and uncertainty scarred her eyes.

Sameer grabbed her by her hands and then clasped her tightly to his chest, breaking down and crying aloud.

'Sameer, relax, you are hurting me. I am here, I am here now,' she pleaded.

Sameer crashed on his knees as he wept. Inara bent down and embraced him as uncontrollable tears started running down her face too.

They could not speak for almost an hour, as they tried to comfort each other. They were at the tail-end of a storm as the ruins of their immediate past lay scattered around them.

As they regained their composure, Inara narrated her miraculous escape from Majid.

'When he walked menacingly towards me, I stood at the edge of the bank as angry waters of the Yamuna raged behind me. I threatened him, but I knew nothing could stop him. The

251

look in his eyes said it all. He would kill me, but not before…you know. So I took a leap of faith. I jumped in the waters leaving it to the Almighty and my swimming skills. As the waters tried to taunt and bury me, I looked back and saw Majid walking away, probably thinking that the Yamuna had swallowed me. I frantically looked around. The strong flow was also keeping me afloat. Ahead of me was a large log that had probably fallen off the paper mill. It was a massive struggle to grab the log but I finally did it. The waters were slowing down too as I pushed the log to the other side of the Yamuna. It was pitch dark as I reached the other side. The only thing in my mind was to reach your home then. There was no way I could go back to the spot we had decided upon. I hoped that you too would come back home when you wouldn't find me there. As I walked aimlessly through the narrow alleys, I was in a total disarray. But I kept asking myself to focus as I had to reach your place. I emerged on the road and saw an auto appearing and suddenly I started crying. I begged the autowallah to take me to Noida. I was not even audible to myself. The autowallah first looked at me in shock as I shivered. People around me started walking towards me in curiosity. It was the attention I did not want or maybe I was too paranoid. So, I jumped into the auto as it drove towards Noida. I reached your home and here I am. I wanted to call you, but I wasn't sure who was with you. Knowing Abbu, I was so sure that he must have gotten your phone tapped too. So we waited.'

As Inara narrated her incredible tale of escape, Sameer was also thinking about the future. He knew that they could no longer stay in Noida. He would have to go some other place and then maybe hide themselves for some time. Sameer's mother knew of a place. Her husband's brother, who was staying in

Gorakhpur. It was a chance they had to take.

By the time they reached Gorakhpur, Inara was rechristened as Shruti Verma, Sameer's wife. The wedding took place in a temple in Gorakhpur before they headed for his uncle's house who was a farmer staying with his son and daughter-in-law and their two kids. The story that they narrated was that Sameer had lost his job and was in a dire financial mess and needed shelter before he could get another job.

Sameer left for Mumbai in a week to seek another job. He had links and he got a breakthrough in just one month. But he decided to stay alone for six months in a rented single- bedroom house in Thane. He was paranoid and wanted Shruti and his mother to shift only after he was confident that nobody was looking for him. It was only after six months that Shruti boarded the Rajdhani express from Gorakhpur to Mumbai. It was nerve-racking for her as she kept looking around for familiar faces, praying hard that no one recognize her. Sameer was waiting for them in the Chatrapati Shivaji terminal. He heaved a sigh of relief. As the train reached its final destination, tears started pouring from Shruti's eyes. These were tears of relief, but deep down, she knew that she was betraying a sense of uncertainty that lay ahead, a future that was going to be riddled with fear at every turn of their lives. She also knew, and so did Sameer, that their only undoing would be if, at some point in their lives together, they realized that they were not meant to be with each other. It did happen with couples who were madly in love and then slowly marriage changed it all. They knew it could happen to them too.

Before they knew it, it was a year since they had moved to Mumbai. As time passed and they settled comfortably in the secure environs of the city, Shruti started to look for a job.

THE KAAFIR'S LOVE

Soon, she started working in a BPO in the Latin American division. It was the normal life she had craved for and the job was the means to give her that reassurance.

Epilogue

Five years later...

At Marine Drive, Prabha looked nervously at the waves rising towards her and crashing with a roar at the rocks. She hugged herself as the unusual chilly air struck her bony frame. She turned her head towards her left and said, 'Shruti beta, ask Sameer not to go further. It's dangerous.'

Shruti looked at Sameer who stood precariously on a rock and sighed, 'What he doesn't realize is that even Suhani wants to emulate him and join him there.'

Shruti held the hand of a restless 3-year-old girl who was trying hard to get free so she could play with her father. She looked at her father, who smiled and shouted, 'Darling, I want you to come here, but your mother won't let you. I guess a few more years and we will be challenging the Arabian Sea's waves.'

'Sameer!' There was an edge to Shruti's voice, 'Come here, right now!'

Sameer winked at her and started walking back as waves

crashed loudly on the rocks behind them.

Shruti knew that her family had limited choices, and she had decided to live with it. The first two years in Mumbai had been quite a struggle as they lived in fear of being tracked by her father. The fear died down first with the job and then with the birth of Suhani which coincided with the assassination of Imtiaz Khan. He was shot dead as he emerged out of his house on his way to the mosque. The police initially suspected the Hindu gangsters but the investigation was a dead end. It had to be.

Imran, the new Imam of Jama Masjid, had never forgiven Imtiaz for the mess he had created and was always uncomfortable with Imtiaz Khan's criminal ways. The financial muscle of Imtiaz was another issue, through which he tried to bully the mosque and the clergy. So, he shut him up.

Imran Khan was now the undisputed king of affairs of the Walled City—in fact, of Delhi and UP—and his power was still rising.

As Suhani slept, hugging her Barbie, between her parents, Sameer gazed at the dark skies through his window. The sound of a Mumbai local train echoed from a distance. He raised his right hand and started caressing Shruti's hair.

'I just realized that you could never grieve for your father properly...'

Shruti turned her head towards Sameer as a film of tears covered her left eye.

'Grieving for him meant that I would have to visit my family...and that is an excitement I do not desire in our lives. Not for us...and certainly not for Suhani...'

Sameer gazed at her intensely and said, 'But some day, we will have to face our moment of truth. Don't you wonder if your mother misses you dearly? Wondering too if she has

256

a grandson or granddaughter?'

'Stop it Sameer! You know this will not lead us anywhere. I have been trying to keep my mind off the temptation to call up Ammi. It's a risk I can't take. But as you said, some day, we may have to face our moment of truth.'

Sameer smiled, 'Well, we came this far. I guess that will be a piece of cake for us, isn't it?'

She smiled back, 'But no more of that excitement, please. I have had it for a lifetime.'

Sameer turned sombre and moved gently towards Shruti without disturbing Suhani who was sleeping between them.

'And I promise that I will always be there for you and for our Suhani...'

'You don't have to say that,' Shruti ruffled his hair, 'my Kaafir in a shining armour...'

THE KAAFIR'S LOVE